W0246889

PENGUIN MODERN CLASSICS
Strangers on the Roof

RAJENDRA YADAV (1929–2013) was among the most important and famous modern Hindi authors and intellectuals. Raised and educated in Agra, he wrote his first and greatest novel, *Sara Akash*, in 1951 (first published as *Pret Bolte Hain*). Never out of print since, it has sold over 500,000 copies, and was made into a film directed by Basu Chatterjee in 1969. Along with Kamleshwar and Mohan Rakesh, Yadav started the Nayi Kahani movement which transformed the Hindi literary scene in the 1950s and '60s. Author of seven novels and twelve short story collections, Yadav reinvented himself as an editor, political commentator and translator. In 1986, he re-launched Premchand's magazine *Hans*, and, with assistance from associate editor Archana Varma, turned it for over a decade into Hindi's most prominent literary journal. Yadav ran his own publishing house Akshar Prakashan, where his office became a centre for literary debate, and he developed *Hans* into a controversial forum for women's and minority voices. He is survived by his wife, well-known Hindi fiction writer Mannu Bhandari, and their daughter, Rachna.

RUTH VANITA, raised and educated in Delhi, taught at Delhi University for twenty years and now teaches at the University of Montana. Founding co-editor of *Manushi*, India's first nationwide feminist magazine, she is the author of several books, most recently *Gender, Sex and the City: Urdu Rekhti Poetry 1780–1870*, and co-editor of *Same-Sex Love in India: A Literary History*. She has translated many works of fiction and poetry from Hindi to English, most recently *Alone Together: Selected Stories of Mannu Bhandari, Rajee Seth and Archana Varma*.

Strangers on the Roof

Rajendra Yadav

Translated from the Hindi by
RUTH VANITA

PENGUIN BOOKS

An imprint of Penguin Random House

PENGUIN BOOKS

USA | Canada | UK | Ireland | Australia
New Zealand | India | South Africa | China | Singapore

Penguin Books is part of the Penguin Random House group of companies
whose addresses can be found at global.penguinrandomhouse.com

Published by Penguin Random House India Pvt. Ltd
4th Floor, Capital Tower 1, MG Road,
Gurugram 122 002, Haryana, India

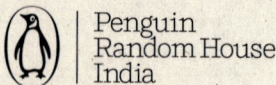

| Penguin
Random House
India

First published in Hindi as *Sara Akash* by Pragati Prakashan 1952
This translation first published by Penguin Books India 1994
This edition published 2014

Copyright © Rajendra Yadav 1951
Translation copyright © Ruth Vanita 1994

ISBN 9780143423829

Typeset in Adobe Caslon Pro by Tranistics Data Technologies
Printed at Repro India Limited

www.penguin.co.in

This is a legitimate digitally printed version of the book and therefore might not
have certain extra finishing on the cover.

Contents

Introduction

Sara Akash was Rajendra Yadav's first novel. Like many authors' first novels, it is also his best. Set in his home town Agra, it was based on a friend's experience of not having spoken to his wife for the first eight years of marriage. Yadav combines keenly observed details of urban lower-middle-class life with the troubled consciousness of a member of that class. These are also the two primary features of the Nayi Kahani (New Story) movement that Yadav pioneered, along with other writers, including his wife, Mannu Bhandari.

The aptly named protagonist Samar (Battle) is inspired by self-contradictory dreams, as is his wife, Prabha (Radiance). Before their marriage, each of them dreams of doing something extraordinary—she of working for village women's welfare, and he of becoming a Nehru or a Dayanand Saraswati. However, they also cherish more mundane visions of a beautifully furnished house, several servants and plenty of leisure. Both sets of dreams, products of the first decade after Indian independence, are extinguished by financial and familial realities that demand endless drudgery epitomized by the proverbial kolhu ka bail or bullock circling the oil-press.

The novel is a modern genre produced by and for the middle classes, and its two great themes are marriage and money. Yadav excels at depicting the inextricability of conjugality and finance. Lack of money causes most of the family's problems. While Samar juggles the merciless arithmetic of budgeting his first salary, Prabha's letters remain unsent because she cannot buy a stamp or an envelope. The only pleasure reliably available to people in these circumstances is that of marital intimacy, which comes with its own high price—that of producing children who entail yet more expense and anxiety.

Samar and Prabha forgo even this pleasure for a year, and Yadav evokes through images of ice, rock and subterranean fluids Samar's deep yearnings that he tries to deny. In the wonderfully written climactic scene in chapter ten, passionate weeping becomes their form of communion. Where words have failed, tears speak. The irony of this is sharper in Hindi, since Yadav uses throughout the phrases bolna or baat karna (to speak or to talk) with their heartland Hindi connotation of sexual intimacy. This meaning was once dominant too in the English word 'conversation', while the word 'intercourse' earlier indicated verbal interaction rather than sexual interaction as it does today. These idioms suggest that sex is a kind of speech and celibacy a kind of silence or shutting off of the self. It is no accident that in the first half of the novel Samar talks incessantly to himself but barely converses with others. After he and Prabha become intimate, he has long conversations both with her and with other friends.

Other finely wrought ironies include the way moonlight, that perennial symbol of love in both literature and cinema, reminds Samar always of Prabha's grief. Sadly ironic too is the way her hands and feet, the first parts of her that he sees at the wedding ceremony, manifest her gradual erosion in the daily grind of family life. The fair and delicate hands he sees when she cooks the first meal, arouse in him a desire to see her face; after they finally speak to each other, he notices how thin, dark and dry her hands have become, while the fair heels he had once noticed are now dirty and cracked. Her wrists, with bangles on them, precipitate Samar's final outburst, when he sees Prabha's capitulation to his family's demand for a child as a betrayal of him.

The second half of the novel, which the film chose to omit, works primarily as a sort of coda, framing the events with analyses voiced by the cardboard character Shirish. Is Shirish just another frustrated youth whose simplistic left-wing views comically mirror Samar's half-baked right-wing ideas? Shirish, unfortunately, is not so easily dismissed, both because his sermons occupy considerable space, and because Samar defers to him and it seems that the reader is expected to do so too.

For there are two Rajendra Yadavs—the imaginative fiction-writer who delights in the mystery of existence, and the ideologue who attempts to explain away complex phenomena such as religion or culture by imposing his ideology on them. Shirish is the mouthpiece for the ideologue, although fortunately Samar, Prabha and the family remain vital enough to prevent him from altogether stifling the novel. The family's turn-about from isolating Prabha before Samar speaks to her, to vilifying the couple when they form a new unit, is particularly well delineated.

Yadav the fiction-writer is at his best when developing

female characters. When I translated his story 'Prateeksha' for inclusion in *Same-Sex Love in India*, I was struck by the depth with which he imagined the psyche of a woman character entirely different from himself, and his ease in sympathetically depicting a same-sex relationship at a time when it was far from fashionable to do so. Likewise, in *Sara Akash*, Prabha, her strength balanced by flexibility, shows up Samar's hot-headed egocentricity when she agrees to wear bangles so as not to offend her mother-in-law and he smashes them, injuring both her and himself. Munni, too, though a cameo, and Bhabhi, the insecure and malicious sister-in-law, illuminate in their different ways women's intractable predicament. Prabha's voice is heard most clearly not in her conversations with Samar, which seem always hedged about by her anxiety not to offend him, but in her letter to her college friend, Rama. The letter shows us a playful Prabha of the past, an only daughter who habitually got up late, so different from the Prabha of the present who has to rise at unearthly hours to cook for a large family. It ends with her dream of lying with her head in Rama's lap, a contrast to her relationship with Samar, where she always plays the nurturer, cradling his head in her lap.

The difference between the two Yadavs emerges in the novel's handling of Hindu philosophy and narrative. Shirish reductively characterizes Hindu philosophy as escapism, and Samar remarks, '[T]hat man is amazing. He has his own way of looking at everything.' Samar does not realize that far from being original, Shirish's contempt for Hindu culture, which he dubs 'cow dung culture', springs directly from colonial stereotypes internalized by the colonized. Shirish's unawareness of the colonial forces that have shaped him is evident in his laughing at the nawabs of Lucknow who, he says, now pull handcarts. Samar's own experiential insight, however, into the oneness of all things comes closer to the advaita philosophy that Shirish dismisses. Embracing Prabha, Samar looks up at the night sky: 'And in a flash I felt, this star-laden sky, these many directions, all are part of ourselves, our being, they too are us.

Similarly, when Shirish berates Hindus for celebrating the mistreatment of Sita, Samar responds from his own experience: 'I felt as if I were standing before Prabha, my head bowed like a criminal. Did King Ram, the ideal for all men, never in his own heart, stand thus, his head bowed by the weight of his crime? Did he never find himself speechless before Sita?' These questions indicate precisely how the Ram–Sita story has functioned in the Indian imagination as a site for critiquing male oppression of women. For Ram has indeed repeatedly been rendered speechless before Sita, from Valmiki's epic where she has the last word before she returns to the earth-goddess, her mother, to numerous regional and folk retellings that recent commentators have examined.

Sara Akash was first published in 1951 under the title *Pret Bolte Hain* (Ghosts Speak). This refers to Shirish's view of the past as a ghost that insists on haunting the present and needs to be killed once for all. As Hamlet found, though, the past is not so easily silenced. The new title, *Sara Akash* (All the Sky) is drawn from a poem by nationalist poet Ramdhari Singh, pen-name 'Dinkar' (Sun). This more expansive title reflects the ordinary small-town dweller's most direct access to nature—the sky seen from the rooftop where he or she sleeps, relaxes and conducts chores that may include cleaning grains, washing hair or drying clothes. Here, Samar, the morning after his reconciliation with Prabha, rejoices in the sunrise. Prabha, though, has to struggle for even this access, as the family objects to the way it exposes her to the public gaze. Metaphorically, the title resonates with the post-Independence generation's optimism:

Senani karo prayan abhay
Bhavi itihas tumhara hai
Ye nakht amaa ke bujhte hain
Sara akash tumhara hai

Soldier, march on, fearless,
Future history is yours
These stars in darkness are quenched
All the sky is yours.

It contrasts ironically with Samar's final view of the sky, seen from the narrow perspective of one trapped between two trains moving in opposite directions, which seem to incite him either to commit suicide or to run away from home and his responsibilities. Yadav is good at conjuring up such characteristically modern endings, where a character is left as it were on the knife's edge. Several of his stories, such as 'Kinare se Kinare Tak',[1] simultaneously frustrate and satisfy the reader by refusing easy resolutions to the quandaries that torment the protagonist.

In his later years, Rajendra Yadav was best known as a public intellectual, a champion of the underdog. His desire to *epater le bourgeoisie* (both right-wing and left-wing),

---

[1]Translated as 'From One Shore to the Other', *Indian Literature*, 2014.

often embroiled him in controversy. That he was getting something right is indicated by his having been paradoxically and simultaneously accused both of misogyny and of being anti-men. Under his editorship, *Hans* continued its original founder Premchand's commitment to bring excluded groups into the literary arena. Opening up the journal to Dalit and women writers, he also opened himself up to accusations of encouraging pornography and low-quality writing, accusations which continue even after his death. Fearlessness of the kind displayed by Yadav both in his political critiques and in his challenges to political correctness is reminiscent of the bygone era of Nirala, Ugra and Ajneya and alien to the world of social media where conformity rules.

Reading Yadav's editorials in *Hans*, I did sometimes wonder, though, why one with so great a gift for fiction-writing would choose to expend his energies on the passing debates of the day. Of late, though, both from experience and from observation, I have come to realize that in a world replete with egregious injustice and irrationality, this choice may be forced upon one. Even that most reclusive of novelists, Vikram Seth, has found himself compelled to take up arms of late in defence of liberty.

The sympathetic and imaginative passion for liberty and for justice that animates *Sara Akash* has enthralled readers for over six decades and will continue to do so.

First Half: Evening

Ten directions but no answer

1

All of a sudden, the untuneful drumbeats and the twittering of women's voices came to an abrupt stop. 'What's happened? What's happened?' people cried as women and children came crowding out on to the balconies to peer across the alley. The eunuchs at the gate, who had been swaying their bodies and clapping, singing, 'May you live long, O bridegroom,' stopped and gaped, bewildered.

The daughter-in-law in the house facing ours had doused her clothes with kerosene and set herself on fire. Neighbours, alerted by the billowing smoke, ran to save her, but by the time they broke down the door, it was all over. What a thing to happen at such an auspicious moment! Everyone felt oppressed by a sense of impending doom. Screams and cries, people running to and fro, as happens in an earthquake!

No wonder then that I found it hard to believe that this was my wedding night.

In the turmoil, I somehow managed to slip away. Behind me, the screams and cries of women faded into the damp, filthy, narrow alley. Hard to make out whether these were the sounds of joyful singing at someone's wedding or of mourners weeping over someone burnt to death . . .

The whole world knows that tonight is my wedding night. The youth who used to go around speechifying, 'The country needs courageous young men dedicated to action,' has joined the common herd. Is it to be believed that Samar, whom fire and flood could not deter from going to the shakha, has not shown his face there for two weeks now, and slinks around, avoiding his own comrades? That, right now, he has slipped away, evading the accusing eyes of guests, friends, acquaintances and strangers, and is threading his way through the alleys as he heads for the temple? That is the only place where he can sit for a few moments and think in peace about this great change before he returns home late at night. By then, the din will have died down. But the voices pursue him.

'One more, one more, Thakur Saheb! How can you hesitate on the day of your second son's wedding? But the bride's father seems to be somewhat miserly—will you provide only local liquor to the bridegroom's party? At least today, foreign . . .'

My father, face burning and eyes swimming, straightens his turban and roars in a liquor-sodden voice, 'We have been cheated . . .'

'Get up, get up, it's time for the wedding ceremony. How can you sleep here like this—what will people say? A fine bridegroom's party this is! Get up, I say . . .'

'Look, look, that one standing behind the bride's mother. The girl with the long plait and white jewelled flowers in her ears. What eyes—I declare I'll collapse here and now!'

4

'Yes, repeat after me—whatever I build, a well, a tank or a dharmashala, I will build only with your consent and counsel. Now the girl vows that . . .'

Outside, the pipes squeal and the drums beat.

Run, run—run far away from this mess—someone keeps chanting inside me. Look at that boy walking ahead, he looks familiar. Turn around at once, otherwise he'll chatter on for two hours, and crack foolish jokes: 'How did you like your wife? What, no sweets for me? You didn't even take me along in the barat.' Run away.

What a burdensome way to start life!

I feel like leaving it all behind and running away to some distant, unknown place. Tomorrow, the newspapers will carry a notice: 'Son, your mother is seriously ill. Come back, all is forgiven.'

Nothing stirs, all around. As if a huge truck has got stuck in swampy ground. The engine groans, the wheels spin but the truck does not move, and mountainous clouds of smoke shut out the sky. Nothing to be seen, all sense of direction lost. My strength has given out. My breath falters—dust, motionless dust, everywhere.

In the gathering gloom I stood, leaning my forehead on the temple pillar. My head felt heavy. A beautiful, marble, black-and-white chessboard floor, two rows of pillars leading to the shrine, a vast hall, a few devotees with musical instruments sitting before the Lord and singing: 'Mine is the cowherd, the lifter of mountains . . .' Followed by cries of: 'Victory to the flute-player, to the son of Nand, we bow to you, O lover of your devotees.' Echo-filled evening, perfumed with incense, dimly lit. Can no one tell me what I should do?

Still leaning against the pillar, I sank down on the steps.

I do not even have the courage to run away. If only I had escaped at that time, just for fifteen days, to Calcutta or Bombay, Pune or Haridwar—just anywhere—none of this would have happened. But all I could do was cry and plead: 'Don't tie this millstone round my neck, don't tie this millstone round my neck.' Even while I sat, silently clasping the green-bangled hand in one fist and a ball of flour in the other, two voices kept repeating within me: 'There's still time, get up and run!' and 'O God, who is this they are tying round my neck!' Walking round the fire seven times with faltering steps—God only knows what the priest was saying—I remembered, just so had the priest said, 'Careful!' and taking it for a warning, the Samarth Guru Ramdas had fled from his wedding pavilion.

'It's time a bride came to this house—it's more than eight years since the eldest boy was married,' all our relatives had said. And my mother would say every day, 'O for the day when the younger daughter-in-law's feet will cross our threshold!' My father would grumble, 'We've been in debt to the tune of seven to eight thousand rupees ever since Munni's marriage. These boys must do something. It's beyond me now.' One's own comfort, one's own self-interest, one's own satisfactions, that's the keynote in our house. Never mind if others suffer in the process. No concern for anyone else's wishes or will. The old people think the world must run as it did in their youth, else it will descend into hell. 'What wishes can these boys have? What do they know of life? We have seen the world, after all.' And the truth is they know nothing of what lies beyond their noses. For them it is: What can a boy want more than to get married, to have a wife and children, to become a clerk, and to smoke his father's hookah after he is gone? O my lost aspirations, my dreams of becoming someone out of the ordinary—they will be suffocated to death, one by one. Those dreams of my future, fed on sleepless nights, nourished on blood, will die an untimely death.

I feel as if all that I thought this morning was thought not by me but by someone else. How irrelevant it appears now. I wrote in my diary: 'Why do I give up so easily? Why do I feel that my aspirations are doomed to die? Gold has to pass through fire in order to be purified. Life tests everyone—this is my fire ordeal. One should not be so easily perturbed by hardships. I must keep my head in times of crisis. This is the first secret of greatness—to be calm in the face of trouble. Napoleon used to write letters on the battlefield. I must never forget that I am going to become someone—someone before whom the world will bow its head. One whose every word will be a command for the nation, one who will free Mother India from the clutches of these foreign wretches. India is a land of great men. The blood of Rana Pratap and Shivaji runs in my veins, I must be worthy of it. It is we who are to continue and keep alive their tradition, their culture. We, the youth. Today too there are among us thousands of Buddhas, Mahavirs, Krishnas, Rams. We must awaken them, bring them forward. It is the forces of youth who can give birth today to Hanuman, Bhim and Bhishma Pitamah. Today is my moment of truth, it will not continue forever. These are the pitfalls and hurdles beyond which lie greatness, dignity, self-respect—the land of immortality. This is an obstacle race challenging me to reach the goal. God has placed these hurdles here in order to refine our powers. Yes, we will stride ahead, stepping over these obstacles and difficulties. Even today I am resolute in my vow of lifelong celibacy . . .'

That diary written this morning! But right now I feel as if I'm being carried along on the current of a fast-flowing stream. Who knows where it will take me? What shall I do with this present moment? Let myself be caught in this web of illusion, of enchantment, or break out of it? I am resolved, as far as is possible, not to get caught in it. O God, strengthen my spirit in this hour of crisis, make me firm so that I do not bend, do not let me be defeated.

Well, the marriage has taken place now. But I am still the same at heart. I will not get caught in its pleasures or pains. Perhaps I am demanding too much of myself but I will try with all my heart and soul to live up to this resolve. This is the time for me to forge myself, the time for self-construction.

Someone said Prabha is a matriculate. I have seen nothing of her but her hand. When we were walking round the fire and she was ahead of me, I saw her feet too. But, whatever happens, I will not establish any relations with her. I won't speak to her. If I have to, I will speak just the few words that may be necessary. Right now, I'll try to send her to her parents' house. Everyone is self-obsessed—why shouldn't I be too? I won't be lured by anyone. I was pressured into getting married. That's bad enough. I don't care whether or not she gets anything out of it. I have to build myself. I want to apply myself with all my heart and soul to my studies. Four years to go. I must do my M.A. I don't know what she will do, where she will live till then. Why should I try to find out? Why count the miles of a journey you don't intend to undertake? Obstacles sometimes present themselves in a very beautiful form; to refuse to be allured by them is wisdom. My wife is welcome to do as she likes. Why should we act as obstacles in one another's path?

Someone said she was very well-read, very intelligent. Can I not explain my point of view to her? If ever in the future we are to lead a domestic life together, she too can use this intervening time as a time of preparation. I should at least take a look at her face. My sister-in-law says there are faint pockmarks on it. What are her features like? Tonight is the wedding night. I have slipped away to escape being teased. Who knows what I am expected to do or how it is to be done!

Well, however it may be, what have I to do with all that? I have to take a major resolve today—this is my most difficult examination ever. If I falter today no force in the world can save me, and if I get through safely, I will rid myself once and for all of all anxieties. It may not be possible not to speak at all. I will say to her: 'Look, we both are intelligent people. Our parents have done whatever they could, but it is we who have to plan our lives. First of all, we have to complete our education . . .' But what if she starts crying at this? Will her tears wash the ground from under my feet? No, no, no—Yashodhara's beauty could not bind the Buddha, the milkmaids' love could not stop Krishna from becoming a king.

But, after all, is a wife always only an obstacle? Had Ram any strength apart from Sita's? Did not the Rajput women themselves send their husbands into battle? But I—I am very weak. Such things would be possible only if I could cast myself in that mould. Until then, indifference must be my weapon, and detachment my shield. I will have to tread carefully in this swamp of tears and lust. May this image of Krishna be my witness ...

O God, give me strength, self-control, wisdom, to take the right path. Let those who can walk with me accompany me; may I not halt, allured by those who fall behind. I began to hum to myself: 'Give us strength, O sea of compassion, to stand firm in the path of duty ...'

Then I noticed with a start that the bhajans were over and the kirtan had begun.

2

Laughter, jokes and giggles, the loud wail of the shehnais, the pipers turning their heads towards one another and playing ever louder—I felt as if I was trying to contain a tempest and it was struggling to find a way out—reverberating, circulating, growling.

I wonder if what has happened is a good or a bad thing. The wedding night is over and I actually have not spoken to her. I'm confused—is this God's fulfilment of my prayer or the beginning of my misfortunes!

I am very sentimental, very weak. I get easily carried away and swayed by emotions, by weaknesses, and lose my footing ...

Bhabhi had gently pushed me into the room and shut the door behind me. Prabha was standing at the window, leaning her head against the bars, as if she had fallen asleep standing there. I stood for a while and then went and sat on the edge of the bed, as if afraid of something. I had thought I would quietly lie down and go to sleep ... and once I go to sleep I never wake up till morning. But my heart was beating loudly and all the rocks of my strength seemed ready to burst. I had to gather all my resources of self-confidence and firmness. How eager the boys had been to give me all kinds of advice. Idiots! They think I'm like those thousands of fellows for whom a woman, any girl they see passing by, is a flower of heaven for which their souls have been yearning for countless ages. They see a girl going by in a tonga and fall behind, following her for miles, merely for the pleasure of watching her! I was never like that. My path is not theirs.

I kept repeating to myself: Woman is darkness, Woman is a temptress, Woman is illusion. Woman binds a man who is rising to divinity and drags him down into the deep, dark pits of hell. Woman is man's greatest weakness.

My path is not the path that thousands of boys take. I may not look different from them, but I am different in every way. My future is in my hands. Every moment I tread on a sword's edge. All I must do is steady myself so that I do not falter. I have always found myself much above these people.

Before I entered this room, I thought that I would find Prabha sitting huddled, like any shy new bride, all decked up to welcome me. I would have to be vigilant in those first moments. But I was startled to see her now—she was wearing the usual brightly coloured clothes brides wear, but she continued to stand silently at the window even after I had sat down on the bed. When I came in, a number of other women, neighbours, relatives, God knows who all, were at the door with my sister-in-law, giggling and whispering. I paid no attention to them. Now the only sound in this silent room was the whirring of the fan standing on a stool. Each time one of the fan's blades touched a wire it would make a harsh rattle. We had borrowed the electricity line from a neighbour for the wedding. I wanted to appear utterly unconcerned and indifferent. I tried to imagine that my face was radiating lustre due to the purity and nobility of my feelings. After a while I wondered whether she had fallen asleep. But when I sat down on the bed, she raised her head slightly to look at me and then leaned against the window once more, as if nothing at all had happened.

I kept sitting there like a fool, looking at the fan. What should I do now? Slowly, I sank further down on the bed and put my head against the wall. The minutes slid by. I was afraid that she would burst into tears at this hard-heartedness of mine, would catch hold of my feet with both hands, lift a tearful face pleading for reassurance, and ask, 'My lord! Tell me, what offence has your slave girl committed?' Then she would lay her head at my feet and ask forgiveness a thousand times. It would be very hard to retain my composure at that point. Yes, surely, this drama would soon occur . . .

But then I realized that a long time had passed and apart from the occasional tinkling of a bangle, the silence of midnight stretched between us like a poisonous mist. Suddenly I felt that my heart, which had been expanding and contracting like a sponge in a sea of emotions and doubts, had now congealed into a piece of stone. A voice inside me asked: 'Why did I come here? Not a word, no welcome—have I not been insulted?' I admit that beneath the motionless, icy sheet of ambitions, hopes and firm resolve, I had also felt the stirring of a warm, flowing spring. Perhaps much lay concealed in some dark corner of my mind—eagerness perhaps, or sweetness. Despite my firmness I was also afraid: what if this spring of hot blood were to burst forth, sweeping aside all my icy resolve, and drown me.

I felt as if I had been struck—how insulting! I have been insulted! My blood froze. Why did I come here? Could I not have gone elsewhere tonight? At worst, my family would have got upset—so what? My family is uneducated and she is a matriculate. Perhaps she feels superior to us. Certainly she is arrogant and thinks no end of herself. She kept standing there, and, enraged, I sat up. Shameless creature! So this is modern education, is it? No modesty, no respect for anyone! She thinks I will flatter and coax her, as most boys would. Huh, she can think again. She'll have to wait till doomsday before I act that way. I had thought since both of us are educated and intelligent we could converse sensibly and decide to concentrate on self-improvement. But no. If this is what she wants, well and good. I will not bend; if I bend today, I'll be finished for life. Today, it is I who must kill the cat. Madam must be thinking, as she stands there, that I will go to her and say, 'Come, why are you standing? Come and sit down.' Then she will blush and act coy, enact a drama of coquettishness. Just then I realized how rude it was of her not to have greeted or bowed to me when I entered. I had thought she would fall at my feet and I would gently lift her by the shoulders. Is this the courtesy, the manners her family has taught her? How proudly they had announced that their daughter is a matriculate!

After sitting there a few moments longer I stood up abruptly. My head throbbed and the room seemed to dance at my humiliation. Still, I had the feeling that as I left the room she would come up and catch hold of my hand or my shirt. Then I would hesitate and consider forgiving her. But when I took a few steps towards the door and she made no move, my self-respect flared up like a petrol fire. I decided that now even if she did come to stop me I would go off without looking back. Impudent creature!

I felt as if she had raised her head, startled, when the door opened with a loud creak. By then, I was outside. I paused a moment, I don't know why, then climbed the stairs to the roof. Everyone lay asleep there, on string beds or on the floor. Moonlight rained down, and the air was heady with the smell of queen-of-the-night. But I had no eyes for all this. I threw myself on the bare floor in a corner and lay there, fighting an inner battle.

Would I be able, ever, to forget the way I had been treated? Never, never. When Vidyotama behaved like this, her doltish husband was transformed into the king of poets, Kalidas. Now it was to be seen how I would avenge this insult. But why, after all, had I gone there? Was this not weakness on my part? Had I not received divine punishment for having strayed off the path? The kick I had been dealt should serve to steady me! I had read somewhere: 'There is no force in the world as powerful as an insult to draw out a man's inmost being.' Now the strength of my inner being would be tested. I would remember it, this gift given on my wedding night! What had happened was for the best. That was not my path, after all.

I felt as if I could clearly see the working of my fate—it was opening one definite path for me and closing all others. Certainly that would be the path to great things, to the heights.

And suddenly, in the midst of this mental turmoil, the tears began to flow, rolling down uncontrollably as I gazed at the sky. O God, what is this you have tied round my neck?

Where have you cast me? And a familiar despondency rose up and overshadowed my mind—I am alone on this desolate path, absolutely alone. No one is with me. No one to dispel my exhaustion with words of consolation, to wipe my despairing tears and say, 'Never mind, I am with you.' What kind of girl is this they have bound to me? How is life to go on? And all this while the tears continued to pour down as though my eyes were drawing moisture from every pore in my body.

A thought floated up: what if I get up now and go away without a word to anyone? I'll go anywhere—Calcutta, Bombay, Haridwar—run, run away!

All night I simmered and roasted on fiery coals.

3

Like a forest fire the news spread through the house: Samar has not spoken to Prabha.

I sat on the doorstep of my room, head in my hands, as depressed as if I had just returned from a cremation. Evening shadows had begun to emerge from the corners and spread through the house. My depression grew with the shadows; I felt as if a dark sea, a vast void, lay before me. What should I do now?

Since morning many people had questioned me. Perhaps they had questioned Prabha too. But both of us had shown such unwillingness to speak that they had not dared to repeat their questions. Bhabhi had asked, first sarcastically, then seriously, what was wrong. Amma too. But I evaded all questions. All day I mooned around, avoiding everyone. No doubt I was annoyed with that so-called wife of mine, yet I wanted to know what she had said against me. So far I had not heard anything, and was rather surprised. Looked as if they hadn't managed to get anything out of her. Whatever they had guessed was from my behaviour! Sometimes I would check myself—perhaps this too was a way of impressing me! But now I felt within me an indifference, a cold, hard detachment, as if I had no ties with anyone in that house. Perhaps I wouldn't have cared even if she had gone around talking about me to all and sundry.

Babuji had asked, as if investigating a great mystery, 'Did something happen?' I was silent. 'Did you have a fight?'

I had panicked when Munni came to say, 'Babuji is calling you.' Why was he calling me? With a sinking heart, I went.

I have always been afraid of coming into Babuji's presence. For about three to four years now, he hasn't hit me, but the memory of those blows and bruises is still fresh. And these memories seem to double and redouble my terror of him. One never knows how he will react. In the days when he used to hit me, I felt a certain obstinate freedom from anxiety—at worst I would get a beating. After all, one gets hurt while playing hockey or football, and one doesn't make a fuss. But of late I have begun to feel a strange, mysterious fear of him. When I expect to be scolded or beaten for some misdoing, and he lets it be, I feel as if penalties are accumulating in my account. To shrink from his presence has become second nature. However rebellious I may be at heart, the terror of Babuji is so ingrained in me that I am struck dumb in his presence. And I do exactly as he says, even when my whole soul revolts against it.

Yet, terrified as I was, I had prepared a speech in my defence. He was sitting silent, smoking, as if sunk in philosophical speculation. The chairs and stools clustered around him suggested that some people had been there and had just left. When he indicated with his eyebrows that I was to sit down, my courage evaporated like so much smoke. I sat down carefully, as far from him as possible.

'What's the matter? You don't like the bride?' he asked very gently. This gentleness unnerved me completely; I felt every word of my speech slipping away.

Seeing that I was silent, he inhaled deeply and asked, 'Speak plainly, why are you hesitating? I hear you didn't even speak to her?'

I sat silent, studying the lines on my palm. All the questions and answers I had prepared had fled. My mind seemed filled with a deep sadness.

Babuji went on, 'Think of it like this: that poor girl has come into a strange house—on whom is she to rely? Is this the way to treat someone who comes into the house? What will she tell her family? It's true you didn't want to get married, son, but this is the way of the world. One has to do one's duty. Suppose—'

He was interrupted by my suddenly bursting into tears. The fact is that I was not prepared for this truth-telling. I couldn't control myself. I began to wipe my eyes and nose with my fists like a child, and when he said kindly, 'Go, don't be a baby,' I quickly came away.

For a long time I sat at the door of my room, thinking foolish thoughts. I could not see where I was to blame. Even though I knew this marriage would destroy my high ideals and ambitions, I had felt somewhat hopeful at the thought that the girl was educated and intelligent. We could try to understand one another, help one another grow. Had I wished I too could have dragged her to bed and launched into blind praise of her beauty, or, like a savage, killed a parrot or a cat in her presence to establish lifelong mastery over her. But I wanted to behave like an educated, civilized and courteous man; I wanted to introduce myself to her, and get to know her. Then I would have told her all my dreams and aspirations, explained to her my way of looking at life and the world. And afterwards, I would have asked gently, 'In what way would you like to help me in all this?' But her behaviour gave me no opportunity to say any of this. No, I am not at all to blame. Babuji is wrong to hold me responsible.

Suddenly it occurred to me: How does Babuji know that I didn't talk to her? I was startled. Who told him that? I hadn't mentioned it to anyone, but she must have. Since morning I had been wondering how she could treat such an important happening so lightly, why she had not said anything to anyone? But no one could have known of it, had she not said something. After all, she's a woman, she may not have told Amma, but she must have told Munni or Bhabhi. Should I ask them? No, that will expose my weakness. They'll go and tell her, and she will think me a weakling. Weak? So far she has had only one glimpse of my strength . . .

'Lalaji, why are you sitting here lost in thought?' Bhabhi suddenly appeared. 'You're behaving as if instead of getting married you have been saddled with all the world's woes. Why are you sitting with your head in your hands? Do you have a headache or what? Anyone who saw you would think you have a son or daughter to marry off!'

I started, as if I'd been caught committing a theft. To show one's griefs and anxieties is also a sign of weakness. Controlling myself, I said, 'Nothing, Bhabhi, I'm not worried about anything. Just sitting around.' I felt as if everyone in the house, every acquaintance, was pointing at me with each word, each gesture. And I felt deeply afraid of this targeting, of having to respond to it.

'Lalaji, don't put me on! As if it's not as clear as daylight. You haven't eaten or drunk all day.' Then she smiled mischievously and asked, 'Why, didn't you get along then?'

I understood her joke but answered gravely, 'There's no question of getting along, Bhabhi. I can't put up with arrogance even from my nearest and dearest, however beautiful or educated a person may be. I will trample such arrogance under my feet.' I can't say whether I was speaking so forcefully in order to answer Babuji or to address Prabha who was somewhere in the house, or merely in response to my sister-in-law.

'I think so too, Lalaji!' Bhabhi looked around cautiously before she replied in an undertone. 'Prabha is somewhat stuck-up on account of her education and her looks. If you ask me, she's no such beauty either. After all, who's not beautiful at a certain age? Wasn't I? Wasn't Ammaji?' She blushed as she spoke.

'Huh!' I tossed my head. 'This is the way she behaves with the little beauty she has. Had she been really beautiful, what would she have thought of herself?' I spoke loudly so that she might hear.

Bhabhi understood what I was up to. She said coaxingly, 'I beg you, Lalaji, speak softly otherwise someone will think I'm turning you against her.'

'Where's the question of misguiding me, Bhabhi? Do I have no sense? Am I blind? I kept saying, don't push me into this well. But at that time you too were determined not to let

21

me escape the noose. Well, what am I to do now?'

'Forget it, Lalaji, why do you get so upset about little things?' Bhabhi said tenderly. 'Come, come and have your dinner. Everything will be all right soon. You are hot-headed and she is still a child. I'll tell her how to behave. Of course she should not have behaved that way. But the worst part is that she thinks no end of herself. Doesn't think any of us worth talking to. She doesn't cover her head or her face, no matter who's around. She's brought a book from her home and sits reading it all the time. That's all she seems to have brought with her! Her education is more for display than genuine, I think. Anyway, Lalaji, why let yourself be distracted from your studies by all this!'

She paused and then said thoughtfully, 'She'll prepare the lunch tomorrow. Your brother says she's a superb cook.'

'How does he know?' I asked, surprised.

Bhabhi was startled. Then she said in normal tones, 'He must have had a meal when they went to see her. He's been praising her to the skies ever since. You'll see tomorrow.' She turned to leave, 'All right, come and eat something now. I'm going to serve the food.'

Since morning the atmosphere in the house had seemed so burdensome that far from eating, I had not even felt like having a drink of water. But I felt better after talking to Bhabhi, and after a while I got up and went to the kitchen.

At night, my parents and my sister Munni indirectly, and Bhabhi clearly, said to me, 'These things do happen. One can't have a lifelong fight over such small things. You have to live with her, you are married to her, after all. What is the poor thing to do? Even if she is at fault you should forgive her. In two days her brother will come to fetch her. What will she say of us? We'll be disgraced before the whole community. Our relations with her family will be soured. Let her ask your pardon now.' But the whole atmosphere worked to make me more obstinate. I said plainly to Munni, 'If you people want to let me sleep here tonight, fine, otherwise I'll go and stay with Diwakar or some other friend.'

'Lalaji, once you get an idea in your head you refuse to listen to anyone! Is this any way to talk! Once in a while you should obey your elders.'

'No, Bhabhi, no. Obedience has landed me in this mess—please let me alone now.' Something unspoken in everything everyone said was acting to increase my resistance, and yesterday's incident came before me with heightened intensity.

Just then I noticed a shadow at the door. She was standing there. Bhabhi went to the door and said, 'What have you brought? Milk? Why did you bother? Wasn't anyone else around? Munni is really the limit! She should at least have let the new bride relax for a couple of days. She could have brought the milk herself. Well, now that you've brought it, give it to him! What's there to be shy of?' Just then, Munni called from the kitchen, 'Bhabhi, Amma is calling you. Come and tell me how much dal to soak for tomorrow.' 'Coming.' Bhabhi smiled mischievously at me and left. As she went, she said softly to her, 'Say you're sorry, what's the use of prolonging it? You might as well be the one to humble yourself.'

The same room as last night. Lit by a dark blue bulb hanging from a red wire. A strange dreamlike atmosphere. I sat silent, gazing at the bulb as if I were unaware of the world, lost in deep contemplation. But my entire consciousness was focused on the doorway. I could see a hand with a glass of milk and part of a figure in a silk sari. I was waiting eagerly for her to come and ask my pardon and persuade me to drink the milk. I would forgive her. I too wouldn't like her to speak adversely of us to her family. And I had demonstrated to her what a man of resolve I was.

A minute passed ... two ... five ... ten ... a long time had passed and it seemed idiotic to keep sitting there. I sat up with a jerk and half-rose as if recalling something. Then I got up and walked to the door as if unaware that anyone was there. With a fine show of indifference I avoided touching her as I went past, and she stood there silent, holding the milk.

As I came out, I heard a tearful hesitant voice, 'Listen!' But I didn't wait to listen to anything. I ran up the stairs as if totally unconcerned. Tonight, too, the open sky lay spread above the roof.

That night I made two decisions. First, whether she spoke to me or not, I would not speak to her. I would not have any relations with her or show any weakness at all. Second, I would concentrate on my studies and follow my old routine as if nothing whatsoever had happened. The marriage was a nightmare which was over.

Next day, she cooked the meal. My decision not to speak to her was as firm as ever. But the decision to have no relations with her seemed somewhat excessive now. I wouldn't speak or show any inclination towards her but there could be no harm in eating the food she cooked—at least once, just to try it out. Of course, I'd go there only after much persuasion. Not that she'd come to persuade me! If only . . .

The custom was that I should be the first to eat the food she had prepared. I had nothing to do with all the other customs and rituals that were being observed. Every day hordes of women from the neighbourhood descended on the house, and from three in the afternoon to eleven at night, they sang to the accompaniment of dholaks. Handfuls of laddoos and batashas were liberally distributed. Munni's throat was sore from singing too much. Bhabhi was constantly grumbling about how many old women's feet she had to touch and how many paans she had to prepare. She would go and dump the paan box near Prabha, who would be sitting alone, reading or talking to the girls of her age who had come to see her. And if she heard anyone say that the younger daughter-in-law was prettier and better mannered than the elder, she would mutter to her, 'You haven't yet prepared the paan, and Amma and all the aunts are demanding it every minute. Here, give it to me—I'll do it faster. You're a new bride so you're shy, aren't you?' And she would take out the ones that were ready and join in the conversation about how much work this wedding had entailed.

I had clearly told Bhabhi that I wouldn't eat anything prepared by Prabha. I wanted to see how she would react. But Amma spoke for the first time. 'No, son, that's not done. It's a custom in this family. God who provides food cannot be insulted.' I was surprised that Amma didn't scold me. Somehow, my family's unexpectedly civilized behaviour gave me the feeling that they enjoyed the way I was behaving. Amma, who generally scolded me about every little thing, was abnormally silent, only sometimes murmuring to my aunt, 'What can I say, Poono, all my pleasure in arranging this marriage has been destroyed.' And she seemed to swallow the rest with a deep sigh.

When I was called to lunch, Amma, Munni, Bhabhi and Amar were all sitting in the kitchen. The kitchen was divided into two parts—one for cooking, one for eating—by a chest-high brick wall, in order to screen the women from the elders. She was behind the wall. I could not see how she sat to cook, but I could see her hands arranging the bowls in the plates. I noticed, as if for the first time, that her hands were fair, the palms and nails coloured with henna. She had large gold rings in a new boat-shaped design on two fingers, gold bangles between the glass bangles on one hand, and on the other a small wristwatch with a black silk strap. I thought the hands quite pretty, the fingers slender and delicate. For the first time I felt like having a proper look at her face. I also felt annoyed with myself for being foolish.

Two trembling hands held out a plate; Bhabhi took it and put it before me. Everyone leaned forward to look at me as if I were about to perform some magic. Two small, thin rotis lay folded on the plate, three kinds of vegetables, dal, curd, two kinds of chutney, papad and pickles. My mouth watered just looking at it all. Smiling, I swallowed and pulled the plate towards me. Delicately, I dipped a piece of roti in the dal. Everyone was eagerly waiting to hear me praise the food. But as soon as I put the morsel in my mouth I rushed out, shouting 'O, O.' Outside, I spat out the whole morsel. My eyes were watering badly.

'What's happened? What's happened?' Everyone was looking at me in horror. I heard the rolling pin slip from Prabha's hands and fall to the floor.

'Happened, indeed! The dal is bitter as poison. I'm not going to eat this fine feast!' I bent down like a martyr, broke off a piece and raised it to my brow, then sent the plate flying with a kick and stormed out without a backward look. I heard a tearful voice say, 'But I'd tasted the dal.'

A huge uproar ensued. 'The bride doesn't know how to cook, now she'll have to be taught this too.' Bhabhi said tauntingly, 'Who knows who cooked the meal the day she was shown to us. Setting out to cook wearing a wristwatch! What good will a watch do you at the stove, pray? Either be a fine lady or learn to work properly—you can't do both. You might have cooked well the first day at least. Now even if you serve nectar ever after, this will never be forgotten.' Amma could be heard muttering, 'She'd tasted it indeed! Maybe in your family it is the custom to consume undiluted salt, what have we to do with that? Here you might have put a little less. No one would lose face if they had to ask for a little more. Now we'll have to teach her everything from scratch. We've got nothing out of this wedding. Neither a girl worth the name nor . . .'

For some reason Munni said nothing at all. I felt as if she was on Prabha's side.

The next day her brother came and she left with him. Life had gone through a turbulent phase, and now returned to normal. By the next day, the smell of clarified butter and special delicacies wafted from the kitchen had become as remote as an event that happened years ago.

4

'Samar Bhaiya, just come down a minute,' Amar called from downstairs, where he was cleaning our elder brother's cycle. I looked out. Two RSS volunteers were at the door. I went down. 'You haven't been coming for several days. We wondered if you were well or . . .' I had started going to the shakha in the mornings in order to get some exercise. In the evening I attended their lectures. But after my marriage and all the mental turmoil it caused, I hadn't felt like going. With great difficulty I managed to get rid of them and returned, dragging my feet. Now I began to dread their coming again to enquire about me.

Truly, she had come like a tempest and left like a retreating tide. But I felt as if someone had badly shaken up the normal routine of the house. As if some terrible mishap had occurred, the true effect of which my mind was as yet unable to grasp. I told myself it was a crisis which had come and gone. Someone has rightly said: 'From a distance a crisis may look terrible and forbidding like a vast mountain, but when you are close to it, roads and paths can always be found to negotiate it.' One day Amma said to someone, 'There's no dearth of girls for our sons. We'll get Samar remarried.' When I heard this, I rebuked her for perhaps the first or second time in my life, 'One marriage has given me enough bliss! Now please allow me to study.' She said nothing. I know that at heart she believes that even if I don't talk to Prabha for two months, four months or a year or two, she is after all my wife. Now that our fates have been bound together we will have to adjust to one another.

I had insisted that there should be no bargaining for dowry, and what came was not up to my family's expectations, so Amma would often remark, 'What can I say, Chandan, I have lost all my pleasure in this marriage.' Chandan is my maternal uncle. He had arranged the match. She would taunt him, 'Did you consider anything else at all besides the girl's education?'

The show put up for the wedding was long over and we were back to harsh reality. Every day an epic battle would be fought in the house over paying for the wheat or the sugar. Often, Babuji would remark to Amma or Bhai Saheb, 'How are we going to manage now, have you thought of that?' He gets a pension of only twenty-five rupees. Bhai Saheb's salary is ninety-nine rupees, including all allowances. He is still pulling on with the cycle he got at his wedding. Amma is worn out with illness and sits in bed, muttering over her rosary. Three children still studying—Amar in class ten, the youngest, Kunwar, in class six. Munni is also around. And I am appearing for the intermediate exam.

Munni is the most unfortunate member of our family. She's two years younger than me. A couple of years ago, when she was about seventeen, she was taken out of school and married off. Driven by the constant taunts of 'How big she's grown,' we somehow scraped together a dowry by selling some household articles and giving away some things Bhabhi had brought in her dowry. Oh, how the bridegroom's party harassed us at the wedding—we should be entertained like this, we want this, we want that. Munni began to write pathetic letters from her in-laws' house. When she came to visit us she would weep. She couldn't tell anyone how her mother-in-law and her husband joined hands to torture her. It was only later that we learnt just how bad-charactered the husband was and where he spent his nights. For a year-and-a-half, she somehow carried on, but then her mother-in-law died and a mountain of troubles descended on her head. Now there was no one to restrain the husband. He brought another woman into the house. We heard she was a Brahmin. Munni was made to work like a servant for him and his mistress, and was not given food for days together. God knows what tortures were inflicted on her—she didn't tell us the half of it. She would be pinned down all night, her palms under two legs of a cot, while they disported themselves in her presence. One morning she reappeared, her body covered with bruises from caning. Since then she has been with us.

Whenever I look at her, I wish I could get hold of her husband, and beat and kick him in public, right in the bazaar. 'You bastard, did we give you our flower-like sister for this? This is how it feels to be beaten up—how do you like it?' And, grinding my teeth, I would imagine thrashing him till he foamed at the mouth. I don't know what goes on in Munni's mind. She has become very quiet, removed from happenings around her. While all of us are sitting together below, she'll sit alone upstairs, gazing into space. When she comes down she'll shrink into herself, avoiding all eyes. As if something is crushing her to pieces within. We all notice that she is growing paler every day. At this bright, pearl-like age of eighteen or nineteen she is withering and wrinkling in grief. But what is to be done? Perhaps she will have to live here all her life. Babuji has written many letters to that man, has tried to put pressure on him through elders of the community, but all in vain. She is not educated enough to do any work. If she studies for five or six years she will be able to get a schoolteacher's job for thirty or thirty-five rupees. Even to learn tailoring would take her a couple of years. And where is the money to come from? The boys' education is a major financial problem for us. When Munni first came everyone sympathized with her, consoled her. Now no one thinks about her any more. It is only she who remembers that she is a burden on the family.

I don't know why, but after my marriage I have become much more conscious of the family's predicament. I don't feel as if it was I who got married. That perhaps was someone else. No one even talks of the bride now. My unwillingness seems to have been taken more seriously than was necessary. They seem to have forgotten that an outsider has become a member of the family. Once or twice Bhabhi laughed and said, 'Don't worry, Lalaji, everything will be all right. A woman should be kept down, otherwise she gets too uppity. Specially if she's uppity to begin with! My father used to say that a woman is a wooden monkey. A man should not get too enamoured of her. However beautiful or educated she may be, she has to do the same work after all. It's the work a man values, not your

31

looks. What's the good of reading thousands of books if you know nothing of housework? Look at me—you can wake me up at midnight and without opening my eyes, I'll put all the spices correctly in the dishes. Cut my nose off if I put less or more!' Then she would begin to talk of her own family. 'My elder brother too got a wife of that kind. She thought herself too good for us. My brother wasn't going to stand for it! He taught her a lesson soon enough. Some women are like that, Lalaji—they need to be given a beating. My sister-in-law is just fine now. She trembles like a leaf if she sees my brother frown.' And she waved her hands to mimic a trembling leaf.

I don't know why I feel so unhappy and sick these days. This constant harping on the scarcity of money! Constant hints that I should contribute. I'm afraid to go anywhere near these people. One day I asked, 'Do you want me to appear for the F.A. exam or not?' Bhaiya immediately replied, 'Who's forbidding you to study?' I felt like saying, 'Then stop this complaining night and day. You want me to feel obliged for being allowed to study, yet you don't want me to study.'

Sometimes I have a fierce yearning to immerse myself in my studies and pay no attention to their talk. Let them chatter as they wish. Another strange development. My former carefree cheerfulness, my dreams of a bright future, all are gradually being suppressed. Now I can see before me what I will end up doing. A strange despair is in me, solid as an anvil, on which all that they say falls like hammer strokes—my inner world reverberates to these blows, stunned, anguished. I don't feel like staying at home. I'm forced to eat two meals and sleep here. I was always quiet and am still so. But the earlier silence was a silence of satisfaction and fulfilment; this silence cuts at me like a saw. Nothing interests me. The board exams approach at their slow, cruel pace, hanging over my head like the sword of Damocles. Whenever I remember them I tremble like a goat beneath the butcher's knife. Whether or not classes are on in college, I spend the time from ten to four roaming around. Sometimes with friends in the hostel, or else in somebody's house. What was it I had in me which I have lost? I have also begun to realize that people have started thinking of me as an idler who does nothing but hang around, sour-faced.

The disrespect in their eyes works like acid on my sensitive soul. When I can't bear it any longer I go and sit in the park. I lie there for hours and just don't feel like getting up. Thoughts chase one another through my mind. Either that or I do not think at all. Suddenly I realize that I've been lying there a very long time, then I get up and drag myself home. I have no desire to find out who may have come or gone, or what may have happened at home. I reproach myself, and try my best to return to my former carefree state, but I just cannot rid myself of the burden that weighs me down.

In vain, in vain—my whole life has been wasted. The days I have lived have been meaningless, aimless, and a wall of terrible darkness blocks out the days to come. I see no path before me. Whenever I begin to do something the question torments me—why do this? What is the use? As if everything in the world is purposeless and unnecessary. As if some cruel fist has wrung out the last drops of juice from life's nectareous sponge. A mist hangs over my mind, rendering it numb with its icy touch.

Like a fly in a web whose life is being sucked out drop by

drop before the spider discards the skeleton, I can see, I can feel the light of my eyes, the smile on my lips going from me, melting away, but how to stop them? This constant domestic bickering, the guilt and self-reproach in my heart, the burning of my dreams like a house of lac.

I see many boys at college who roar with laughter for no reason. They are carefree, they tease each other, joke and horse around. I feel as if I do not know any of them. How false and artificial it all seems—whistling and gesturing at girls going by, boasting of their exploits with the poor refugee women who come to beg for help at the dharmashalas, chattering about film stars, arguing about cricketers. I don't even feel like joining the intellectual ones who discuss politics, the dangers posed by communism to Indian culture. I feel all their talk is of things that have nothing to do with life. They irritate me— why can't they ever shut up? Why must they chatter non-stop, jumping around like a pack of monkeys? What's the use of all their talk? Fine, Madhubala is the world's most beautiful actress and Ashok Kumar does a great job even though he's old, but what has it to do with you? So what if the running commentary is better than the live game, and if Stalin's daughter's deeds are coming to light? What is it that you want, after all? This life of externalities appears hollow, joyless and futile to me. Sometimes I envy them and wonder why I can't laugh and talk as they do, why I don't feel like leaping forward to kick an empty cigarette tin on the road. But my heart seems to have died in me. Hearing my classmates constantly label me 'deadly dull', I feel I have aged by twenty years. A deep despair, a subtle but diffused exhaustion has settled into me.

That saffron flag waving beyond the clouds retreats from

me every day. I feel as if I haven't seen a movie for years. I saw a couple at the time of my wedding. I don't know why I feel as if, now that I am married, I don't have the right to ask my parents for money. Depressed and dejected . . . I am utterly alone! Sometimes I gain momentary peace by reading the Gita. I like to sit alone in the temple and think. That is the only time I feel I can forget everything. The perfumed incense soothes and lulls my taut nerves that are ready to snap with anxiety and worry. On the way back I feel I'm returning to that world where a man is like a bullock bound to an oil mill. But an incident took place which made me stop going to the temple. An extremely weak and emaciated Punjabi refugee had gone into the temple to ask for prasad. The priest picked up a smouldering stick and beat him out like a dog—that sight broke something in me. I said nothing, I merely watched like a spectator sitting in the balcony, but that was my last day at the temple.

I feel as if everyone has entered into a conspiracy to leave me alone. They do not say anything: it is done indirectly, through their insulting neglect and loaded gestures, and it eats away at me every moment. As if all of them are fed up of me and disgusted with me. Their faces show utter contempt for me. I feel afraid. A strange panic seizes me as I approach the house. My marriage did not fulfil your expectations—is that, too, my fault? Sometimes I feel an intense yearning for my mother to call me and ask what's wrong. My brother has no time even to look my way. My fear of Father grows by leaps and bounds.

I have not the slightest desire to think about Prabha, but when I constantly hear her being criticized, a mild feeling of protest rises in me. Have these people nothing better to do? Did I ask you to tie this millstone around my neck? You brought this proud girl and bound her to me, and now I get all the blame for it. I have repeatedly called up her image in my mind and am convinced that pride lay at the root of her behaviour. But when I try to think objectively, I ask myself: how is it possible that my wife stayed four days in my house and I did not speak a single word to her?

And when I can no longer bear all this, I wish I could sit alone somewhere and cry and cry till I fall unconscious, and never emerge from that state. But what is this weakness which makes me desire that while I am crying, the dirty pillowcase should not come into contact with my lips, the cold marble of the temple pillar not touch my brow, and the dry grass on the lawn not prick my cheeks . . . I don't know what place, what world, would bring me peace!

5

One day, while serving my food, Munni asked, 'Brother, did you not talk at all to Bhabhi?'

I looked at her, trying to assess her meaning, and replied briefly, pulling the plate towards me, 'No.' My tone was expressionless, but I was curious to know why she had asked me this.

'Will you marry again?' She was sitting in front of the stove and doodling on the floor with a piece of coal.

'Yes, yes, why not—now that you've torn one marriage threadbare, whom do you want to ruin next?' The words flew out of my mouth. And suddenly, for the first time, the thought flashed into my mind—how much Prabha must have suffered when all of us behaved as we did. Everyone had forgotten her now, as if she was dead. I wondered whether she might, unhappy as she was, have written to say that if I didn't like her I should marry again. I remembered hearing and reading about girls doing that kind of thing. I felt like asking, 'Has Prabha written or what?' The morsel I had swallowed seemed to be working its way upwards. The food was tasteless, I had lost my appetite. Sipping water to keep down the rising nausea, I asked, 'Who talked about it—Amma?'

'No. I just asked.' Munni evaded my question. Then she looked at me and said, 'At night, after dinner, when Bhabhi presses Amma's feet, that is when they generally talk about it.' And, holding her arm to the light, she began to slide her bangles up and down.

'Munni, I'm telling you, I'll leave the house and run away. I want to study. They find it hard to educate me, but are ready to marry me off any number of times,' I said in a tearful voice.

She was quiet for a while, then said, 'All right, Bhaiya, tell me something.' She sounded as if she was about to reveal some secret.

I looked at her questioningly. Just then Bhabhi appeared at the door. She had rushed back from her bath in order to complete the cooking. Dozens of washed and wrung-out clothes lay rolled up on her shoulders. 'Oh, so Munni is serving the food today! I came running because I thought Lalaji would be sitting quietly, waiting, and then he would leave without eating. What has happened to our Lalaji these days?' She sat down and leaned against the wall. She was panting. Pregnant. Taking the clothes off her shoulders, she held them out to Munni and said in a wheedling tone, 'Munni, be a good girl and hang these out to dry.'

'Wonderful—must I do all the work? Why don't you dry them yourself,' pouted Munni.

'I swear by you, sister, my hands are nearly broken just washing them. I fall at your feet, do go, please,' Bhabhi said with exaggerated tiredness, and then looked meaningfully at

Munni. Then she laughed and blushed. Munni also laughed and went off with the clothes.

I kept nibbling at the food though I had no desire to eat. Bhabhi sat watching me, her head resting on her hand, as if seeing me eat had reminded her of something. Then she said as if to herself, 'This year it's quite cold already though it's a long way yet to Diwali. How many more days to Diwali, Lalaji?'

'Must be ten to fifteen days,' I said indifferently.

Counting on her fingers, she said, 'On Diwali it will be exactly six months since your wedding.'

Six months! Each day had seemed to suffocate me, but now it seemed as if time had sped by. What could have become of Prabha in all this time? Surely a letter or two must have come? I'd ask Munni later, I thought. But what was it Munni wanted to tell me? Why are all of them talking about my marriage today? These days I have lost all enthusiasm, all desire for pleasure. The desire to know rose in my mind and died as quickly. I told myself something must have happened here, at home.

'What a marriage yours is, Lalaji!' Bhabhi said, sighing deeply, in a tone of great sympathy and sorrow. 'Cold water on all our dreams. As for the give and take part of it, that's unimportant, it's forgotten in a year or two. But that queen has been tied to you for life. It seems her family has written to suggest sending her back here.'

'It was you who were so taken with the idea,' I said. 'You were the one who kept singing her praises.'

'Listen to him! What could I know of her—I repeated what I'd heard!' She sighed deeply. 'There should be some limit even to arrogance. I swear, never in all my life have I come across such an arrogant woman. If one has great virtues one's tantrums may be overlooked, otherwise who'd put up with such behaviour? She thought she'd get away with everything on the strength of her looks and her education—but she was no such heavenly nymph either.' Bhabhi paused to see how I was taking this. Then she went on, 'I felt like laughing when that princess went into the kitchen wearing her watch. I didn't say anything, but when she said, "I tasted the dal, Ammaji," I could have raised a furore. I thought, never mind. No one should eat before the person who is supposed to eat first. Who was she to taste it?'

I was sick of all this. I was getting late for college. I said, 'Bhabhi, I'm getting late. I can't finish this. Munni's given me too much.' And I stood up.

She kept calling out, 'But you've eaten next to nothing, Lalaji, do finish it.'

'No, Bhabhi, I'll eat it when I come back after class.' As I was leaving I heard her say with an artificial laugh, 'She's coming, but I'm warning you, keep her under control, Lalaji, otherwise you'll repent.'

The men silent and the women acting so strangely. What meaning should I put to all of this? But, since morning, I have been feeling out of sorts. Today, all of a sudden, a question keeps arising from the sadness in my heart: What could have become of her? Shouldn't she have written me a letter? Perhaps I would have read it uncaringly and torn it up. Yet should she not have written? How must she be? What effect could this blow have had on her? For some reason my heart clamoured irresistibly to find out something about her. What could she have told her family?

40

Sometimes a shudder runs through me. How will I spend a whole lifetime with this arrogant girl? What is to become of my future and of hers? And this foolish talk of remarriage? Was it that Munni was about to talk of?

When I went to ask Amma for the board exam fees, she gasped at the mention of twenty-five rupees, 'O lord, where am I to get so much money? Ask your father.' I had gone to her in order to avoid having to approach Father. Now my heartbeat sped up. I thought of approaching Bhaiya and Bhabhi, but I knew they would either not have the money or would not want to part with the twenty-five or thirty rupees they may have laid by for a rainy day. 'Babuji, the board exam fees have to be paid tomorrow,' I mumbled, as if I was talking to myself. I had sat down quietly, then spoken with bowed head, as ashamed as if I were asking for money to buy liquor.

Babuji was repairing a string bed. At first he kept staring at me, then asked in a loud voice, 'How much?' 'Twenty-five.' I brought out the words as if I had but twenty-five breaths left to draw in this life.

'Hmm.' He grunted and tugged at a rope, pressed it beneath an elbow and said, 'My twenty-five rupees pension has come—take it. Don't worry about me—I have to toil all my life for you and I'll do it. I'm fated to keep feeding my sons until they grow as large as camels and oxen. Yesterday Amar was demanding his fees. Money flowed like water at Diwali too. The only one earning is Dheeraj and you fellows will suck him dry, that's clear.' He reached under his shirt into his vest pocket, drew out the notes and put them before me without counting them. 'Here, take it. What are you standing there gaping at me for?'

I didn't have the courage to pick up the notes. I felt like going off somewhere—my studies could go to hell—and somehow making a pile of money to satisfy these people. O to be able to say, 'Here, take this money, how much do you want—money, money, money . . . !'

Babuji bent his head again, then said in altered tones, 'You have no idea how many problems there are, Samar. What am I to do, tell me? I don't have the strength to take up a job again. Dheeraj's wife is about to deliver—another problem. An eldest son's first child—do you know how much expense that will entail? And all of you still studying! You have to be fed and clothed on time. Your mother is worn out with cooking all day. She too is old. The poor woman has toiled long enough. She needs rest now. For thirty years she has been labouring without rest. You might at least go and fetch your wife—she'll be of some help. Those who are going to work or to college will get their meals on time. Munni will help her. Munni too has to stay here. The whole community spits on us, but what to do? Our problems are endless.'

At that moment, looking at the whole situation from Babuji's point of view, I really felt very sorry for him. Are my parents to blame if they have become cross and ill-tempered? How long are they to carry on like this? Swallowing, I managed to say, 'Babuji, send Amar. I won't go.'

He suddenly changed his tune and said harshly, 'Fine, Amar will go. You die a thousand deaths when your wife is mentioned. Is she a wolf waiting to devour you? Nice set of sons I've produced! Each one thinks himself a crown prince. You people are beyond my comprehension. I'll see how long you hold out and don't talk to her. I did my best to explain to you—she's a girl from another house, what will she think, what will she tell her family? After all, we have to get your brothers married too. People gossip—can you stop them? But you think you're too smart to listen to advice. If you're a man of your word, don't speak to her all your life.'

Something Bhabhi had said flashed into my mind. She had said one day, jokingly yet in an admonitory tone, 'Lalaji, do you know what Babuji was saying to Amma today?' When I didn't answer, she went on, 'He was saying, tell Samar to see a doctor. Let him have a check-up, we'll pay the fees.' When I didn't understand and asked, 'Why, what's wrong with me?' Bhabhi stuffed the end of her sari into her mouth to stifle her giggles while I tingled with rage.

Babuji kept tightening the strings, tight-jawed and angry, and I picked up the money and came away as fast as I could. What filthy minds do these people have! Babuji was still muttering to himself and his voice was fanning the fires of wrath in me.

Keep doing as they say! If they say, get married, one must get married. If they say, go leave her at her parents' house or fetch her back, one must leave her or fetch her. Just because I asked for twenty-five rupees I had to hear all these fine speeches. Thank God I had managed to get my tuition fees waived else there would have been an epic battle every month. Why did you produce us if you can't give us a decent education? I don't ask for money for books. My clothes are old and threadbare, yet I manage somehow. I have to get through the winter in them. I never ask for money to see a film or to have a snack. Yet I am reproached and called a camel and an ox.

Fetch your daughter-in-law if you want to, don't call her

43

if you don't want to. Why ask me? Do you always consult me before you act? As if you always abide by my wishes! Did you listen to anything I said when you were getting me married? At that time it was, 'You're a child, keep quiet. We'll break your head if you talk too much.' Break my head indeed! Why don't you break it now? Am I the only one left in this house who can go to fetch her? Why can't Amar go? You've spoilt him thoroughly by always saying, 'He's a kid, he's a kid.' What is it to me, you'll suffer the consequences. Yes, I'll show you whether I talk to her or not all my life. That's up to me. No one can force me to talk. This is not a wedding which can be forced on one. This is a matter of one's feelings—I won't speak to her. You're disgraced in the community—huh!

6

On my way back from college I met Amar. He was rotating a football in both hands—probably off for a game. As soon as he saw me he said, 'Samar Bhaiya, I've brought sister-in-law home.'

I had been walking along with my head down. I looked up with a start. 'Really?' And I suddenly stopped. I stared at him, then asked, 'Anything special happened?'

'Nothing special. They were reluctant to send her. Bhaiya, her family is very rude. I'm telling you plainly, I'll never go there again.'

'Why, did they beat you up?' I asked in a low voice, smiling malevolently.

'Is beating the only form of rudeness? They were constantly criticizing Bhabhi and our parents. We may be very bad, but I'm not willing to hear my family criticized.' He spoke boldly, quite unconcerned how I might react.

'And they didn't say what Samar was like?' I suddenly asked. Unconsciously, a sort of tenderness had crept into my voice. What could she have said about me?

'Well, I have to admit that all of them had nothing but praise for you.'

'Praise?' I was astonished, completely taken aback. Then I said disbelievingly, 'You must have misunderstood.'

'That's possible,' he agreed. 'We didn't talk much about you. They only asked a few times—how much further is he going to study and will your taking Prabha back now not disturb his studies? They also said, the more you studied, the happier they would be. But they were not too pleased that you hadn't gone to fetch her the first time—that's the custom. I explained that this was not the first time she had left her house—that was at the time of the wedding itself. And that you are working very hard these days.'

'No other problems?' I halted him midway. The curiosity aroused by the word 'praise' was not assuaged by his talk. By saying 'You must have misunderstood,' I wanted to provoke him as well as be sure that he wasn't speaking sarcastically. What could I ask now? That word was creating a storm in my mind. I was overwhelmed by a powerful desire to find out what she had said of me. At that moment I suddenly felt my behaviour had been grossly improper. If I were to be put in the dock and asked why I had not spoken to my wife on my wedding night, what would I say? Merely that she had not sat huddled up at the sight of me but had remained standing? Or that I had great aspirations and I thought a woman would prove an impediment, or that I had been married against my will? Are these any reasons for not speaking? How could I justify my behaviour except as the outcome of emotional agitation? I felt as if my behaviour throughout had been not only wrong but foolish. I was filled with self-reproach.

'No, nothing else. They asked when she would come again. She has become quite weak, so they said that if she needs any medicine we should take care of it,' Amar said and prepared to go.

'Was she unwell?' I asked, and at the same time felt ashamed of my weakness.

'Yes, perhaps she was,' Amar said philosophically and made off, tossing his football.

They said we should take care of her! And here, Babuji was saying the meals would be served on time when she came. The bride has just come and they plan to make her do all the work. Strange attitude my family has! So, did she really praise me, then? No, no, Amar could not have understood.

I was feeling very hesitant about going home, yet I also felt as if the sadness that had settled over me like a scummy layer had been cut away, and the clear moving water beneath had once again become visible. I could hardly believe that she had not talked against me to her family. Surely she must have said something. How could it be otherwise? Some taunt would definitely have been flung at Amar. After all, she had talked about the others. At that moment, I was exasperated at my folly in not having looked at her properly even once. How would I face her now—the thought embarrassed me no end. What was the point of this vow not to speak? Right now I felt ready to laugh off even the greatest offence done to me, or to ignore it. I was surprised at myself—was all this freshness, this light-heartedness, really in me?

But when I entered the house I pulled a long face, and behaved as normally as possible, as if I had not met Amar and did not know of Prabha's arrival. A tired expression and dry lips. Munni saw me and yelled, 'Samar Bhaiya, Bhabhi has come!'

'So what am I to do?' The words escaped my lips, and at that moment I remembered the taunt about showing myself to a doctor. For no reason I felt irritated. I went to my room as if I were very tired and in a hurry to put away my books. But only I knew with what effort I controlled myself at that moment.

Through the open windows, I saw her trunk in my room. A wave of pleasure ran through me. I was eager to see what other new things the room contained. I felt a certain satisfaction in the knowledge that Prabha had nowhere else to go; she had to stay in my room. The room we had been given at the time of the wedding had been reclaimed by my older brother. So she would have to talk to me, sooner or later. This time I too would not act so standoffish. Her shawl hung on a peg in the room. Next to the trunk was a cane basket— the things needed for the journey must be inside it. I looked around and then cautiously lifted the towel that covered the basket. A copy of *Maya* lay rolled up there. She must have bought it at the railway bookstall. I opened it—on the first page was written in clear, pearl-like letters: Prabha. I had an impulse to write my name next to it. Then I hastily put all the things back. What would she think if she saw me?

It was evening. I slipped out of the house, avoiding Bhabhi's and Munni's eyes. I didn't feel like encountering anyone: they would begin to tease me. Where to go? I didn't feel like going and lying in the park. After that incident I had stopped going to the temple. I thought of going to Diwakar's house but gave up the idea. He might delay me too long. I roamed the streets. Punjabi refugees were hawking soap, vegetables and other goods. Boys were selling roasted gram and peanuts; some had set up wooden stalls to sell clothes. One had to acknowledge the courage and self-reliance of these people. After going through such terrible hardship, such an inferno, we people would have been fit for nothing but begging alms. What had they not suffered and witnessed? They remember their lost land, their forfeited glory, mourn their dead, and then start labouring afresh. The women sit at taps, washing clothes night and day. After many days, today I remembered that I had not attended any of the RSS lectures. Should I go there? But what excuse would I give for having stayed away so long? It would be embarrassing. Not today, I would go some other day. I was surprised at myself—where was all my despair, my anxiety and sorrow? Yesterday, at this hour, when I was crossing this bridge, my nerves were ready to burst with tension. What a sensible and understanding girl Prabha is! Any other girl would have told such tales of me to her family that I would have been disgraced for ever. She must simply have said that I'm busy studying because the exams are approaching. That's the difference between an educated and an uneducated girl. Huh, what an uproar we created that day because there was a little extra salt in the food. She's a human being, so what if she put a little too much salt? Should we never forgive her? Poor girl, a new bride, she must have been nervous. A new place, new people and fearsome critics like Amma and Bhabhi. She must have been terrified. Why, if I'm told to stand up and read before the class, I won't be able to read a single line properly, I'll stammer and get bathed in sweat.

I have always been too hasty in my judgments. I barely set eyes on a thing before I make up my mind about it. This is a great weakness in me. I must shake it off. I am to blame in this whole affair, she is not at fault. Standing on the bridge and watching the railway lines far below, I felt surprised at myself—what were those foolish anxieties which made me sit in a corner of the temple and weep? Were they really worth worrying about and crying over for hours? I forgot her neglectful behaviour, her impertinence in not having written a letter, everything.

When I returned home quite late, Bhabhi said, 'Lalaji, aren't you going to eat? Your wife is waiting without eating. All of us have been waiting anxiously and you are nowhere to be found. You left in the morning and didn't even return after class.' Her voice was rich with suppressed laughter.

Of late, I had stopped reacting to meaningless remarks; I would reply only when necessary. I'd generally answer Bhabhi's jokes in a low voice and end the matter there. I didn't feel like conversing with anyone. I wanted to continue behaving like this so that no one would sense the sudden change in me. So I replied quietly, 'Yes, Bhabhi, I had some work . . .'

'Didn't you know Prabha had come?' Bhabhi asked. I looked at her as if I didn't understand, then said as if in haste, 'No, I didn't. Give me food now, I'm hungry. Then I have to sit down to study.'

'You will get food later, first give us sweets,' came Munni's voice from somewhere afar.

Bhabhi laughed in reply, 'He, give us sweets! He'll be very quick to eat the sweets that have come from his in-laws.' She looks pretty when she laughs.

'Forget sweets, Bhabhi, just give me dry roti. That'll do for me. You and the in-laws are welcome to the sweets!' I said, as if preoccupied, and added, 'Hurry up. I want to get to work for the board exams.'

Bhabhi seemed very pleased.

After dinner I sat down with the lantern to study. Winter was just beginning. When I study I start feeling sleepy, so I'd begun to sleep on the floor instead of on the cot. The cot was covered with my old, filthy quilts and mattresses. Every day I'd vow to myself that I'd study till twelve or one, and wake up at four or five, but this programme never took off. Since of all the sons, I was studying in the highest class, I had the right to a separate lantern. The other two boys shared one. But every other day there would be a fight over this too—how could the whole family manage with just one lantern? And when my older brother caught me sleeping with the lantern still burning, the uproar that would ensue over waste of oil is better left undescribed.

I sat before the lantern, head bent over my book. It was Matthew Arnold's *Sohrab and Rustum.* Try as I would, I just could not read it. Defeated, I gave up and settled down to wait. Occasionally, I would turn a page. I wanted to see what she would do. I knew when all the housework was done, when she and Munni and Bhabhi had exchanged all the news, she would come. I was awaiting that moment. How much longer would they keep talking?

I heard the sound of footsteps. The murmur of voices downstairs had ceased. I had noticed that Amma was absolutely silent. Clearly showing indifference. She felt the cold very much, so I guessed she must be sitting wrapped in a quilt, telling her rosary. I had an impulse to look out and see what was causing the delay. But Bhaiya might see me, and in any case the living room and Amma's room were not visible from upstairs. Cautiously, I went and peered through a hole in the parapet. I imagined the scene—Munni in bed, the quilt drawn up to her nose, Bhabhi pressing Amma's feet, and Prabha sitting close to Munni's bed, head bowed, unobtrusive, listening to their talk. She must be wishing their talk would end so that she could go and get some rest.

I sensed that someone was standing at the door. By the shadow I knew it was she. Either she was watching me study or she was hesitant to come in. After a while she came in, timid and afraid, and opened the trunk so quietly that there was no sound at all. From a slight rustle I guessed she had taken out some clothes. For a while she sat still, thinking, then put her hands on her knees, rose to her feet and left. She is tired. Perhaps she has gone to change her clothes. All my senses seemed to have got concentrated in my ears. The faint tinkle of bangles, the rustle of clothes, the strange perfume of a healthy young female body entered the room in a wave and withdrew. My heart yearned and my nerves echoed like taut wires responding to a touch. I could not understand this strange bliss spreading through me, this warmth that was creeping into every pore. All that had happened so far fled from my mind, and golden pictures of a happy married life danced before me. Scenes of dalliance seen in hundreds of films and read in stories: how we would play, tease and tickle one another, quarrel and make up; Prabha would mischievously run away with my book to make me talk with her, and I would chase her in mock anger. Peals of merriment and flashes of laughter, joy pouring down like a raincloud: the images danced tantalizingly before my eyes.

My eyes secretly followed her feet to the door. Feet coloured with henna. Silver anklets swung over the fair heels. When she put her foot down the sari covered the anklet, when she raised her foot, the anklet appeared once more. As she crossed the threshold the words almost rose to my lips, 'Listen, Prabha!' I don't know how I managed to hold down this tender and irresistible wish to call her. With difficulty I told myself that she must have gone to change her clothes and would soon return. Books, papers, studies—all swam away from me. All that was left was 'I', drowning in a sea of emotions, every moment losing command over myself. I felt as if the ground I sat on was swaying and tilting towards her.

Just then I heard Bhabhi's voice from the other end of the roof, perhaps from Bhaiya's room, 'No, Prabha, go and sleep there. If there's no bed, I'll bring you one. Your Jethji will be coming here any minute.'

She answered in a low voice, then Bhabhi's high voice could be heard again, 'But why don't you want to sleep there?' Something in her voice reminded me of the doctor business, because she added some joke in a lower tone. Prabha answered swiftly, as if she didn't like the joke. Then silence. Then Bhabhi again, 'Listen, Prabha, don't act this way. You are a bride. If you start like this how will you go on? You have to spend your whole life here. These things do happen.' Then I heard Prabha, this time quite loud, sharp and determined, 'Am I to go and force myself where I'm not wanted? Where am I to sleep there? I can't keep wagging my tail when I'm kicked, or lick the feet of one who rejects me. He has his board exams—

why should I disturb him? If anything happens, I'll be blamed. He sees my coming here as hell for him and you tell me to go there!'

Each word like a poisoned arrow tipped with pride and arrogance! Something pierced my brain like a bullet from a gun. I felt as if someone had ruthlessly pushed me down from a high tower. I sat up straight, my brows pulled together. 'So that's it, is it?' With sharpened vision I glared at the lifeless letters. That one sentence threw itself around in my heart like a powerful, caged tiger knocking itself against the bars, 'So that's it, is it?'

Oh, what a narrow escape! How close I had come to calling her! The words were on my tongue, I had thought out the whole sentence. I was nearly swept away by a terrible illusion, by the force of sentimentality. If I had called, I would have been shamed for life.

What pride! Each word dripping with acid. This was perhaps the second time I had heard her voice clearly. What a bold manner! Had I been about to bow before this sharp, dagger-like voice? It was God who saved me! I would have regretted it all my life. I have much to understand yet, I must understand this pride. Studied a little and thinks herself a goddess! What's the use of her studies! Bhabhi was right— she's very proud of her education and her looks. After all, only a woman can understand a woman. A man can't. She was absolutely right—I must keep her under control.

And I felt my arms throb with the desire to go and beat her, kick her, till she forgot all her pride. Sometimes Bhai Saheb gives Bhabhi a slap. I feel bad for hours after I see it. But at this moment I felt he was quite right. However idealistic we may be, what Tulsidas has written of woman sums up the wisdom of centuries. Woman? Woman has made many great ones dance to her tune. She is a monkey who will dance only when shown the rod.

What follies I was lost in a moment ago. Thoughts of future marital bliss, of play and laughter, with this woman? No, no, today I swear by all the deities and by God himself that never will I establish relations with this woman, never compromise with her. It's impossible. How can I get on with one who thinks she's the smartest in the world? Never, never.

What a prize idiot I am! Amar said something (who knows if it's true or false) and I began coupling earth and heaven! What does he understand of sarcasm! How terrible this world is! How slippery—the slightest slip and one is down. Impossible to recover one's foothold in that fast-flowing current. That is why our philosophers have termed it illusion and a snare.

Again light footsteps and a rustling—someone was coming. My thoughts were halted. Who could it be? That princess again—or was it Bhabhi, eager to read me a lesson? If it was Bhabhi I was in for a three-hour-long sermon. I repeated to myself several times—not even *Brahman*, Vishnu or Mahesh in person, no force on earth, can effect a compromise between us today. I know she will not bend. Her pride will not let her bend, and I too am not made of such clay. Iron against steel—let us see which breaks first.

She had reached the door—not Bhabhi—she. Without hesitating she crossed the threshold and went straight to her belongings. I sat stiffly, pretending to notice nothing. The trunk was opened and the basket, things were taken out and replaced, and I sat, watching all this from the corners of my eyes or guessing from the sounds. Something was spread out on the floor at the other end of the room and she lay down with her back to me, an old sari rolled up under her head.

Lie down! What do I care! Tossing my head, I returned to *Sohrab and Rustum*. Who does she think she is, after all—a heavenly nymph or an incarnation of Saraswati? How does her mind work? Madam must have realized what kind of person she has to deal with. I am not made of wax to melt at the slightest heat. Otherwise, could any other man in the world have shown such firmness and self-control on his wedding night? Her pride must have taken a beating that day itself. She must have planned to keep her husband under her thumb, to have him wag his tail like a pet dog. When she found things otherwise she must have thought I would come running after her in a day or two. And I? I say I can spend any number of lifetimes like this. Has studied a bit and thinks no end of herself! Lying there so stiff—lie there all night, lie there all your life! I won't ask why you're lying there! When you die I'll pick you up and throw you out, I don't even put up with my father's pride, and you—just who do you think you are?

Who needs you? My family entrapped me otherwise none of this would have happened. You would have been happy in your own house. I thought you would be sensible. But you have never known what good sense is. What a swamp Babuji has pushed me into—how happy I was, playing and enjoying myself! Anyway, now that I'm in it let me play the game.

And the night deepened. Sometimes the watchman's long-drawn, rhythmical cry would sound from one end to the other of the empty alleys and marketplaces, raising echoes that quavered and then drowned. Sometimes, far away, a train would growl and shriek, and compared to those terrible, demonic sounds the dogs' barking would seem like the mere scraping of mice around a garbage heap. Or a carriage would go by with a heavy rumble, the horse bells tinkling, and then the night, wrapped in deep silence, would again turn over and go to sleep. Immune to all else, I was engaged in an imaginary, heated debate with Prabha. I was in the grip of a desire to lecture her. I kept angrily repeating all my earlier arguments in her favour, answering each one with redoubled energy, abusing their futility and my folly. Grinding my teeth with rage I would say, 'Prabhaji, you have not yet realized whom your fate has confronted you with! When you realize that, you will understand what kind of man I am!' Then I'd quote some lines from *Sohrab and Rustum* as if they had been composed especially for this occasion. These were the lines in which Sohrab challenges Rustum, saying, 'I have fought in countless battles but never have I had to leave the battlefield vanquished nor has the foe ever escaped alive.' 'Remember, Prabhaji, "Never the field was lost nor the foe saved."'

I was absolutely right to act as I did that first day. My behaviour was not in the least improper. That is what a person like her deserves. From today, my foremost aim will be to crush her pride.

And the black stream of darkness ran slowly over the mountains and valleys of night; the night passed. The wick had burnt unevenly in the lantern, so the flame was rising higher on one side than the other. I sat still, thinking, oblivious to sleep or rest. Sometimes I would look with hatred at Prabha lying shrunken in a corner, and then get lost in myself once more. I'd pull a face and repeat with mockery, 'I won't go there.' Why had she come here then? Why didn't she go drown herself?

The wick was burning out, smoke gathered in thick folds around the edges of the lantern, and its clean glass chimney was overlaid with layer upon layer of blackness . . .

7

Next day I felt as if I had narrowly escaped some terrible mishap or avoided committing some grave offence. I kept congratulating myself on the fortunate chance that had saved me from being swept by emotion into so serious an error. Surely some god had protected me! Now I would see to this fine lady. Whenever I thought of Prabha's behaviour, I would clench my teeth and repeat in amazement, as if some truth were being revealed to me for the first time, 'Such arrogance? Taunting me about the board exam just because I mentioned it to Bhabhi at dinner?' Very well. All that had happened yesterday seemed today like a dream—a dream in which I had nearly died, and the memory of which still made my heart race.

That day, when Bhabhi was serving me food, I said to her, 'Bhabhi, do you want me to pass the exams or not?' Bhabhi took a roti off the fire with the tongs and replied, 'Why, what have I done, Lala?'

'It's not a question of what you have done. The question is, what do you people have in mind for me?'

'Say plainly what you mean. Don't talk in riddles,' Bhabhi said, bending her head as she prepared the next roti, though she had understood what I was getting at.

'As if you don't know what I mean! I said right from the start, don't get me into this mess. But no one listened to me. Now, if I fail, you can all sing your usual song about how good-for-nothing children are these days. I managed to get a separate room for myself so that I could study in peace, and now you stuff every Tom, Dick and Harry into it—how do you expect me to study? Only three months were left yet you couldn't wait.' I spoke loudly, conscious that she must be somewhere within earshot. Later, I thought with satisfaction that I had paid her back for her remark last night.

Bhabhi replied in the tone of an older person explaining things to a younger. 'It's like this, Lalaji, all of us want you to be happy. How can an outsider mean more to us than you? But you can see my condition for yourself. I will soon have to stop working, and then it is you who will get late for college every day. Now, she and Munni will manage somehow. I have no great hopes of that princess, but if she does at least this much, I'll be happy. I wouldn't be surprised if even this is too much for her. Let's see what kind of food she prepares.'

'What you're talking about is a general problem, it concerns everyone, why should I alone have to pay the price? It's my studies that will suffer the most,' I said angrily.

'It's not as if Ammaji is very happy either. Amar has told us the way she has talked to her family about us. We are greedy for money, we are like this, we are like that. This is her home now, after all. Isn't she shamed too by talking like that? Who's not greedy for money? Isn't her father greedy? She's his only daughter yet he couldn't give a decent dowry. To hell with such money! Will you take it with you to the next world? Finally, everyone has to go empty-handed. What's the use of having money if you don't spend freely even at a wedding? There are only a few occasions when you have to spend, after all.' At this point, Bhabhi suddenly fell silent. I understood—everyone must be discussing how much her parents would send if she had a son. That thought had suddenly silenced her. Silently, she continued cooking and I continued eating. I've never been interested in all this give and take—it's women's business. After a while, I asked, 'Bhabhi, all this is fine, but what am I to do?'

'But Lalaji, tell me, what other place is there in this house? There are just those two rooms.'

'What do I care—let her go to hell or go burn herself in the kitchen, just let me alone. Allow me to study.' I was exasperated.

'No, Lalaji, that's no way to talk,' Bhabhi said sympathetically. 'Your bride has just arrived and you talk like this?'

'When I have nothing to do with her why should I have this headache?'

'Oh, Lalaji, please don't talk so loud or Munni will say I am misleading you.' Then she asked in a gentle, intimate tone, 'Why are you so annoyed with her?'

'Shall I tell you?' I replied unhesitatingly. 'First, I didn't want to get married right now. This burden was imposed on me against my will. And second, I can't stand the sight of her. Am I to be forced to like her against my will? You did what you could. But you can't control every action of mine.'

61

'I don't know why you don't like her. Munni and Amma may be angry with her yet they say that she's the most beautiful bride who has ever come to this house.'

'Maybe. I didn't notice anything special,' I said in an indifferent tone.

'Her father said he couldn't give much cash because he'd spent twenty thousand rupees on her education; she was taught to play, to sing, to do fine needlework and embroidery. Well, now we'll see what revolution she brings about here.' Then she added, 'Why don't you allot her the duty of waking you each morning by singing "Awake, beloved Mohan". . .' And she was convulsed with laughter at her joke.

Downing a glass of water in one gulp, I said, 'This is no time for jokes. I beg you, allow me to study.'

'All right, I'll tell Amma. I can't think of any other place, though.'

'Tell Amma or Bhaiya or anyone you like—all I want is peace . . .'

As I collected my books and set out for college a thought came to me. Everyone said Prabha was beautiful. I should at least take one full look at her face. But someone immediately seemed to say, 'No, never, never.' I should not foster any such weakness in my breast. Once I let myself soften I'll be destroyed. All day I kept thinking, it was good that things turned out the way they did. I had escaped being burdened with another problem, an unnecessary nuisance. Now I could study with a free mind. This is the time to concentrate on building a firm base for myself. Who in this world ever dies for another? Each one looks out for himself. And I must also keep in mind that my path is not the path of common people. My path is that of making, of doing, of becoming. I will think of nothing but my studies, I'll work very hard. Let the whole world go to hell, I couldn't care less.

All day I was very cheerful, yet something kept simmering inside me: such contemptuous indifference—never before have I been treated in this way.

That night she didn't sleep in my room. I don't know where she slept, perhaps with Munni or with Bhabhi. I didn't bother to find out. Munni's posture of neutrality and my mother's silence did puzzle me, though. I got the feeling that Munni sympathized with Prabha. She must have slept with Munni. She was welcome to sleep anywhere she liked. For a long time, I kept thinking of ways to teach her a lesson. I did not want to miss any opportunity to treat her with disdain, even to insult her. It would not be enough merely to ignore her. How else would she realize that she was being punished for her offences? I must humble her pride. I felt as if I had arrived fully armed into the battlefield.

When I emerged from my bath next morning I said to Bhabhi, 'Bhabhi, why do you strain yourself now? This is the time for you to rest. After all, there's Munni, there are others in the house too, why should you be the only one to toil? If everyone has the right to eat, they must work too.'

I had seen her sitting near the pile of dirty dishes and scrubbing them, one by one. She touched them as if they were burning hot. I laughed to myself with cruel pleasure: an only daughter! She would never have had to wash dishes. Served her right!

And, after this, she was given the task of cooking for the

63

whole family. Bhabhi had been awaiting this opportunity. Munni helped out for a day or two, then gave up. She preferred to sit by herself, moping and crying. However, she was always ready with verbal sympathy for Prabha. If anyone complained about the food, she'd immediately speak up for her. 'She cooks all day. Isn't she a human being too? And on top of it, you find fault.' A couple of times she and I fell out sharply over this. I told her plainly, 'If that's how it is, why don't you help her with all the work?'

'Bhabhi, if you have a son I'll take a full set of new clothes. No excuses! It's decided in advance.' I heard Munni's voice as I was passing by. She saw me and said, 'I've made a bet with Bhabhi.' Bhabhi blushed deeply. She had turned pale of late but today she had acquired a strange, grave beauty. I had never seen her look so appealing.

Pushing Munni aside, she pretended to be embarrassed. 'How can you talk that way in front of the menfolk! Have some sense, do.'

An air of expectation hung heavy over the house. The sweeper woman had already announced that she would claim a sari and blouse. All who entered the house could talk of nothing else. Everyone wanted a boy and perhaps that is why they talked of a boy all the time. But Bhabhi and Amma would deliberately suppose the worst, as if fearing that the sweet dream of a son might be affected by the evil eye. They would say, 'It's God's will. If it's a girl, can anyone prevent it?' By talking of a girl they seemed to want to steel themselves for the pain they might have to endure; in fact, they had full faith that it would be a boy. Amma and Babuji were eagerly awaiting a first grandson, yet they also feared the expense it would entail. 'God knows what will happen,' they would murmur, thinking of the big feast that would have to be given. The days slipped by in these speculations. Bhabhi, clad in loose clothes, moved about as little as possible and sat smiling to herself, lost in her own thoughts.

And finally one night, after a great deal of commotion in the house, my brother became the father of a daughter. Amma hit her forehead with her hand, 'So Goddess Bhavani is the first to come to this house!' The expected joy seemed to have been blighted by untimely frost, yet everyone tried their best to appear happy. The midwife looked crestfallen. The nurse was grave-faced as she washed and bathed the child. The nurse had been called because the midwife had said that complications had set in. The room reeked of carbolic. That night all of us stayed awake. There was much running to and fro—heat the water, fetch this, fetch that. I don't know how Bhabhi felt, but Babuji did heave a quiet sigh of relief: the immediate expenditure had been forestalled. Now we could evade all demands by saying, 'No one distributes sweets or gives a feast at the birth of a girl!' But all he said was, 'Well, the house has been awarded its first degree!'

Munni teased me, 'Aren't you going to give me a treat now that you are an uncle?' I don't know whether or not I was pleased at having become an uncle, but I thoroughly enjoyed the thought that now there would be much more work to be done in the house. And who was there to do it but Prabha! Bhabhi needed someone to serve her, Amma was too old and unwell to be of any help. All she did was sit around telling her rosary and keeping track through Munni of all that went on in the house. Or she would keep issuing instructions to the barber's wife who had been appointed to look after Bhabhi for a week or so. Earlier it was Bhabhi who used to press Amma's feet at night after completing all the housework, and that was the time all the family affairs would be discussed threadbare.

According to our customs, parents cannot eat food cooked by a married daughter, so now all the work fell on Prabha.

Prabha would get up at some unearthly hour in the morning and prepare Bhabhi's special diet. By six in the morning she'd have finished that. Then she would wash the previous night's dishes, clean the kitchen, have a bath, and hurriedly start preparing breakfast so that those who were to go to college or to work should not get delayed. By noon, lunch would be ready; then she would wash the dishes and spend an hour or two sifting wheat or dal, or sitting with Bhabhi and stitching and mending Amar's and Kunwar's clothes. Preparations were afoot for the naming ceremony. At least thirty to forty people had been invited. Lentils and spices were being cleaned and ground. By three in the afternoon the stove would be lit again and she would be bending over it, blowing on the wood and wiping the tears from her eyes as the smoke billowed out. Her face would turn bright red. She'd be busy in the kitchen till eight or nine at night. Then there were all kinds of little tasks to be done for Bhabhi. Often, when I returned at night from Diwakar's place, I would see Prabha sitting near Amma, pressing her feet. Probably she didn't get to bed before midnight.

What surprised me most was that she did all this quietly, like clockwork, as if it caused her no hardship at all. She would take up each new task piled on her as if it were perfectly natural to her, and she never showed the slightest unwillingness or weariness. And this irritated me. If only she would show some unwillingness, some weariness, I could exult in her pain and think to myself, 'Well, madam, how do you feel now?'

Gradually everyone had begun to notice that Prabha did not cover her face in front of elders. In the beginning, as long as she kept her head bowed, it hadn't been noticed. Babuji always coughed before entering. A couple of times he found Prabha with her face uncovered but thought she hadn't observed him coming in. But when he realized that Prabha merely turned around and did not veil her face, he said to Amma, 'What's the difference between a daughter and a daughter-in-law if both go around with unveiled face and open hair?' This caused a big uproar. Bhabhi flung taunts as usual, and Amma too paused while telling her rosary to say in exasperated tones, 'Bahu, perhaps your family does not observe parda, but you have to follow the customs of our family. You need not veil yourself before me if you don't want to, but behave with some modesty before the elders of the community. I've never heard of such shameless behaviour. The whole community is talking of it. Whoever sees you condemns us. Lots of people will come for the naming ceremony, what will they say? What is it to us if it is customary to dance naked in your family?' My brother rebuked me a couple of times, 'Samar, why don't you make your wife behave herself? Amma and Babuji don't like it at all. She ought to do as they say out of respect for them. Not that I think parda is a good practice, but it's a tradition in our family. What metal is your wife made of—she turns a deaf ear to all of Amma's reproaches and scoldings, as if it's the mere barking of a dog.' And this was true too. She never answered back but she never once veiled herself, despite all the scoldings. She behaved as if she hadn't heard anything that was said. This refusal to react irritated Amma even more, but on this issue Prabha was like a stone. All Amma could do was keep repeating, 'Bahu, of what use is such shamelessness? How will it hurt you to cover your forehead? Till today, the women of this house have never lifted the veil above the chin.'

On principle I am opposed to parda. As a student of history I know that parda increased after the advent of the Muslims. But when I saw this opposition put into practice, I was shocked. It was a novel sight for me to see Prabha walking with uncovered face in front of my parents. After all, in what other way can respect for parents-in-law and elders be expressed? True, she walked with her head bent, but is respect merely a matter of lowering one's head and eyes? But how was I to communicate this to her? A couple of times I said loudly to Munni, 'Munni, this sister-in-law of yours is very rude. Has no one taught her how to behave respectfully and politely?' But she turned a deaf ear to this too. Finally, everyone had to compromise on this question and get used to her behaviour. Now, in fact, they notice it only when some visitor arrives. At such times Amma tried to keep Prabha out of the way.

In the beginning, everyone was surprised at the way Prabha took on all the work at once, but gradually the fault-finding began. Even Munni would say in kindly tones, 'Bhabhi, don't use so much ghee. You'll run short of it later.' The advent of one more member had further weakened the already tottering economy of the household. Babuji was often to be seen pacing about near Amma's bed, running his hand over his head and saying, 'Mother of Dheeraj, expenses are piling up day by day. What is poor Dheeraj to do? He's working himself to death. Is it his fault the family is so large? If Samar somehow manages to get through and finds a job, Dheeraj will get some relief. I feel miserable when I look at him, anxiety and work have reduced him to a skeleton. He never sits down to talk, never goes to see friends. How long can he keep up this pace? How his youth is being destroyed, the days when he should be happy and carefree! What times we are living in! Could we ever have foreseen this? And this wretched Munni is another burden on us. She must go back. I've tried talking to the other elders and I was somewhat hopeful, but these days no one is willing to talk straight. Each one wants to be recompensed in advance.' Seeing Prabha pass by, he would turn away and say huskily, 'Be a little thrifty, daughter. Sacks of rupees used to lie around in this very house. Ghee used to flow like water but what is left of all that now . . .'

Despite all this moaning and groaning, I was well looked after. Whenever I returned from college I would find my room neat as a pin, all the things I had left scattered were tidily arranged, and the lantern gleaming. When I saw this, a mild depression would seize me. But I would dismiss it as exhaustion caused by hard work.

Sometimes I would get exasperated with myself. Why was I so obsessed with Prabha? How she eats, where she sleeps, how she works; she doesn't rest for even a moment! I constantly find fault with well-cooked vegetables, complaining of too much or too little salt and spices; I keep flinging taunts at her while talking to Amma, Bhabhi or Munni in her presence; I make sarcastic remarks. The fact is that my attention is focused on her. As if I have nothing better to do. Shouldn't I be studying? Why don't I concentrate as much on my studies? If I fail this time I will not only be disgraced but also find all roads closed to me. I have decided to ignore her, why then am I so entangled in thoughts of her? It's become a habit with me to keep track of all her movements. Why give her so much importance? Why not treat her as just another dog or cat in the house? Time and again, I decided to think as little as possible about her, but somehow or other my thoughts would get diverted towards her. When I returned in the evening to find my dirty vest washed and hung out to dry and, later, neatly folded and put away, I would forget all about my studies and start thinking of Prabha once more.

Another change had taken place. Formerly, whenever some new and difficult task was imposed on Prabha, I would be heartily pleased—good, let her suffer. I would eagerly wait to see how she reacted. Deep down, I also wanted to find out where and when she sat down to cry. If only I could catch and shame her at such a moment! When I shivered in the cold late at night or early in the morning, I would wonder how she must be feeling, washing dishes or cleaning the kitchen. But as she continued accepting each fresh task with ease, and doing all the work without a reaction or a murmur, my enthusiasm gradually began to wane. And in place of that earlier satisfaction, unease and perplexity beset me. As when a weapon fails to hit its target and the question arises: Now what? What is to be done next? Defeat could not be accepted so easily!

Sometimes, while he was eating, Bhai Saheb would say, 'Bahu, why don't you go and sit with your sister-in-law for a while? The poor thing must be feeling lonely—she may need something or other too.' Although Prabha didn't cover her face before them, she never spoke to my father or elder brother; she would keep working with her head bent low. Her lips would flutter, wanting to tell Bhai Saheb that she sat with Bhabhi every afternoon. She would look up as if to say something but then bow her head again.

The day of the naming ceremony. When I reached home in the evening I found a scene in full swing. Amma was yelling at the top of her voice, 'Because we keep quiet she's getting totally out of hand. Must the whole world run as you want it to? Do we count for nothing? All of us are fools. You are the only learned one. What a thing to do on an auspicious day! I had no idea what she was up to, and before I knew it, she had done this!'

All the others were standing around as if in a state of shock. Bhabhi, lying on her bed in her room, was sobbing loudly, 'To hell with such education! Is education for one's own improvement or to take the life of another? O God! Who knows what will happen now?' Munni was standing quietly, looking on. I realized that something serious had happened. One look at Prabha, standing frightened and shocked in a corner, was enough to tell me that she was the offender. Making an effort to control herself, she said in a husky voice, 'Ammaji, I'd never have done it if I'd known. I thought it was an ordinary lump of clay.'

'Of course it is only an ordinary lump of clay,' Amma replied, getting even more enraged. 'Look at her answering back as if she's my grandmother. Why should you bother to see what it was? Had you gone mad? Were you blind? Couldn't you see the sacred thread tied round it? Look at the way she keeps on talking back. Your parents have certainly brought you up well, taught you to argue with elders. Roams around with her face bare as a frying pan, regardless of who may be coming or going, and to top it all, has a tongue as sharp as a pair of scissors. If my daughter talked back the way you do I'd pull out her tongue and bury her alive.' Amma's fury kept growing, and being talked back to made her feel so insulted that she began to cry.

I only half-understood what was going on. In a loud voice I asked, 'Munni, what has happened?' Seeing how angry I looked, Munni said nothing. Kunwar told me, 'In the morning the priest prepared and worshipped Ganeshji, and Chhoti Bhabhi used the clay image to wash the dirty dishes.' This reminded Bhabhi afresh of her wrongs and she burst out crying with redoubled vigour.

My heart beat loudly. I could still hear Amma whimpering. Bhabhi was saying, 'If anything happens what will it matter to her? She'll wash her hands of it. O God, you see everything. You understand everyone. The world is full of envy and spite. O God!'

I drew in my breath, clenched my teeth and went thundering up to her, glaring at her with unblinking eyes, like a cat about to pounce on a mouse. I relaxed my right hand, weighed it and *wham*! All five fingers fell on Prabha's left cheek. The slap was delivered with all my might. She tottered, nearly fell, righted herself, and sat down on the floor with a thump. I said, 'You bitch, if you want to live here behave properly. Otherwise get out right now and go wherever you want to. Fancy yourself an atheist, do you?'

Still glaring at her, I returned to my former position with the air of a football player who has scored a goal. Everyone was stunned. Amma's anger and tears both vanished in a moment. Bhabhi too was silent.

But I was now shaken by such a wave of self-hatred and guilt that I could not stay there. I quietly turned and left. I don't know what happened next, whether or not she cried, whether she continued to lie there or if somebody picked her up and took her inside. All I remember is that the slap was delivered with all my strength and each finger throbbed with the impact.

As I entered my room, someone began chanting in my head, 'What have I done? How could I have done it?' For the first time in my life I had raised my hand against a woman. I felt as if my hand was becoming paralysed and beginning to rot away. I remembered how harshly I had criticized my brother from time to time for hitting Bhabhi. What excitement was it that had blinded me? I had spoken to her for the first time in seven or eight months, and in abusive language! Communicated for the first time with a slap! For a long time I could not believe what had happened.

Then a voice of poisonous loathing spoke up, 'You low-down coward, you scum! Is this your idealism? Are these your dreams of becoming great? Are you the one who is studying for the intermediate exam and goes around mouthing all kinds of platitudes?' And before it could go further, the storm that had been building up within broke. Racked by sobs, I wondered—what madness was it that had carried me away? If only my whole being could flow away in these tears! I was so overcome by guilt that I felt like slapping myself again and again until my fingers fell off...

8

'When do your exams begin, brother?' Munni asked. 'Exams?' I scratched my neck. For the life of me I couldn't remember when they were to begin. Although I had been in the habit of reminding myself daily of the date of the exams and their overwhelming importance, right now I could not even take in the meaning of what Munni had said. In fact, at first I had difficulty in making out who was speaking to me. Then, once the idea of the exams sank in, I sat still, thinking about them. I forgot Munni's presence and her question.

Was I slowly going mad? As soon as this occurred to me, I told myself forcefully, 'No, no. I never behave in an incoherent manner, my thoughts proceed in an orderly sequence. I go through the day's routine in a normal manner.' The more I tried to convince myself that I was not going mad, the stronger grew the belief that I definitely was. And if I was, when had it begun?

The slap delivered with all my force, the head slamming against the wall, Prabha swaying and falling—each time the scene rose before my eyes as if revealed by a flash of lightning, my heart would feel like a dam about to burst. I was constantly gnawed by remorse and guilt, conscious that I ought not to have acted as I had. How could I have raised my hand against her? How could I have descended to such savagery? Had it really happened? Was it not a fantasy, a dream of mine?

But she should not have acted that way, either. Couldn't she tell the difference between a lump of clay and Ganeshji? Who gave her the right to insult other people's faith? Just because she is educated? I am also educated. But never will I put up with any sort of disregard for our culture and our deities. It is good that she was taught a lesson. By exaggerating the extent of her offence, I would try to tell myself I had acted justifiably. After all, if something untoward did happen, who would be responsible? True, after reading books like *Satyarthprakash* I had lost faith in all these gods and goddesses, yet I respected the faith of others. Why should I insult what I do not worship? So I would argue and try to convince myself, but a voice within me would insist that it was not right for me to have hit her.

The day after this incident, I did not have the courage to appear outdoors. When I awoke, I felt as if I'd got up after a long illness. My body ached abominably. How would I dare look people in the eye? Or face the light of day after having committed such a crime? What if she should cross my path and I should see the mark on her cheek? How would I endure that sight? Oppressed by these perplexities, I stole out like a thief and roamed about aimlessly all day. Sitting under a tree in the park I asked myself: what is happening to me? Why am I so absorbed in myself all the time, why have I become so irritable, why do I delight in hurting others, why do I lose control of myself, hit out at people, fight and burst into tears? Whatever explanations I may offer myself, wouldn't anyone, judging by my behaviour, decide that I am losing my sanity? A fine marriage it was indeed! What is this that has happened to me?

After many days, I once again went towards the temple. I didn't go in, though, but sat in my usual place outside. O God, what a dreadful thing I have done. What shall I do now?

Every now and then, I would feel exasperated with myself—why had I taken on this headache? How detrimental it was to my interests to be constantly thinking about Prabha or my behaviour towards her! Was this all that was left for me to do in the world? In class I sit dumb as a dodo, outside it I walk around long-faced. Night and day, only this one obsession! In the last eight or ten months I've forgotten how to talk, how to smile, how to laugh.

That day I once again resolved to let bygones be bygones. Now I would not think of anything except the exams. It was wrong to keep brooding over the past. I have nothing to do with anyone in the world, no one belongs to me. I have not wronged anyone nor am I responsible for anyone. All come into the world with their own destiny, all choose their own path. O God, be my witness, forgive the errors I have committed. In future I will keep to myself, and concentrate only on my studies.

And after that day I actually began to find a strange change in myself. Whether inside the house or outside, I now was quite unperturbed by things that formerly used to destroy my mental peace for hours. I would see what was going on and then return to thoughts of my studies, my exams. I compelled myself to wrestle night and day with the demon of study. If I stayed at home I was bound to get distracted, so I generally stayed outside. I would glance at a newspaper in the shop of some news agent, and spend the rest of the day with Diwakar. We did not waste time chatting. Only occasionally, if he started off on some topic, we might get talking. He often spoke with great respect and affection of a friend of his called Shirish. He promised to introduce me to him whenever he next came over. I was not particularly enthused by the prospect. Everyone was astonished at the intensity of my involvement with my studies.

At home, no one talked about what had happened that day. Babuji and Bhai Saheb heard about it; Bhabhi seemed quite pleased. My younger brothers stayed out of my way as if afraid that I might pounce on them for no reason. This made me wonder—did I really have a frightening appearance? Huh, what of it? I would toss my head and go back to work. Nowadays, everyone seemed to be self-absorbed. I didn't see much of Bhabhi. Whenever I came home, she would be sitting alone, busy with her child. Nursing her or oiling her or bathing her. After the child's birth, she had completely given up doing housework. Munni was free to do as she pleased. She spent her time playing with the child or lying around, lost in thought. All the housework fell to Prabha's share. But this did not seem to me anything worthy of notice or at all strange. I had long ago given up thinking about when she ate and when she rested. Whenever a letter came for her, one of us would always open it. The letter would be given to her only after we had read it. And when she wrote a letter and gave it to someone to post, it was always read before it was posted. The envelope would be moistened with water and opened. What if complaints or criticism of the family were being transmitted to her or by her? And, gradually, she seemed to give up writing letters altogether.

One day I heard Amma say to her, 'Bahu, don't you ever write to your parents? Your father has written to enquire whether you are ill.'

'What to write, Ammaji? As you see, all is well,' Prabha said, pausing while grinding the chutney.

'I know, I know. But even so, daughter, you could write a couple of lines now and then. Only a parent knows a parent's heart. They say they have written you five or six letters and you haven't replied to a single one.' It had been a long time since Amma had talked to Prabha in so mild a tone.

I was emptying a shopping bag before leaving to get the rations and I saw her eyes fill with tears. She was quiet a little while, then she swallowed and said softly, 'I'll write, Ammaji.'

I left without a second look. I don't know if the matter was discussed further. That little conversation kept coming back into my head but I forced myself to concentrate on my studies.

I began to feel that my sensitivity, my capacity to feel, was gradually being eroded, paralysed. Nothing seemed worth considering long or deeply. For instance, now it was she who did everything for me. But I was as indifferent as ever. At night she would keep a pitcher of water next to my bed. If Amma, Babuji or Bhai Saheb ever asked for jaggery tea, a cup would quietly reach me too. Without looking to see who had brought it, I would drink it. Since, these days, it was generally she who was in the kitchen, I had some difficulty at meal times. I used to call out to Munni to come and serve me. But, gradually, Prabha began to do the serving. If I wanted more, I would push the plate towards her and she would ladle out whatever was needed. At first this seemed a very strange and even amusing arrangement, but then the novelty of it wore off and I stopped feeling awkward. I felt things could go on in this way all life long. Just as one uses a machine or takes water from a tap, I would get what I wanted and not give it a second thought. And, after all, except for talking, everything else was normal, all the work was done as required. I had forgotten to think of Prabha as a live, sensitive human being with whom I had any relationship. I looked at all things as if they were remote from and unconnected to me. So I went on, oblivious to everything.

This process of oblivion grew so accelerated that it frightened me. Could it be the prelude to madness? Each day that passed became dim and untrue as a dream, and all that was to come was overshadowed by a disinterested dullness. I felt as if I were growing oblivious not only to the world and everything around me but even to myself; I could barely remember to bathe and to eat on time. Suddenly a whim would seize me and I would sit down to read the Gita. I would forget to keep my clothes and other things in order. I would put down a book I was reading, forget where I had kept it, and spend hours searching for it. And when, finally, I found it right there, in the pile of my books, I would slap my forehead in frustration. I would constantly lose my pen, pencil, keys or money, or rather forget where I'd kept them. Things came to such a pass that by evening I would have forgotten what

I'd read that morning. Whichever book I picked up appeared entirely new to me. I felt dazed. As if my consciousness was slowly dying, or as if that inner being which used to be turbulent like the surface of a lake was freezing and becoming hard, immovable, lifeless as ice. Whatever fell on it would bounce off and fall some distance away, leaving it unmarked.

All I still remembered was that I had to take my exams.

As a stream of water flows over a hard rock, the waves of time, of days and nights, flowed over me, and I, unmoved, saw that the rock remained just as it was.

It was nearly ten and the dal had not yet begun to boil. Prabha was hurriedly kneading the flour. I had looked into the kitchen and was thinking of leaving without eating when Munni came running up. 'Prabha, you haven't taken Bhabhi her milk. She's very angry, she's started crying.' Prabha, still kneading the flour, replied mildly, 'The milk is ready but I want to prepare the meal because it's time for everyone to leave for work.' Then she said coaxingly, 'Won't you give it to her, please? It's in a covered bowl near the stove.'

Munni went towards the stove and then cried out, 'Oh, the milk is spilt! Now what?'

'Spilt?' She grew pale and leapt up. 'I kept it very carefully, what could have happened?'

'Now Bhabhi will create a real furore.' Just then Amar was heard complaining to Amma, 'Look, Amma, it's ten o'clock and the food is not ready. When is one supposed to eat, and when is one supposed to go to school?'

'She'll work at a snail's pace, never mind if you get late,' Amma replied tauntingly. She would interrupt her prayers to make these remarks and then pick up her recitation where she had left off. 'If it were a new job one could understand the delay. But not to be able to manage the work you do every day . . .'

Amar came into the kitchen, still grumbling. 'The flour is still being kneaded and the dal . . .' He leant over the partition in the kitchen to see what stage the dal had reached. His eyes began to water with the smoke. Munni was standing near the spilt milk, and a frightened-looking Prabha was mopping it up with her floury hands. Amar at once yelled out, 'Rivers of milk are being spilt here!'

Amma forgot all about her prayers. The gunpowder caught fire. 'Spilt the milk? Very good! What does she care? Her father sent us a buffalo to provide milk so she can spill it and let it boil over as she pleases. And the dal boiling over too with no one to bother about it. She's gone blind. The proverb is right: when a slut moves, the whole house shakes. Whenever she walks around she knocks something over or breaks something. God knows what's wrong with her limbs. Goes around with her head held high, like a rogue elephant. Drank up two and a half kilos of milk herself, and the poor older one will have to go hungry. She has not one good quality, not a single one. To hell with such education! Has studied up to class ten, indeed! Look at the mess the kitchen is in! The rolling pin lying here, the board lying there. Anyone would feel sick having to eat in such a place. O God, a nice curse you have saddled us with . . .'

I took my books and left for college at this point. Had this happened some time ago, I don't know what I would have said or done. Now I felt none of this was worth bothering about.

81

I felt no need to think about what Prabha did or whether she was right or wrong. I felt as if nothing at all abnormal was happening. I had begun to feel as if I had no relationship with Prabha and as if my family did not belong to me.

When I came home in the coffee break, I found a covered plate in my room. I quickly gulped down the food and rushed off. It didn't seem strange to me. I did sense that an epic battle had taken place in the interval. Huh, what is it to me . . .

It was early February and bitterly cold. The exams were to begin in early March, so I was on preparatory leave. I used to go and study at Diwakar's place because there was just no corner of our house where one could study undisturbed in the afternoon and evening. Some row or other would be on or I would be sent off on an errand. 'Just go to the mill and get some flour, Bhaiya,' Munni would say. Or Bhabhi would ask, 'Please get me a good tonic from the doctor, Lalaji.' Also, when we both studied together, we understood things better. Sometimes we'd go to a teacher's house for help. I wouldn't dare go alone. Diwakar had his own room, quite separate from the rest of the house, so sometimes I'd spend the night there. I felt much more at peace in his house than in my own. Whenever I went home everyone would be grumpy, either because a fight had just occurred or else one was in progress. Amma would be in tears or Bhabhi would be muttering to herself. One thing which sometimes shook me was that Prabha's face was always unchanged, emotionless, as if made of stone. Always serious, almost inauspiciously death-like. There were dark hollows round her eyes, and her lips were chapped from the cold. Her heels too were cracked, the fissures encrusted with dirt.

Returning from Diwakar's house one morning, I heard

Amma affectionately chiding Prabha, 'When did you last wash your hair? Look at it—it's matted with dirt. You silly girl, can't you wash it now and again? Or if you can't, let me burn it up and solve the problem for you! It must be full of lice—they must be falling into the food too.'

For once, Amma's voice didn't sound angry or sarcastic. Perhaps this led Prabha to pluck up courage and reply, 'You tell me, Ammaji, where's the time to wash it?'

One can never say what will make Amma flare up. Immediately, her voice grew sharp. 'Oh, so now you want to tell me how overworked you are, do you? Wonderful! A fine daughter-in-law you are, you want to taunt me with the work you do! So you have no time to do anything for yourself? You find time to eat, don't you? Just count and tell me how many tasks you perform. Cooking two meals a day—that one task is all you do. If you choose to take all day about it, that's up to you. And tell me, in which home do daughters-in-law do no work? Perhaps in your father's house there are a dozen servants to do all the work, but in this house, madam, all the work will be done by the daughters-in-law.'

I was at the tap, cleaning my teeth with powdered charcoal. Rocking her crying baby in her arms, Bhabhi looked at me and said, 'Look what a fuss she makes every day just because she has to do a little work. Didn't I do all this work? Did I ever complain of it to Ammaji? She's barely begun to do a little, and is already telling us what a great favour she's doing us! Don't throw it in my face, Bahu, I'll return all the work you've done with interest. Or next I'll hear—'

At this, Bhaiya growled, 'What is this constant bickering in aid of? What a way to start the day! Have you nothing better to do? Look at the time—it's nearly nine.'

But no one was impressed by his argument. Amma retorted, 'She behaves this way despite all our bickering. If we kept quiet, all the housework would come to a standstill. She's the kind who gets moving only when kicked. Say nothing, and not a leaf will stir. If I don't say anything do you think she'll ever mend her sari? Look at it, caked with dirt. Why, madam, can't you see how dirty and torn your sari is? The truth is, she's too lazy to wash it. All she wants to do is sit on the bed with a book . . .'

One quick glance while washing my face was enough to tell me that the sari was worn so thin that it wouldn't stand up either to mending or to washing. Through the rents, I could see the hairs on her legs, stiff with cold. 'Huh, what is it to me?' I thought and walked off, towelling my face and neck. I felt not the slightest desire to find out how the quarrel proceeded. I felt as if I had never had the ability to think or to feel.

When I returned that afternoon Babuji was berating her. 'You don't veil yourself before us, fine, we'll steel ourselves to bear that. But don't cross all limits in your shamelessness. Didn't you give a thought to what all the neighbours would say when you went up on the roof and washed your hair there? In winter, everybody goes up and sits on the roof to bask in the sun. What else would they do but gape? And this Munni— she's a big girl now but has no sense. There she sat, pouring water over her head!'

Munni pulled a face and replied, 'What funny things you say, Babuji! It's so cold these days. You men pour a couple of pitchers over yourself and that's it, you've bathed, but can our hair be washed that way? It takes ages. How can one get drenched in the cold down here in the yard? The water's icy cold. In the sunshine on the roof it's tolerable—so what if she went up there?'

'Well, winter can't be escaped.' Babuji cooled down at Munni's intervention. Amma said, 'I can't afford firewood at three rupees a maund to heat water all day. If it was a matter of one person, it could be done—two maunds of wood would be required just to heat water for this whole army.'

Amma had become amazingly articulate of late! Bhabhi always hung around, holding the baby in her arms.

And my whole being was benumbed as if someone had injected opium into me. Sometimes I felt I had been encased in a thick sheath where no sound could reach me and nothing could touch me. I wasn't even sure whether I was a speaking, feeling creature. As though all sensitivity had been suffocated in me. Everything, without and within, seemed unreal. The outer crust had grown hard, and inside too something was solidifying and growing harder every instant. Would all of me, outside and inside, harden and turn to stone . . .?

No, I must not think this way. My exams begin in a week's time.

9

I was feeling very lighthearted and cheerful when I emerged from the hall after completing the last paper. I was satisfied with my performance. A big load was off my head. Now that the task which used to keep me obsessively occupied was over, what would I do? Before I could consider this problem, Diwakar said, 'Come on, let's go and see a film. It's been ages since we went to the cinema.' I would have been in a quandary as to how to respond had he not continued, 'It's my treat today, and if mother allows, we'll take Kiran along too. God knows when the poor girl last saw a film. She must be cursing herself for having got into such a black hole!'

When we parted he again reminded me to be sure to reach his house on time that evening, and not lose myself in philosophical speculations. Poor fellow didn't know what awaited me at home!

Munni's husband had suddenly turned up. For some reason, I had never been able to stand the sight of him. The whole house was in turmoil; everyone was astonished. He had been put up in the outer sitting room. Babuji and Bhai Saheb sat there with him most of the time. As soon as he arrived he said he had come to fetch Munni. We had had no word from him for about two-and-a-half years, he had never tried to find out whether Munni was dead or alive, he'd ignored the dozens of letters Babuji wrote to him, and turned a deaf ear to the community elders. Naturally, all of us were taken aback to see him here all of a sudden. I was stunned when I heard that he had come to fetch Munni. Everyone in the house walked around with a sort of furtive excitement, eager to discuss it with each other. Only Prabha and Munni were silent, busy in the kitchen. Bhabhi and Amma conversed in undertones, making all kinds of speculations, and every now and then sending Kunwar out with instructions, 'Go quietly and hear what your father and he are saying.' Bhabhi herself would tiptoe up to the door, hide behind it and listen, then come back and give Amma a full report, with embellishments. Everyone was eager to know the reason for this unexpected change of heart. The conversation in the sitting room appeared to be of a serious nature.

After dinner had been served, Babuji appeared and informed Amma, 'Munni will leave tomorrow morning, by the ten o'clock train.' A stunned silence fell over the house.

All of us gathered around to find out what was happening. Amma was already annoyed at having had to wait so long to find out. Exasperated, she exclaimed, 'Sit down and tell me what it's all about. What do you mean, Munni will go tomorrow? What's come over the wretch now? What kept him away all these years?' Amma kept her voice low, to prevent its reaching the sitting room.

87

Babuji sat down at the foot of her bed, a small lantern at his feet. All of us gathered around. We squatted in a circle, chins on knees, shivering in the cold. Munni was already there, in a corner, leaning against the wall. Bhabhi had put the child to bed early, and appeared with her face veiled. Prabha was not to be seen. The light of the lantern was dimmed by the shadows of the four of us sitting around it. Kunwar was hesitantly warming his hands above the lantern, afraid that someone would rebuke him. But no one took any notice.

Babuji explained, 'He has come to fetch Munni. He's begging to be forgiven, regretting his mistake and saying it will never happen again. He says if we hear of any misbehaviour by him he'll suffer any punishment the community decides. What could I do—he was almost crying!'

'But what's making him cry now? Why has the rascal suddenly come to his senses? What's become of that witch?' Amma's style of talking about her son-in-law had changed.

'It's because of that witch that he has come to his senses. About six months ago, she suddenly made off with a lot of clothes and jewels. He reported it to the police but she is not to be found. Now he has realized his folly.'

We were startled. So that was it! His lordship had arrived because he was in need! Kunwar said angrily, 'Babuji, you should refuse to send Munni.'

But in that atmosphere of high seriousness, no one took any notice of him. Bhai Saheb said, 'He says she has ruined him. She had blinded him so that he didn't know where his interests lay. She misled him and his wits went astray!'

'Went astray indeed!' Amma tossed her head in anger. Then she sighed deeply and added, 'How can one rely on such a man? Tomorrow he'll be misled by someone else. I won't send my daughter with him. The first time he beat her half-dead, this time he'll finish her off altogether.'

'But he's vowing to behave himself, he's swearing and promising,' Babuji tried to convince her. 'The way he talks he seems to have learnt his lesson. After all, mother of Dheeraj, what if he made one mistake—he won't necessarily keep repeating it all his life. At that age, a man may get carried away—I've had a plain talk with him.'

Amma was not convinced. She said dismissively, 'Your talk! Anyone can lead you by the nose.'

'This is precisely what I don't like about you! This is what angers me. You refuse to understand the situation and keep singing your own song. You might listen to others too, sometimes.' Babuji went on in troubled, defeated tones, 'True, he's driven by his own need, but at least he's come himself to fetch her. The way he talks one can make out he's sorry and won't harass her again. If that's how things are, why not send her? In any case, what do you plan to do—keep her here all her life? We can't afford to educate her or get her trained in any trade—it's hard enough to afford the boys' education. And then, each one has his own responsibilities. How long can we keep her? Or else, let's get her married to someone else.'

Amma interrupted at once. 'Shame on you. How can you talk that way before the children? Get her remarried indeed! The whole community, the whole city will spit on us. Not that we have such a great reputation to begin with! It seems your hobnobbing with the Arya Samajis has turned your wits!'

'Then tell me, what am I to do? When I say something sensible you won't listen. Anything else makes you mad. You tell me what to do. I think we won't get a better chance than this. He's come himself to request us. And think of this, what will become of Munni here? There, she'll be mistress of her own house. There's no point crying over spilt milk. You are one of those who would chase out the snake when it comes to your courtyard and later go to its hole to worship it.'

Amma had opened her mouth to retort when Munni suddenly burst into tears, startling all of us. She had been sitting quietly against the wall, hugging her knees, either from the cold or to hide her face. Now her body shook with sobs. I was sitting closest to her. I put my hand on her forehead to raise her face and said in distress, 'What's the matter, Munni, what's the matter? Why are you crying?'

She pushed my hand away and cried even louder.

'Say something, Munni! Tell us why you're crying,' Bhai Saheb said gently.

After a while, with great difficulty, she managed to say between sobs, 'Babuji, give me poison with your own hands and kill me, strangle me, but don't send me there! Don't send me there, Babuji! I'll die there. I beg you, I fall at your feet, don't send me away.' And she pounced on Babuji's feet, embraced them, and wept aloud.

Our eyes filled with tears. Amma kept wiping her tears as they fell and sighing deeply.

'What are you doing?' Babuji bent down and pulled her into his lap. She lay face down on his lap and kept crying like a cow being led to the slaughter. She tried to stifle her cries by stuffing Babuji's shirt into her mouth but the sobs welled up in powerful bursts, as if they would break her frail ribcage. Her shoulders and her whole body shook with great spurts of weeping. Bent over, with his chin on her trembling, dark-haired head, Babuji too wept soundlessly. Stroking her back, he tried to still the restlessness of his own heart. Tears fell from our eyes too, the sharp, salty acid finding its way to our lips. Trying to repress our emotions and the water flowing from our noses, we would repeatedly draw deep, shuddering breaths. Finally Kunwar could bear it no longer. He went and clung to Amma and cried, 'Amma, we won't let Munni Didi go. Don't send her.'

We were tormented by the memory of our frequent neglect and even occasional ill-treatment of this unhappy girl. I resolved in my heart that I would keep Munni with me, no matter what. Couldn't we afford to provide food and clothes for one girl? After eight or ten minutes, when the weeping had somewhat subsided, Munni said again, 'Babuji, I'll work as a maidservant or I'll grind grain and support myself, but don't send me there with him.'

Babuji had regained his composure. He said persuasively, 'Have you gone mad, child? Are we strangers to you? If anything goes wrong you just come back here any time, even at midnight. You have first rights over this house, we come later. But believe me, nothing will happen this time.'

'No, Babuji, no!' The words burst from her as if she saw a terrible demon before her. 'Don't push me into that well, Babuji . . .'

This time, Babuji groaned like a wounded man, 'It's for your own good, child! That's your house, if you don't look after it, it will go to ruin. It's for your own good! If you stay here, no one will respect you, everyone will point at you. How can we stop people from gossiping?'

'The day you hear that I have misbehaved, you can poison me with your own hands!' she said, still crying. It seemed as if nothing could stem her tears.

Babuji too began to cry again. This time it looked as if he would continue for some time. His lips were trembling uncontrollably. Then he gently pushed Munni to one side, got up and hurriedly went out.

All of us sat there for about an hour, silent, stupefied. As it grew colder and we began to feel sleepy we got up and left, one by one. Only Munni remained, lying on Amma's bed and whimpering softly.

Next morning, Munni was sent on her way. She cried aloud, she sobbed, she clung to us and wept. She said nothing more, she just kept crying as if in a fit of hysteria. She held on to Prabha and wept as if they were parting for many lives to come. They seemed unable to let go of one another. It was time for the train to leave so they had to be separated. Babuji had absented himself on the pretext of some work.

Munni was closest to me in age so I was the fondest of her. She put her arms around me and wept passionately. My throat was tight and I felt as if my body would explode, my ribs burst apart and my heart leap out through my mouth. All she could say was, 'Bhaiya, talk to Prabha, she hasn't done anything wrong . . .'

And after that, she left. She seemed barely conscious, she simply cried and cried. I watched the train till it was out of sight. When we got home I shut myself in my room. Tears flowed ceaselessly from my eyes and fell into my lap, and I sat motionless, as if in a meditative trance. Something which I could not comprehend reverberated in my heart.

The house was like a house of death. One sat gloomily here, another was sobbing there. It was as if we had just returned from a cremation. Every wall of the house seemed to wail aloud.

10

It was past eleven when I left Diwakar's house after dinner. I hadn't informed them at home that I would be late. Now I was in for a good scolding: 'Can't you at least let us know before you go out?' Even to get the door opened at this time of night would be difficult. Whoever came to open it would consider it his prime duty to deliver a lecture on the inconvenience caused to him by my irresponsibility. My heart sank as I neared home. The road and all the bylanes lay deserted. Obstructed by the houses, moonlight fell in patches on the road. It created a strange, unreal effect as it mingled with the mist.

For some reason, I felt very uneasy, and something tugged at my heart. Munni's husband's arrival had prevented us going to the cinema the day we had planned. So we had decided to go a couple of days later. The film had ended around ten o'clock. I hadn't cared much for the film, but some love scenes between the hero and heroine did have an impact on me, and I felt a pang, wishing I too could experience such feelings. It was a long time since I'd last seen a film. On the way back, Diwakar and I walked together, and Kiran walked at a slight distance from us. Many other people too were walking home, discussing various aspects of the film. Kiran rarely spoke to me or in my presence. The embarrassment I had felt on the way to the cinema arose afresh in me. My clothes were shabby compared to theirs. Outgrown, much-mended shirt and trousers, and worn old sandals. Strange to relate, I had never felt so awkward because of my topknot as I did at that moment. Somehow I managed to undo it and spread it out in the rest of my hair. Every now and then, I would pass my hand over my head to check that it hadn't sprung upright. The thought came to me, what if it were to be cut off? Immediately I reproached myself—what ideas I have these days!

Just then Diwakar drew closer to me and said, 'Well sir, how are things with you? What are you up to?'

I remembered Bhai Saheb's remarks. That morning in the sitting room he had said, 'Well, what do you have in mind, now that the exams are off your back?'

'I will do as you say.' I understood that he was suggesting I find a job.

'Try to do something now. Ask that friend of yours.'

'Let the results come first.'

'The results will take at least two months. What will you do till then? Just waste time?' Bhai Saheb said in anxious tones. 'You can see the state we are in. My ninety to hundred rupees is a drop of water in a bottomless well. You have to do something or other. If both of us educate Amar and Kunwar, they too will get good jobs.'

'Yes, I'll find out,' I said, trying to be tactful.

'Tell that friend of yours, he'll find something. He must know dozens of people.'

'I'll ask him.' My attention was diverted by the sound of Babuji's raised voice from inside the house. To change the subject I said, 'Why is Babuji getting angry?' In fact it hardly mattered to me. He was scolding someone as usual, why worry about it? But I wanted to evade Bhai Saheb's proddings.

'Let's go and see.' As we went in, he reminded me once more, 'Don't forget to ask him. Just mention it.'

Now Diwakar's question reminded me. I replied, 'Nothing. You tell me what to do.'

'Forget it, pal, enjoy yourself. Rest is a great thing—sleep all you can!' Then suddenly he remembered something. 'But you're not the resting kind! You're a sworn enemy of rest. You must have begun swotting over the third year books, or else taken to reading Indian philosophy.'

I replied sadly, 'No, Diwakar, perhaps I won't be able to study any further.'

'Won't be able to? What do you mean?' he laughed. 'Did you hear, Kiran, our Samar has begun spouting filmi dialogues.'

Kiran smiled. Until then, she'd been walking along as if uninvolved in the conversation.

'Yes.' I lost interest. 'Anyway, there's a long time to go yet. Well, what's your news, what are you doing these days?'

'I? What have I to do? Now it's just Kiran and me. She had grown very annoyed with me, saying that studies were everything to me and she was nothing. So now I've put myself at her disposal.' And he burst out laughing. But then, realizing that the joke had gone too far and Kiran was frowning at his talking about their personal relationship, he immediately added, 'So today she has to deal with Mother. Well, Kiran, Mother will be in a fine temper today. She was angry enough when she gave you permission to go to the cinema, and now when she has probably cooked and got her eyes full of smoke, she must be cursing you to her heart's content.'

'Huh!' Kiran sounded unmoved. 'How long can one work oneself to death? If we go to the cinema once in six months and she still curses, what am I to do?'

'Say that in front of her,' Diwakar said teasingly.

I was quite displeased by this. How could Diwakar hear his wife talk of his mother like that! And Kiran—to speak so insultingly, that too before me, of a mother-in-law who is in the place of a mother! If Prabha had talked that way, I would have forgotten all my vows and resolutions and slapped her hard. And as I thought this the scene of the slap flashed before my eyes. I didn't at all approve of Kiran's impoliteness.

'Ah yes, Samar!' Diwakar suddenly addressed me. 'Kiran often asks me why you haven't brought your wife over to our place. Well, Kiran, invite them over, only then will he bring Bhabhi.'

I was in a fix. Kiran was eagerly looking at me, waiting for my reply. I hastily managed to stammer, 'She . . . she's at her parents' place. I'll definitely introduce her to you when she gets back.'

The matter ended there. But that part of my heart which, unknown to me, was still warm below many layers of ice, gave vent to a deep sigh—if only I too could take my wife to the cinema like this! And I remembered how these two had sat close together at the cinema, making comments on the film from time to time. And many of the scenes of the film had also stirred something in me. Yet I was not willing to acknowledge that Prabha had anything to do with the word 'wife' or any connection with these desires that arose in me. I had already decreed that Prabha was a creature outside this area. As if my wife was somewhere else, in someone else's control. She was not Prabha at all.

On Diwakar's insistence I had dinner at his place. And now that I was returning home, the same old Samar of five hours ago was with me. The suffocation and disgust I had tried to escape were revived again. As if I had been wandering in some dream world and had now returned to the real world, I wondered what turn events at home had taken.

That morning, when Bhai Saheb and I had gone inside we saw Prabha standing with head bent like a criminal in the dock, and Babuji like a Durvasa waving his hands about and shouting. Amma was lending him assistance from time to time. Bhabhi, with a veil as long as an elephant's trunk over her face, was standing hidden behind the door.

'Is there no other place to clean lentils?' Babuji started afresh when he saw us. 'It must be cleaned on the roof! Just as that day hair had to be washed on the roof. That day I kept quiet because Munni intervened. So now eating, sleeping, everything has to be done on the roof. Walks around like a dumb creature, won't look at anyone. It's impossible to understand what goes on in the head of this princess. Why don't you tell us why you're so fond of the roof? I'm telling you plainly today, I won't put up with this. Get it into your head, once for all. It's winter, dozens of men are up on the rooftops, sitting in the sun and gaping around. Behave as a daughter-in-law is supposed to behave!'

'How is she to cast amorous glances at the neighbours if she doesn't go up alone on the roof?' Amma's ire increased at the sight of us. 'Why else is she constantly running up to the roof?'

Prabha had been listening quietly with head bent, but at this her head snapped up. She looked sharply at Amma and then bent her head once more. Perhaps a couple of tears fell from her eyes.

'Yes, yes, quite right. Who knows, she may run off with someone, like Pandeji's daughter,' said Babuji, proceeding to the sitting room, head bent as if lost in thought.

'What Pandeji?' asked Amma with a start. 'This one, in our colony? Which of his daughters has run off? The older one? Well, they'd let her grow like an elephant and hadn't got her married.' And she slapped her forehead with both hands. 'O God, what times are these? Religion, piety, all have been abandoned.' Babuji had gone so she asked Bhaiya, 'Whom did she run away with, Dheeraj?'

'Who could it be but that schoolmaster who used to come to tutor her,' Bhai Saheb answered. 'I'll find out when I go out just now.'

'O God, how sinful the world has become! They go to such lengths in an instant and no one gets to know! What will become of this Earth!' Amma's face took on a stricken look. Bhai Saheb turned to go out. Bhabhi came in, uncovering her face, and said to Amma, 'Nothing's beyond these educated girls, Ammaji!'

Amma suddenly remembered the original theme and cried, 'Let the world go to hell, what is it to us? But why does she keep running up to the roof? Who does she have waiting there for her?' She glanced at me and went on, 'Don't you dare set foot there again or you'll have me to reckon with.'

Bhabhi affectionately handed the baby to Amma and said, 'Never mind, Ammaji, why do you upset yourself?'

I turned to go and Amma's voice followed me, 'Why should I not be upset? It is because she behaves like this that her husband won't look at her. And here she is, flaunting her youth! The poor boy is wasting away to a shadow. I just don't know what is eating him. A nice millstone she is round our necks! If only she would die, the problem would be solved. She is like hot milk—one can neither swallow it nor spit it out. The boy's life is being ruined. If only she'd die, I would get the boy remarried tomorrow . . .' And Amma's voice grew tearful.

I came out into the courtyard and began climbing the stairs to my room. There's always some quarrel or other brewing here—best ignore it. Yet Munni's words to me still reverberated. I hadn't quite grasped their import but I felt an unease within me.

And then I had left for the cinema. On my return, that unrest rose in me again as I fearfully knocked at the door. I had gone to Diwakar's house to get rid of it and had managed to forget it till now. The whole scene played before my eyes once more. Fortunately, it was Amar who opened the door so I escaped the scolding I had anticipated. He said, 'Bhaiya, where did you go? All of them were annoyed and worried about you.' I asked softly, 'Have they gone to sleep now?' He said, 'Yes,' and I quietly slipped up the stairs to my room. I dreaded finding food kept there for me but was relieved to find there wasn't any. I began to undress.

It was the end of March, winter was almost over. We slept indoors with the doors open. It was past eleven-thirty. A nearly full moon was blooming outside, its light thickened with mist. I was thirsty. I looked around, there was no water. What had happened today—neither food nor water. Prabha never forgot her work. Perhaps she had overlooked it today. For a moment I felt like doing without but I was too thirsty. Water was kept on a stone ledge on the other side of the terrace.

I got up and went out. Dew lay heavy on the ground. As I crossed the terrace I started—someone was sitting there against the wall. A white figure. My heart gave a loud thump. O God, who is this? Everything from ghosts to dacoits flashed through my head. I plucked up courage and looked more closely. I took two steps forward. It was Prabha. Relieved at recognizing her, I was also overcome with astonishment. What was she doing here alone at midnight, in this heavy dew? Once I was sure it was Prabha, I went with steady steps towards the water. All the way one question hammered in my mind: Why was she sitting here at this time? Had she fallen asleep? But when I passed her on the way back, I heard the sound of crying.

Back in bed, I kept tossing and turning. Again and again, someone seemed to ask: Why is she sitting there alone, crying? Was there no other place to cry? Why couldn't she cry in bed? Outside, and at midnight! What surprised me most was that after all the scenes that had occurred, no one had ever told me that she had cried, nor had I seen her do so. True, she was always silent and gloomy. What had happened today?

But why should I bother my head with all this? Along with this thought came reproach: How low can you sink?

And then all kinds of strange ideas kept coming into my head. The film had one sequence where a mountain was blasted with dynamite. Suddenly that scene appeared before me—I felt as if a bomb had exploded within me and buildings had collapsed all around. Men and women, injured, frightened, panic-stricken, ran about screaming and making a fearful din. So great was the noise that I couldn't clearly make out what anyone was saying. All I could hear was a noise, a confused blind noise which whirled around in my brain like the shock waves of the bomb blast. After a long time, it seemed to me that I could hear a couple of voices clearly through the din. One was Munni's voice, shrieking again and again, 'Bhaiya, talk to Prabha.' The other was my own, emerging as if suffocated, 'No, she's at her parents' house. When she comes back I'll definitely introduce her to you.' And beyond this din, another voice intoning, again and again, like a gong solemnly sounding from a great height, that someone was sitting alone outside in the dew at midnight, crying. It felt as if this voice had been thrown up like the cloud of dust raised by the exploding bomb and then was transformed into a question mark. And the explosion settled like a heavy cloud over my brain, over all my nerves, making them vibrate. I tried to go to sleep, ignoring the whole thing, but I felt as if a huge spider crouched on my breast and it was impossible to sleep until I had wrenched it off and thrown it far away. I don't know how long I was tossed on these stormy waves of conflict and agitation—sometimes half-asleep and sometimes wide awake and fully conscious.

When I could bear it no longer I got up. But now my self-respect popped up like a demon to bar my way. I paused, but then like one under a spell I violently pushed it aside and went out. I was very hesitant, I didn't dare go to her. I went straight to the water once more. Bright moonlight still. The dew still falling. And Prabha still there, crying. Something seemed to squeeze my thumping heart. An hour must have passed and she was still crying. I wasn't thirsty but I drank a little more water. Returning, I paused in front of her. I expected her to be startled or to control herself on seeing me, but she kept on crying, silent, unmoving, as though quite alone. Now I didn't know what to do. Should I cough to announce my presence? And when I couldn't think of anything I started to walk back. But my feet seemed to refuse to move. I took each step with great difficulty, as if walking through a swamp. Or as if someone was dragging me backwards with each step. Finally, I turned around again and stood before her. She still sat as if turned to stone. For a little while I watched her, then my voice emerged, cracked, with difficulty, 'What are you doing sitting here at midnight?'

This time she raised her head and looked at me as if she were seeing me for the first time in her life, and then suddenly buried her face in her sari. Her tears flashed like lightning as they caught the moonlight, then were hidden again. She cried with redoubled vigour. I kept standing there. I felt my presence there was futile, unnecessary and humiliating. Then I said in a bitter but steady voice, 'You can cry in the morning, you'll fall ill in this dew. It's quite late, you know.' I brought out the words somehow, but at that moment I realized what a gulf may lie between feelings and words. As I spoke my throat felt choked. Something began to melt in me, then stuck in my chest. I swallowed.

'What is it to you? Why don't you go and sleep?' This time she uncovered her face, raised her head and said, as if writhing in pain, 'In this one year have you ever cared whether I live or die? What's the need now? Go and sleep.' She looked straight at me, and tears simmered in her eyes.

That glance seemed to pierce through my being and sap all the seas of my strength. As if someone had used a strong enchantment to draw out all my strength, from head to foot. Helpless and broken, I sat down before her with a thump, like one weakened by years of illness. Putting my trembling and lifeless hands on her shoulders I asked in a tearful, broken voice, 'Prabha, are you angry with me?' And as I said this I wondered who it was who was speaking from within me.

Before I could say anything more, she suddenly stretched out her hands, grasped my shoulders, shook me as hard as she could, as if in the grip of intense fury, and said, 'Tell me, how have I harmed you? How have I wronged you? If I am not worthy of you, if you don't like me, then strangle me with your own hands, I won't protest. You are free to marry again but tell me, tell me—' And a violent gust of weeping shook her body again as if about to dissolve it. Forgetting herself, she leaned against my shoulder, embracing me. It was as if a cry could not issue from her choked throat, and her body, shaken with sobs, trembled like a leaf, as if throbbing under the strokes of a whip. A sob would rise and send a shudder through her from head to foot. And without being aware of it I too had begun to cry even more vigorously than she. The lava so long suppressed now burst forth as if from an erupting volcano. As if a glacier had melted beneath that unmoved, senseless stone and was flowing out in fountains of tears, washing away each icy rock in my heart. Embracing each other, we both kept crying—heedless, lost.

Whenever I recalled how I had brought someone's innocent, unoffending, beloved only daughter and tormented her, heaped sorrows on her head, tortured her when she had had no one to turn to for consolation, a thousand daggers seemed to stab me all at once and I wept with redoubled force. What could the poor girl do but gradually waste away? At that moment I felt as if no tears, no sobs, no agonized writhing could ever articulate the remorse in my heart, the unrest in my mind, this throbbing, piercing anguish. I felt like yelling aloud and running through the streets with raised hands like a madman, running until I fell unconscious. Only then perhaps would my heart be lightened.

Had I ever, even for a moment, tried to realize that she too was a living being? That she too might feel happiness or sorrow? That she too might have desires and aspirations? Never! Never! Not once had I wondered what supported her, in what hope she toiled here night and day like a servant. After all, she was not our purchased slave. Stroking with trembling fingers the cheek I had slapped, I felt as if the mark of my fingers was still fresh on that cheek. And that spot still throbbed. In my madness, I tried to turn her face to the moonlight to see if the mark was still visible. I felt like jumping down from the roof and committing suicide there and then. Could I ever atone for my behaviour? Was it possible to wipe out the past? But she had locked her two arms around my neck and my arms bound her.

I don't know how long we both kept crying together. We couldn't manage to say a single word. We'd pause briefly and then again start crying with fresh vigour. I felt as if she had almost lost consciousness. When I lifted her half-senseless form and carried her to my room, I felt as if I had brought her out from a burning house, from beneath fallen walls and rubble, and as if my body was scorched, my clothing burnt.

The moon was hidden and the sky dark.

All night we did not sleep a wink nor could we speak a word or even look at one another. It was as if all that had been suppressed for a whole year had to burst out in one day. We would move slightly apart, look, and then cling to one another again even more tightly.

Caw, caw! The crows had awakened ...

She left the room before anyone else awoke. As she went she said, looking away, 'Get me a postcard, please. I've been wanting to write to my mother for a long time but I had no money.' And wiping her eyes with her sari, she went away. Once again, I felt like banging my head against the wall.

O, how would we face one another in broad daylight?

A network of rays had spread itself outside, like the criss-cross of a knitting pattern ...

Second Half: Morning

Ten directions tortured by questions

1

For the first time I realized how pleasurable it is to stand on the roof, one leg on the parapet, and watch, soak in at many levels of one's being, the moment of sunrise: how in the slate-coloured sky a long strip of purple light gradually turns golden from one end to the other of the eastern horizon, and then, when a radiant face pushes aside the heavy curtains of mist and peers out, a tender coolness fills the air, the leaves on the tree nearby begin to move, and the city slowly awakes. For the first time I realized how slowly the sun rises. Sometimes it looked as if that circle was spinning around like a top, rising with dizzy speed; then again, it would seem to rise very slowly, floating up as though rocked on waves. As I watched, a voice in me seemed to exclaim, 'I never knew that before the sun rises rays spring up like the streams of a fountain, and that the aerial on top of the three-storeyed building opposite our house is the first to be touched by those rays.' I felt as if I were gaining new knowledge every moment and I wished someone were standing beside me, whom I could tell all these new things, to whom I could slowly recount the details of the sunrise.

I felt as if I were seeing the sun rise for the first time. As if I had been imprisoned in dark rooms before this and had never seen what was going on around me. Now that I had come into the light I felt as if the shock, after so many days shut up in darkness, would not let me meet anyone's eyes. Truly . . . how will I talk to Prabha in the light, how will I look her straight in the face? How will I bear the reproach in those accusing eyes? How embarrassed I will feel talking to the others! Perhaps all of them will be pleased now. Now Bhabhi will not hint that I should see a doctor. I smiled at the memory of that hint which used to fill me with rage before.

Prabha had got up and left a short while ago. I didn't look at her nor could she look straight at me. And then I quietly got up and came here. I stood for a long time, looking out. I was not sure what I should do next. I wanted to slip out before anyone saw me. Then I remembered that Prabha had asked for a postcard.

The sweepers were cleaning the streets. Milkmen with canisters of milk tied to their cycles were standing at open doorways, and old men wrapped in shawls with babies in their arms were holding out utensils for milk. At one point I stopped and noticed how, when the milkman took out milk from the canister, white drops dripped from his pitcher and his fingertips. I enjoyed the sight and when I realized this I asked myself—has it ever happened this way before? No, surely not! I felt as if everyone I passed on the street knew what a fountain of joy I had pent up within me. Every moment I was afraid the dam would burst and I would run

110

wild on the streets, shouting like a madman, 'Look, how happy I am! I am very happy!' I just didn't know how to express this joy of mine. The thought of what Prabha must be feeling sent a tremor through me. Wine seemed to seep into every pore of me, as raindrops fall on parched ground and moisten the whole earth . . . After such terrible heat, such sweltering hot winds, I was drinking the coolness and peace of a freely flowing stream, like one who had thirsted for aeons.

After I had yelled myself hoarse Diwakar put his head round the door, yawning, 'What is it? You went at eleven last night, and now you turn up again at seven in the morning?' Then, looking over his shoulder to see that no one was around, he said mischievously, 'Your wife is at her parents' place, so you envy the joys of those who are with their wives, do you?'

This joke about wives sent a ripple of pleasure through me. I felt like saying, 'Which rascal's wife is at her parents' place?' but I kept a straight face and asked, 'What do you mean? Shall I go? Come out and see how far advanced the day is.'

'To each his own, my friend! I've just been awakened by your crowing, I must bathe now. Doesn't one deserve a rest after slogging so hard for the exams? I'm determined to relax. After all I haven't promised God, as you have, that I'll get up four hours before daybreak, plunge into cold water, and then set out to awaken the whole world.' Opening the doors of the sitting room, he said, 'Come along in.'

'I'd better go. You'll take a couple of hours dressing and adorning yourself,' I said, settling down comfortably in the sitting room.

'Your face is shining today. What's the matter? Did you

dream you had passed in the first division? They say dreams before dawn turn out true.' He yawned again.

'Don't remind me of the exams. The thought petrifies me. Who knows whether or not I'll pass. If I fail, I'm done for.' It was true that whenever I thought of the exams or the results, all other thoughts flew out of my head and my heart sank. What would happen? Shrugging off the thought I said, 'Forget it, please, don't talk about it. Whatever is to happen will happen. Why fret over it in advance?' And then I was surprised at myself. This fine carelessness regarding the future had never been characteristic of me.

He was silent for a while and then said, 'My mother's still cross about yesterday. Tell me, what's wrong if I go to the cinema with my wife once in a while I just don't understand these people. Believe me, I haven't seen a single case yet of a mother-in-law being satisfied with her daughter-in-law. Two sons or four—it's all the same. I hope this quarrel's going to blow over today . . .'

'So it's still going on?' But I felt as if I had addressed this sentence not to him but to myself. The memory of Prabha shrinking against the wall, with Amma and Bhabhi confronting her, came back. Suddenly, my eyes filled with tears. I heard Munni's tearful voice, 'Bhaiya, talk to Prabha.' I had ignored her voice at the time, but now every part of my being seemed to reverberate with it. I felt like embracing Munni and chirping joyfully in her ear, 'Look, Munni, I have talked, I have talked to your Prabha.' But where was Munni now? She had been thrown into a pit and her mouth stopped with a stone. I felt as if Munni was inside me, yearning for her freedom. She had drawn me out of a pit and fallen into it

112

herself. If only she had drawn me out a little earlier, I would never have let her enter that hell.

Diwakar was saying something and I came to with a start. What if he had guessed what I was thinking? It really was a very bad habit of mine, this going off into my own thoughts in the middle of a conversation. Diwakar was saying, 'Samar, tomorrow a cousin of mine is coming. That's why I want Mother to get over her annoyance today itself. Last time he came I couldn't introduce him to you. You'll never believe how much he's travelled. Must have been to every city in the country. But look, pal, cut off this topknot of yours. He might pull your leg over it and then you'll get annoyed. He's that type. Doesn't like all these shows of piety.'

'What shows? Everyone has his own beliefs.' I didn't want to enter into a debate.

'A nice sort of faith—as you proceed in one direction, this flag of Hinduism waves in another! It certainly has one use, though! When you're fighting with someone you can catch hold of his topknot, he may struggle but won't be able to get away. And during exams, it can be tied to a post to force one to sit still and study.' And he burst out laughing.

'What would a fellow like you know of faith and spiritual joys? All you know is eat, drink and be merry.'

'Say what you will—that is all there is in the world, Samar. I go to your temples too sometimes—one gets fine delicacies there. That's all there ever has been, weave words around it as you may.'

I remembered that I hadn't been to the temple for ages. Yet I said gravely, 'Look, Diwakar, this is a matter of one's faith. Every country has its own culture, its way of living, dressing, thinking. We don't study our culture. That is why the country is in this condition. We are sinking lower and lower. We laugh at our deities and try to ape everything foreign.' When I began I intended to deliver a long and forceful speech, but halfway through I suddenly remembered how Prabha had taken Ganeshji to be a lump of clay and washed dishes with it. I still did not think Prabha had acted rightly, yet ever since then I had been constantly plagued by the consciousness that my behaviour had been grossly improper, indeed inhuman. And it suddenly struck me: if Prabha were to ask me why I had behaved as I did, what would I say? Perhaps I could not honestly defend many of my actions.

Diwakar grew excited and said, 'I don't like your way of getting yourself up like a cartoon in the name of Indianness. Don't mind my saying this but what's so Indian about wearing such unironed, uncreased trousers, such a shabby, crushed shirt, and dangling a topknot when your hair is cut in Western style? Is it Westernization to appear well turned out? If you really want to be Indian then shave your head and wear a dhoti and kurta of coarse homespun, so that when the wind blows your dhoti will flap like the flag on Independence Day, and you will run behind it trying to bring it under control.'

My face grew red. He had often made such remarks about me, and each time I had evaded the question by talking of personal preferences and beliefs. Sometimes we had even stopped talking for days. How to explain to this idiot that I had no clothes besides these? I thought of Prabha's torn and patched sari. But as soon as Prabha's face came before me I forgot all of Diwakar's nonsensical talk, and replied, 'All right, all right, enough is enough. This is not a college debate. Don't spoil my mood early in the morning.'

'But tell me, why are you suddenly in such a good mood today?'

The truth rose to my lips. I suppressed it and said, 'Nothing special. All right, you go have your bath now, and I'll be on my way. I have to write a lot of urgent letters. Give me a few postcards, will you?' Suddenly a tremor ran through my body. I had remembered Prabha's way of asking for a postcard.

'Whom are you writing to, tell me? Keep my roll number too in mind, will you? Whom have the scripts reached?' He laughed, and then grew grave. 'Seriously, don't you have any contacts? I've heard that lots of boys are out for the kill. They go and threaten people they've never met and force them to do as they say. It seems we won't survive this time unless we play some trick or other.' A frown of worry appeared on his brow.

The demon of worry reappeared in my breast too, and I once again began to think of all the consequences of failure in the exams. I asked, 'What are your plans? Are you going to join the third year or will you go into some other line?'

'Time enough to think of all that if I get through. If I fail it means another year at the grind. All those vows and visits to the temple will go to waste. You'll get a first division, why should you worry? It's I who am in a mess.'

I was pleased at his opinion of me but I dissembled and said, 'To hell with a first division, if I manage to pass I'll make a thanksgiving offering to Hanumanji.' I was sure I would get a first division. The thought came to me, if only I'd had the slightest support at home, getting a first division would have been no problem at all.

'All right, all right, no need to put me on. What do you plan to do next? My father insists there's no need to study further. He wants me to join the police. Lots of influence and extra income. But I don't like the idea, Samar. They may dump me in some remote village or district town where I'll yearn for the sight of a human face. Kiran will cry herself to death.' Diwakar sighed deeply and said, 'And as for extra income— Babuji's still living in his own times.'

Diwakar's words touched me. Yet I said, 'What have you to worry about? It's I who am in a fix. I just don't know what to do. This is the end of my education. Only if I find a job can I make both ends meet.'

'Don't be so stupid. Look, forget all this nonsense—let's both join third year,' Diwakar said consolingly.

'No, Diwakar, one must cut one's coat according to one's cloth. My family can't afford it, this time I must get a job. I can't see any other way. I'm on the look-out for something. Tell me if you know of anything.' I remembered what Bhai Saheb had said.

'But there's no point, Samar. You'll get a good job only if you are well qualified. Otherwise you'll end up as a trader's clerk at forty rupees a month. No one wants to employ an intermediate.'

This left me speechless. True, who would give me a job? This glimpse of reality frightened me. To get away from it I said, 'All right, forget it, pal, let the results come first.' And I stood up. How could I keep pestering the poor fellow to get me a job? If he knew of one, he would surely let me know. Coming out of the sitting room I said, 'All right, go have your bath.' And I remembered again, 'Oh yes, those postcards.'

'I bathe only at Holi and Diwali, friend.' He went in to get the postcards. He had his worries too, yet how cheerful he always was! I felt embarrassed to ask for one postcard so I'd asked for four or five. Taking them, I said, 'I'll return these.'

'O yes, I forgot to bring the stamped paper to draw up a contract for their return!' He laughed. 'All right, tell me now, why are you so happy today?'

This time I smiled broadly. As I came out on the street, I said, 'Prabha has come . . .' and walked off.

'Oho, I see, sonny!' Diwakar's voice followed me.

But the embarrassment that had gripped me since morning vanished by evening, and a firmness unknown to me took its place—yes, I have spoken to my wife, what is it to anyone? I was annoyed with myself too—what reason had I to be embarrassed or feel shy?

When I returned from Diwakar's an unfamiliar sweetness possessed me. I had not felt so light-hearted for years. As if I had just been released from prison. Every now and then, a strange compassion would melt my heart. How much the poor girl had suffered! Not a single soul to sympathize with her, but for Munni. She couldn't dare ask anyone in the house for a postcard. What a shame! It was Bhabhi who surprised me most. If she behaved like this now what would she do when she became a mother-in-law? Didn't she realize that she too was a daughter-in-law like Prabha. I was overcome with shame whenever I recalled how I had behaved, misled by her tutoring. I wandered around and went home at two in the afternoon. Babuji was standing at the tap, washing his feet. As soon as he saw me he said, 'Well, your highness, where have you been? Mealtimes mean nothing to you, it seems!'

I didn't like this. What would Prabha think if she heard? I knew the matter would ultimately come round to my being unemployed, so I was scared too. I said in a low voice, 'I'd gone to see Diwakar. I was talking to him about getting a job and it got late.'

Babuji's voice at once grew mild. 'Yes, do something, son, how can we carry on this way?'

When I went in Amma started off. 'Now you don't have to study, still you stay out all day? It's past two, is this any time to eat? No one knows what time you returned last night either.'

Like a cat caught stealing the cream, I slunk into the kitchen, drew up a stool and sat down. When Prabha brought the food, a thrill ran through me. I lifted my head to look at her. A strange equable gravity overspread her face, her eyes were lowered, the faint shadow of a smile played on her lips. It was the same drawn face, but today it was glowing with the lustre of a new contentment, as if, after years, the dust had been wiped off a mirror. I felt like just gazing and gazing at that mirror. I had a strong desire to say something to her but I didn't know what to say. At that moment I felt that I had always been longing to hear Prabha's voice, that I had perhaps never heard it properly. Perhaps it would be impossible for me to recognize her by her voice alone. How could I? I didn't recall her ever speaking. She just worked and worked, silent, grim-faced.

As she gave me the food I noticed how shabby her sari was. With huge tears, sewn up. Was this sari fit to be worn?

118

Why is she wearing it? Has she no other? She must have got some at the time of the wedding. Where are they? I must ask her. I had abandoned her, so the whole family, especially Amma, had not once bothered to enquire whether she needed anything. Amma should be a mother to her. She should not be so prejudiced. Bhabhi's having a daughter has become a licence for her to act like a reigning queen. She spends most of her time in her room, her meals are sent there. She must have kept half a dozen saris aside, unknown to Amma. But why would she give Prabha one? And I shivered when I recalled that Prabha had suffered the terrible cold of January and February in this kind of sari. How she must have felt! No one to support her, no one to talk to her or hear her woes— and that dreadful cold when one doesn't feel like taking one's hands out of one's pockets!

Tears came to my eyes again. Prabha was sitting behind the partition in the kitchen. Today, after so long a time, I remembered that incident of our wedding. She was sitting like this in the kitchen, I could see just so much of her arm stretched out, and I kicked the plate and stormed off. How the small wristwatch with its narrow black strap bloomed that day on her fair, round wrist. Today, I was stunned when I looked at her arms. The skin had darkened with working in the kitchen and turned dry and brittle. No more rounded, the wrist was mere flesh over bone. My eyes fell on her feet. They were black with dirt and lack of care, the heels cracked and fissured. This girl, reared with tenderness and joy, amid hopes and dreams, had been brought to our house with music and rejoicing, and today . . .?

Very gently, so as not to offend Prabha, I slid the plate

aside and got up. Prabha was startled. She raised her head and looked at me eagerly. The same way she had looked the night before. What big, innocent, unpretending eyes! But there were dark circles round them. Prabha's face with those dark circles seemed so terrible to me that I turned my eyes away. I heard a very hesitant voice ask, 'Why?'

There was a lump in my throat and I felt if I spoke I would burst out crying. Biting my lower lip, I managed to reply, 'I ate at Diwakar's place, I'm not hungry.' And I hurriedly left.

Amma was sitting outside, silent, her thick glasses on her nose, reading some religious book. I began to climb the stairs to my room. Through the window of Bhabhi's room I heard her voice. She was saying, 'Those two have started talking to one another.'

'Who?' Bhai Saheb's voice. I remembered today was Sunday.

'Samar and Prabha.' I sensed a tinge of sarcasm in her voice.

'Really!' Bhai Saheb sounded surprised, as if he had turned over and sat up. 'How do you know?'

'Kunwar came to get some cardamom after lunch. He told me.'

I rushed to my room without waiting to hear more, flung myself on my face on the bed, and wept bitterly.

In the evening I again slipped out like a criminal and wandered about aimlessly. The morning's intoxicated bliss had worn away. Now I was seized by reproach and self-disgust. Again and again I prayed, 'Punish me, O God, punish me. I have been terribly cruel to a helpless woman. Hellish tortures were inflicted on her and I was a silent spectator. Where were

120

my eyes? I was a mere boy, but why did Amma and Babuji behave that way?'

And these feelings of remorse drew me to the temple. I sat there a long time, gazing into space. I analysed all that had happened as if I had returned home after a long stay abroad and had now discovered all that had occurred in my absence. Along with feelings of remorse and compassion, and the process of looking at everything afresh, my mind was also eagerly awaiting nightfall. And finally, when I could bear it no longer, I returned home.

And I realized that in this interval everyone's attitude to me had changed. Prabha was in the kitchen. Bhabhi was sitting near Amma and talking to her in an undertone. As I entered the house I somehow sensed that now everyone in the house knew about Prabha and me having talked to one another. They were looking at me as if I were some creature escaped from the zoo. I had been imagining how shy I would feel to meet their eyes when they all got to know. But instead, their piercing glances filled me with exasperation. What was so unique about my talking to Prabha that it should become a topic of speculation? Why make such a fuss about it? If a husband and wife didn't talk to each other yesterday and have started talking today, why should anyone else be so intrigued by it?

Trying my best to ignore the atmosphere, I behaved as if nothing new or important had occurred in my life. As I finished my dinner, Amma said, 'Oh Samar, just go and call your father. The food will grow cold if he doesn't come soon.'

'Where is he?' I asked.

'He's taken the baby out. Must be sitting with Pandit Navalkishore. The child too must be hungry.'

My annoyance grew. Amma was talking in a conciliatory tone, as if anticipating that I might refuse to go. Then I was amused at my readiness to take offence. What had happened to me?

Babuji was sitting on a chair with both his legs drawn up, and Navalkishore, who was always ailing, was reclining on a cot. A couple of other people from the neighbourhood were also there. Babuji was delivering his usual, oft-repeated lecture, 'The truth is this culture is nothing compared to our Indian culture. Nowadays, one doesn't know which way the world is going. But whom have we to blame? Only ourselves. These boys of today term the path laid out by our ancient sages uncivilized. They are not ashamed to call their ancestors savages! But in fact each of our ancient laws is a wonder—the castes, the separate spheres for each one. If all followed the rules prescribed for them, there would be none of this chaos—' Navalkishore felt he had a right to speak on this subject. He broke in eagerly, 'Bhagwan Manu says in the Manusmriti . . .' I was waiting for Babuji to pause so that I could intervene. Now I said, hesitantly lest he rebuke me, 'Babuji, you're being called.'

'All right, I'm coming. Go in and fetch the baby,' he said.

I've been in and out of this house all my life. Panditji's daughter-in-law was playing with the child. I said, 'Bhabhi, Babuji is asking for her.' It was her husband who had beaten up the refugee and chased him out that day. Hearing my voice, Panditji's wife emerged, 'Who is it? Samar? Well, son, haven't seen you in ages. Exams over? Very good. And I heard you have started talking to your wife. Very good, son, who will talk to her if you don't? One may quarrel but one can't stop talking. But, son, don't put up with such improper behaviour as our Bisnu does. He gives all the offerings from the temple to his wife. Doesn't give us a single paisa. They both eat all the good sweetmeats and give us the leavings. These two are out to shame us in our old age—they don't know the difference between night and day. No matter what the hour, it's nothing but giggling and playing. They couldn't care less who might be looking on or overhearing. They don't give us any inkling of what is offered in the temple. Morning and evening, we ask God to take us away. But Samar, you can be sure of this—all the fine sweets offered at the temple are because of the respect Panditji commands. They won't get a single paisa later. They'll learn their lesson then, right now they think they've got it made.' And the thought of Panditji's death, or else some other personal sorrow, brought tears to her eyes. She put her sari to her eyes and whimpered.

Bisnu's wife pulled a face at her mother-in-law and, smiling, handed the baby to me. For some reason, as I was carrying the baby back, I remembered Bhabhi's suggestion that I see a doctor. And I smiled to myself.

2

Eyes wide with surprise, I asked, 'Did you see it yourself?'
Prabha looked away and said, 'I didn't see it myself but
Munni told me she saw it. She said she'd tell you. I'd put the
dal on to cook and turned aside when Bhabhi put a handful
of salt into it.'

'Hmm.' Lifting myself on my elbows I cupped my face in
my palms and considered this. Then I asked, 'Why didn't you
talk to me the first day? Why did you insult me like that on
the very day you arrived?'

Prabha was sitting with one leg drawn up, both arms
wrapped around her knee and her face resting between her
palms. Absolutely calm and unperturbed, she sat thus, answering
my questions. Moonlight rained on the terrace outside and an
oblong of milky white lay beside our bed. With great difficulty
I had persuaded her to talk about the past. She spoke normally,
without emotion, 'I didn't insult you. Did you feel I had insulted
you?' Then she sighed deeply and said, 'Let it be, what's the
use of thinking of all that? It was fated, so it happened.'

'Don't talk of fate, Prabha! Prabha, I'm very anxious to know. Tell me, see how I'm coaxing you,' I said persuasively, and gently took her hand in mine. Her soft hand was so cold and lifeless that it made me shiver.

She let her hand remain in mine. Laughing softly, she answered in the tone of one very experienced and wise, 'What if you do coax me a little after hurting me so often?' And without waiting for my reply she went on, 'I was exhausted after weeks of wakeful nights, my body was aching. And I was very sad. I missed my home. Then Munni told me her story and I grew even more disturbed. She was the only one here who talked to me. And then, by chance, that wretched neighbour's daughter-in-law was burnt to death that very day in the house facing ours. A couple of other incidents also occurred so that altogether I was not in a mood to do anything except cry. I didn't at all feel like talking. And then I heard that you didn't want to get married. All my strength left me. What could I have said to you?'

'Look, Prabha, now that you have started to tell me, don't hide anything. I really do want to know. You promised you would speak plainly, why are you being so cautious now?' My soft, pleading voice suddenly trembled and grew unsteady. I put my head on her lap and lay down. I felt as if she might push my head away and say, 'So now you are putting on a display of love!' My brain was soothed by a soft warmth. 'Let it alone now!' I could only see the outline of her face in the darkness, but I was suddenly startled by two warm drops falling on my forehead. Taking her chin in my hand I turned her face towards me and said affectionately, 'What is this silliness? Are you going to cry round the clock now?' And

I gently tapped her cheek. The shy smile on her lips came before my eyes in imagination, but I hastily withdrew my hand. I had remembered how this hand had slapped the same cheek and how dazed she had been. All for a lump of clay that the pandit had made into Ganesh. I felt that Prabha too had remembered that day. Feeling awkward, I changed the subject. 'Prabha, tell me, why are Bhabhi and Amma so hostile to you?'

Prabha didn't answer. Then she swallowed and said, 'How do I know? It must be my fate, what else can I say?'

'Look, Prabha, tell me truly what I want to know. You and your fate—to hell with fate!' For the first time in my life I had spoken against destiny.

Her hands had been lying still on my warm forehead, now they began to move slowly through my tangled hair. I felt as if I were downing bottles of wine. Fingers still moving, she said, 'The reason for Amma and Babuji's annoyance was plain. They were not satisfied with what my parents gave. I couldn't bring cash or many clothes and jewels. My education became another disqualification. Then Munni made a big deal of my looks, and Amma too remarked that even though I hadn't brought much I was much better looking and better mannered than the older daughter-in-law. That was enough to anger your Bhabhi. Day and night she'd tell tales on me to Amma. I could only listen and keep quiet. To whom could I complain? You too were angry. Many times I thought that like the neighbour's daughter-in-law I too should . . .' She stopped and more tears fell.

I put my hand on her lips. Lovingly, I said, 'Prabha, never say such a thing again!' Then I put my arms round her neck, drew her head down and gently kissed her cold dry lips. I felt

126

as if I had taken a sip of brandy and it was burning its way into every nerve. In a trembling, tearful voice I said, 'Prabha, forgive me this one time. I don't know what demon had taken possession of me. This is the last such offence of my life. Let's resolve today that we will never fight with each other, whatever happens, whatever anyone may say . . .'

Prabha pressed her cheek against my lips and I stopped. Her tears flowed again. I chided her, 'Again! You are very weak, Prabha!' But something silenced me. Was she who had stood unmoved through such storms and tempests weak? Then I remembered that yesterday, for the first time, I had seen Prabha cry. I asked, 'Prabha, tell me one more thing.'

'Hmm.'

'Why were you crying yesterday? I had never seen you cry before. Perhaps you didn't cry even the day I slapped you.'

This time Prabha's voice grew hard. 'Anyone would have cried yesterday. No one has ever accused me of immorality. What I had to hear yesterday . . .' She fell silent. Then she said tensely, 'The day you too cast such aspersions on me I will take poison . . .'

I was quiet. I felt dwarfed by her resolution. In an anxious tone I said, 'The atmosphere in our house gets fouler every day. What should be done about it?' Then I added consolingly, 'You must be feeling you have fallen into a dark well where all your education is wasted.'

She didn't answer immediately. Then she said, 'Troubles don't continue for ever. Once you finish your studies, things will improve. If I'm with you I won't be afraid anywhere, in a well or in a pit. One feels disturbed only when one is alone.' I felt each quiver of her voice in the depths of my heart.

'Well, now that you've asked so many questions, may I ask some too?'

'No, Prabha, no. I won't be able to answer a single question of yours. Take it that I was mad in those days, my brain was not working.'

Early next morning I said to her, 'Prabha, forget all that has happened. I alone was to blame for it. If you can understand my compulsions, then forgive me. You can see the condition of this house. You are intelligent enough to understand it. Now we have to decide how we are to live under these conditions.' I was pleased with myself for talking and thinking so seriously on an important subject.

'What can I say? I'll agree to whatever you say. Have I ever opposed you in anything?' she said. Her head was on my arm and she was looking up at the ceiling.

'But I want you to oppose me. We should discuss everything, thrash it out and reach a conclusion.' As I said this, someone in my mind asked me—Will you be able to brook any opposition? Hastily, I continued, 'I won't do anything without consulting you. Don't you think the conditions in this house are a topic fit for discussion? Why are you afraid of voicing an opinion? After all, you are educated and intelligent.'

'Again a taunt about my education?' Prabha's voice grew sharp. 'Will you too speak the language your family speaks? Tell me, how can I help being educated? My parents educated me—what could I do? I've forgotten all that I studied. Have I ever behaved arrogantly towards anyone in this house because I am educated?' Her tone was angry and tearful.

I realized my error. The poor girl had had to silently hear so many taunts in this regard that she could not hold back her anger now. Gently turning her face towards me, I said, 'Am I reproaching you, silly? Looks as if you're going to pay me back with interest for all those days of silence. You're ready to snap my head off at a moment's notice. You've become sharp like old wine.' To please her I added, 'Once a man sips it he gets addicted and remains intoxicated all his life.'

Crossly, she said, 'I understand the meaning of your words.' Then she seemed to realize that her tone had been too harsh. Looking shy she said, 'In just two days, you've become more expert than any film actor. You've forgotten what you were saying earlier and started speaking nonsense instead!'

She said the word 'expert' in English and it caught my attention. That Prabha was educated had been repeated so many times in so many ways that it had lost its meaning. Her use of this word made me realize for the first time that she was not a girl from the narrow environs of a village or small town but the only daughter of a truly urban family. Noticing Kiran's way of dressing and style of talking I had wished that I too had such a sensible woman with such good taste for my wife. Never had I thought of Prabha in that connection. I had never thought of her as more than an unimportant creature doing the housework. Now I realized that let alone a film, she must be yearning even for the sight of a film poster. She must be longing to read even a single line of a novel or story. City girls have so many dreams, so many interests. This poor girl had buried them all in the walls of our house. The difference between Diwakar's house and our house became clear to me. At least, being educated would not be treated as a demerit in his house. Would our house ever become like his? Would I ever be able to say to Prabha, 'Let's go out this evening.' Or tell her that Diwakar and Kiran were coming over to tea? But . . . but . . . I could think no further. A deep sigh escaped me.

Prabha shook me when she heard me sigh. 'What's eating you?' Then she bent over me, stroked my forehead and said, 'Go on with what you were saying. Are you upset by what I said about your being like an actor?'

I kept quiet and studied her face. For some reason I felt her heart was not in her words. She must be thinking that she has to put up with me now that she is bound to me. Certainly in her heart of hearts she must think me unworthy of her.

'Tell me, please,' she said again. 'Look, I'll do whatever you say but you must agree to one thing I say. I have a habit of chattering. I say whatever comes into my head. Don't get upset by anything I say, I beg of you. I just don't realize what should be said and what should not. Later I regret it. Now that I've been silent so long I keep thinking of things to say. Rama too says that I talk too much.'

I wasn't upset by what she had said but I was growing depressed at my own thoughts. Truly, I did not deserve this girl! I asked, 'Who's Rama?'

'A classfellow of mine.' And she plunged into telling me all about Rama. Finally, she said, 'This time when I went home she wanted to know all about you. We were the naughtiest girls in our class. She's my very close friend. Girls don't normally form such lasting friendships. We used to tell each other that we would never marry, we would finish our studies and then go to a village and teach women there. Sometimes we would plan to tour the whole of India on foot and keep a detailed account of all our adventures in a diary. We'd get to meet all kinds of people in different regions. We planned to learn to use sticks and knives to defend ourselves from hoodlums. O the things we used to talk about—everything in the world! Everyone used to get annoyed with us for talking endlessly to one another. We used to enjoy teasing and annoying them.'

I interrupted her. 'Prabha, do you very much regret having married?'

She started. 'No. When did I say that?' Then she began to laugh. 'See, I told you I have a habit of talking too much. You should stop me. What to do, I get carried away. That's what happened, isn't it?' And she kept chuckling for a long time. I liked to hear her laugh so freely, and I also felt astonished that she could talk and laugh so easily after having endured so much. I didn't remember ever having laughed like this. Suddenly she stopped laughing, pressed both my cheeks with her hands and looking straight into my eyes, said, 'Look, forget all that I have said. What I now want is that you should study well. I'll do whatever you say.'

I remembered all that Diwakar and Babuji had said. I said, 'Prabha, give me your advice about something.'

'I told you not to ask me for advice. I'll do as you say.'

'But listen to what I have to tell you. Don't act so obedient! I have a friend called Diwakar. He insists that I should join third year. But Babuji and Bhai Saheb say I should find a job so that I can contribute to the family income. I don't know what to do. What do you think?'

She was quiet as if waiting for me to continue. Then she said, 'What advice can I give? Do what you think is right.'

I felt she was not saying what she wanted to. 'If I am to do just as I think why would I ask you? What I decide doesn't affect me alone. So far I had the pretext of studying. Now that's over. It's clear I can't study further. We can't carry on in this miserable state. The family needs help immediately. I don't see any other path.'

Prabha yawned and said, 'Fine, then take up some job.'

'Why are you speaking with such disinterest?' I asked. 'I know you don't like the idea. But tell me, what else can I do? And as for a job, it's easy to talk of one but just step out and see how hard it is to find one. No one cares a straw for intermediates and graduates. At best, I'll manage to earn forty to fifty rupees. It'll mean pushing a pen all day and bringing a bundle of files home at night. Not a free moment. Sit up and pore over files all night. Bhai Saheb got a job during the war. He thinks it's still as easy. But times have changed. Who can explain all this to them? I just don't know what to do. If I were well qualified it would be another matter. What am I to say to anyone as of now? "Sir, I'm an intermediate." What kind of job can I expect to get? Well, why don't you say something?'

'What can I say? Shall I take up a job as a school teacher or something?' She seemed to be joking, laughing at the state of affairs in the house.

I immediately said, 'If Amma or Bhabhi hear you suggest such a thing there'll be such a row that you'll forget all about the day you wore a wristwatch to do the cooking.' Then the situation and my own helplessness began to exasperate me.

'Really, Prabha, sometimes I get so fed up that I feel like running away. You must be thinking you've been tied to a good-for-nothing. I tell you, I can't bear to see your condition. Forget living in comfort, you don't even have decent clothes. Nor do I.'

'Don't worry about me. I have more than enough.'

132

But I ignored what she said and went on, 'Diwakar's wife is always asking me to take you over to their place. But tell me, how can I take you? And now I'm afraid they may turn up here some day.' I was regretting having told Diwakar that Prabha had come back. If they came over where would we make them sit?

Prabha spoke up at once. 'O my! Don't bring them here. What will they think of us? And we have no means to entertain them.'

'That's what worries me. Really, sometimes I feel very angry. Sometimes I feel like ignoring all these people—let them talk as much as they wish, let me study well, then get a good job and live in style. Then I'd easily be able to give them as much as the total sum I'll be able to earn as of now.' I went on, lost in dreams. 'Why bother about all these people? Each thinks only of his own interests, everyone has to work out his own destiny. But then I feel guilty. After all, I have a duty to fulfil to my parents.' And I continued thinking.

The sky was growing brighter. Prabha was stretching and yawning. As she got up, she said, 'But if you get a good job won't you be able to do your duty better?'

I kept looking questioningly at her, wondering what she meant by this.

3

No way out, no solution to the problem. Let yourself be stifled and worn away, rest your head against some pillar and weep, consume yourself like a building destroyed by white ants. Is there no way to shake off all this, to get rid of it with one blow? What if I were simply to keep walking, keep walking straight on and on, without looking back? Ugh, what strange thoughts come to me these days? Surely it is time I realized that someone else's future too is bound up with mine, so I cannot take any decision on my own. Sooner or later things must change for the better—why should I yield to despair so soon?

I was afraid, knowing I'd be scolded for returning home so late. Unwillingly, I turned homewards, leaving the din of the employment exchange behind me. That morning, I had hesitantly asked Bhabhi, 'Bhabhi, do you have any ordinary sari kept by?'

'What'll you do with a sari?' I knew Bhabhi had understood but was deliberately pretending she hadn't.

'If you do, give it to Prabha. What would anyone say if they saw her? One feels ashamed even to look at her,' I said, keeping my voice steady with an effort.

A gleam of cunning satisfaction at having forced the truth from me shone in Bhabhi's eyes. I pretended not to see the malice in her smile. She said, 'I swear I don't have even one, Lalaji. I can show you my trunk if you like.' Rocking the child in both arms, she added, 'Amma may have a couple. Why don't you ask her?'

I had gone to Bhabhi because I didn't dare go to Amma. Now I plucked up courage and told myself there was no reason to be so frightened. After all, she knew I had started talking to Prabha. I went to Amma and asked, 'Amma, do you have any saris laid by?' I didn't dare look straight at her.

'What kind? For a lungi? You just got pants made for yourself.'

'Not for me, Amma, for Prabha. Her sari is badly torn. It doesn't bear looking at.'

'Oh! Then why don't you say you want it for her? Why beat about the bush?' Her face had changed at the mention of Prabha. Looking very annoyed, she drew a bunch of keys from beneath her pillow, threw it before me, and said, 'There, the house is yours. If you can find one, take it. Don't I have eyes? Wouldn't I give her a sari if I had one? If any money is left over this month I'll get one. She must be having one or two with her.'

I didn't know what to say. Turning to go I said in a dejected tone, 'If any are left over from the ones she brought at the wedding, you could give it to her. What would anyone say if they saw her?'

135

This time Amma flared up. 'Wedding indeed! As if you didn't see the treasury that came at the wedding! And how long ago was that, pray? Do you think everything would be preserved in a showcase since then? Didn't we give anything to Munni when she left? Or to Prabha when she went home?' Amma's anger kept escalating as she spoke. Her voice grew ever louder. 'So this is the result of your starting to talk to your wife. Now you'll take up cudgels against us on the slightest pretext. Your wife is not unique—there's another daughter-in-law too. Why don't you admit that you are parroting what she has taught you? I understand her inside and out. She's not as simple as she pretends to be, she's as crooked as they come. What else could she have learnt in school but this "mine" and "thine"...'

Just then Babuji came in and rebuked Amma, 'What's the matter? Why are you raising such a racket? Does it ever occur to you that visitors may come in at any moment or may be in the sitting room. What would they think? There's never a moment's peace in this house. Always the same ...'

Amma replied in an equally loud voice, 'Your precious son is presenting a case on his wife's behalf. He's demanding an account of all that she brought at the wedding. He says, give her the clothes she brought, she feels ashamed in the ones she's wearing. Ask him what rolls of velvet she brought with her!'

Babuji looked at me angrily and said, 'You don't earn a single paisa and you act like a lion on your wife's behalf. What shamelessness! Your brother is working himself to death. We've educated you and now you want us to provide you with clothes in the latest fashion. You don't even realize that you should at least manage your own expenses and reduce our burden to some extent. A man should think of these things on his own . . .' He broke off and returned to the sitting room.

Babuji's anger, or perhaps the realization that her intent had been effectively accomplished, quietened Amma. I slunk back to my room. Why had I gone to Amma? Bhabhi must have known this would happen. I'll pay her back some day. She does not dare act directly but keeps inciting one against the other.

Just then Prabha appeared and said, 'Who asked you to go and create such a scene? I don't need any saris. I have a whole trunkful. I don't wear them because I don't want to spoil expensive saris doing housework. Why did you have to go and start a quarrel so early in the morning? Once you start earning I will wear fine clothes to your heart's content. I have seen out the harshest days of winter in these clothes, I am not going to die in them now. If you can't bear the sight I'll take out a new one and wear it. I had kept them to go out in. I fold my hands to you, I fall at your feet, please don't go and create such scenes. You have a fight and then disappear, afterwards it's me they tear to pieces.'

I answered impatiently, 'All right, Prabha, leave me alone just now. Otherwise I'll say something and you will get annoyed.'

Prabha's voice grew choked, 'Have I ever got annoyed with you?'

Just then someone yelled from downstairs, 'Now where has she disappeared? The dal is boiling over on to the stove. Bahu, you could have taken it off the fire before going to chat with your husband . . .'

Prabha trembled like a leaf and ran downstairs.

I sat and stewed . . . Earn, earn! Dig wells, stoke furnaces, do anything, but bring in money. If only I could find a buried treasure, I would rub their noses in money and say, 'Here, chew it, swallow it.' And my childhood fantasies revived once more . . . I'm walking along and my foot strikes something. I think it must be a stone or brick but then I see that it's the edge of a lid sticking out of the ground. I push the soil aside with my foot and find that it's the lid of a heavy brass jar filled with guineas, or gold and silver jewellery. I glance around and then try to drag it out. Or I hide and wait impatiently for nightfall. And then I started laughing at the impossibility of my fantasy. To begin with, those who constructed the road would have dug down fairly deep. Second, would the police and others ever let such treasure out of their clutches?

Then I was exasperated by my folly—how could I occupy myself with such idle thoughts? The question was, what should I do now? If I were to set out in search of a job without awaiting the results, where should I go? Somehow or other I must make an attempt today. This couldn't go on any longer.

I took out my matric certificate, rolled it up, put it in my pocket and slipped out. Amma was grumbling away, scolding Prabha as usual. She had nothing to do besides her prayers and her constant grumbling. Seeing me go out, she fired a parting shot. 'Now he's set off again. You might at least eat before you go. How long will we keep food waiting for you? Yesterday a whole bowl of dal was thrown away. Every day we have to give away rotis to the sweeper woman.'

Is this a home or a madhouse? Endless bickering! Not a

138

moment's peace. No one has any consideration for others, and if you ask for anything a fight starts.

What was wrong in my asking for a sari for Prabha? And then Prabha came and scolded me—wouldn't I feel bad? Babuji's words had stung me. As for Amma—rotis are given to the sweeper woman indeed! How can anyone feel like eating if you don't give him a moment's peace. The other day I had felt bad when Kiran spoke rudely about her mother-in-law. Today I felt she was quite right. When people ill-treat one so much, one is bound to feel resentful. Amma must have plenty of saris but of course they are all for her favourite daughter-in-law. Her husband earns so she's the reigning queen and can sit around all day with her child. The whole family has a maidservant from whom work is extracted as if she's an animal. They couldn't care less whether she even gets enough to eat. They can scold and berate her whenever they like. Because the poor girl is the wife of an unemployed husband.

Once out on the street I forgot where I intended to go. All I recalled was that no one should see me go wherever I was going. I stood there for a long time, trying to recollect. What has happened to me!

I could hear the hubbub in the employment exchange building from a distance. It was as if the two-thousand-strong crowd there had collected for a funfair. All the doorways and corridors of the building were chock-full. The compound too was full of people. Lawns, flowerbeds, all were crawling with people. They stood two deep on the boundary wall, standing on tiptoe. Using each others' shoulders to support themselves, they were trying to peer into the building. It was as if a big leader were about to come and deliver a speech on how the situation in the country was improving day by day, how many dams had been built, how many factories opened, and how important a place India was gaining in the world. Then I wondered if some mishap had taken place—a fire or a murder. But the policeman directing traffic at the crossing was quite calm and unperturbed. Unable to penetrate the crowd, cyclists stood on the roadside, leaning on their cycles and trying to find out what was going on inside. I had just taken up a position on the outskirts of the crowd when someone put a hand on my shoulder. 'Well, friend, how goes it?'

I turned round with a start. Immediately I heard, 'Sorry, I made a mistake.' It was a person with a fair complexion, his unoiled hair combed back, wearing a fine muslin kurta-pyjama. With an apologetic smile on his thin face, he said, 'I took you for someone else.'

I smiled back. 'Never mind.' Then I asked, 'Do you know what's going on here?' For some reason I found him likeable.

'They're recruiting labourers or clerks today, perhaps,' he said, carefully scrutinizing a black tin notice board nearby. I too bent to look at it. It bore a list of various posts on offer.

Almost all had cross marks chalked in front of them. Before carpenters was written 'ten,' before labourers, 'fifty' and before clerks 'three.' My mouth fell open—sixty-three people were required and three thousand were gathered here! My heart missed a beat.

And, after looking on for a while, I turned towards home, downcast. No, there was no place for me in this milling crowd. Diwakar was right—one couldn't get a good job unless one was well qualified. What would I do here? Nephews and cousins of employment officers must be aplenty in this crowd—would they be recruited first or would I? Walking back with me part of the way, my companion remarked bitterly, 'How shameless these leaders are, crying themselves hoarse night and day! With what solemnity on their apelike faces they say: "We are independent. To reconstruct the nation we need good engineers, doctors, technicians, scientists." But the fact is, all they want are gardeners to water the lawns of their bungalows and drivers to drive their cars.'

His anger was like balm to my wounds. He was right—those who wished to study and become something had neither the means nor the facilities. And the leaders wanted doctors, engineers, scientists and technicians to be produced by magic. I used to dream of becoming great, of cutting a unique figure in the world. I had watered those dreams with my blood through many wakeful nights. Dayanand, Shivaji, Rabindranath, Gandhi and Nehru—these were my ideals. I tried to model my life on theirs. Their life stories filled me with excitement, a sense of adventure. How eager I was to push aside obstacles like so many balloons. Until I got married, it was in these beds of fancy that I had rocked myself. How pleased I was with myself for not talking to Prabha, as if the road to greatness lay open before me and it would take me no time at all to become great! What folly, what idiocy! How fanciful and baseless those dreams were! And I, forgetful of reality, had thought them true!

'And the biggest joke is this,' he said, flicking the ash off his cigarette, 'that we fill our immature minds in school and college with recipes for achieving success and greatness, as if after reading up one of those lessons all a boy has to do is go and become Jawaharlal Nehru right away. The wretch of a schoolmaster, who earns merely fifty or hundred rupees, doesn't remember that he too used to read this lesson and in his attempts to become great, ended up in this school where the headmaster's kicks fall to his share. People forget that those great men were sons of big men. They didn't have to worry about where the next meal would come from. It wasn't as if they rose on their own strength.'

He had reached his street. 'Forgive me if I've said anything wrong,' he said and went his way.

His way of talking astonished me, and at the same time I felt sure I had seen him before somewhere. I couldn't remember where. 'No, no, not at all,' I replied. The truth of his words sank into me. There is no future for me, no place. Enraged, I kept crushing my matric certificate with my hands.

I wandered around for a long time, tormented by the thought that I must, I must do something, for Prabha's sake if not for my own. But then the thought would come like a hammer blow: there is no way out, no one is my own . . .

When I reached home that afternoon, Amar was just going in with a letter the postman had given him. 'Whose letter is it, Amar?' I asked.

He started, taken aback, and stammered, 'It's Chhoti Bhabhi's.'

'Here, give it to me.' I stretched out my hand and took it from him. I looked at the defaced stamp—it wasn't from her home, it was from Jodhpur. But I felt not the slightest desire to open it. I knew very well how many of Prabha's letters had been opened by others. I had made out from Amar's attitude that this letter, too, would have been thoroughly examined tonight and given to her tomorrow only if found fit for her perusal.

I went in. Prabha was sitting in a corner, sifting flour. I was really fed up of seeing her constantly engaged either in the kitchen or in some work connected with it. Could there be so much work in the kitchen that it never showed any sign of finishing? I felt like raising her by the arms and saying, 'Come on, enough is enough, someone else will do the rest of the work.' But who would that someone else be? With dry lips and throat I managed to whisper, 'Here's a letter for you, Prabha!'

'From where?' She immediately brightened up. Taking the letter from me she held it by one corner and scrutinized it. 'It's from Jodhpur, it must be Rama's. After so long! I've written to her too but I didn't have an envelope to post it.' Then, catching sight of my face, she added, 'Are you feeling all right?'

'Why, what should be wrong with me?' I said, walking away. 'Read the letter first. You can sift the flour later.'

Holding out the letter to me she said, 'Listen, just put this in my trunk. I'll read it at night. Here's the key.' Untying the key from her sari-end, she added, 'I have a lot of work to do yet.' Then she remembered. 'Why didn't you have your lunch, mister? I haven't eaten either.'

I replied very gently, 'I wasn't hungry, Prabha. I'd eaten earlier.'

'Eaten indeed! I know how you've eaten. You might at least consider that when you go off in a temper without eating, someone else stays hungry too.'

'You mean you really haven't eaten?' I asked at once. The exhaustion of having returned unsuccessful and the load on

143

my mind seemed to melt away. My eyes misted over.

'What do you care? Time enough to enquire when you have a moment to spare from roaming around,' she said crossly, continuing to sift the flour. I tingled all over. Thousands of questions raised their heads—did you stay hungry like this even in the days when I wasn't talking to you? I cleared my throat and said, 'Give it to me, I'll eat now.' I felt angry with myself for the way I'd spoken to her that morning.

'You'll eat that stale food now?' She got up hastily. 'I'll cook fresh food in half an hour. And look, don't mess around too much in my trunk.'

I went upstairs. I opened her trunk and put the letter in. Then I remembered what she had said and an irresistible curiosity to see what she had in her trunk took hold of me. I looked—four or five cotton and silk saris and blouses and several small boxes. The clothes were of fine quality, not the kind to be worn every day in the house. What especially attracted my attention were two or three books. The copy of *Maya* I had seen before. Books given by some relative of hers—a collection of life stories of great women, Gandhiji's autobiography, a book on things a young woman should know, and Premchand's *Rangbhumi*. All had an inscription from the giver and also written in her own hand in a corner, 'Prabha.' The edge of a paper was visible, sticking out between the pages of *Rangbhumi*. I pulled it out—it was somebody's letter. I looked at the sender's name first and was startled. A letter from Prabha! Why was it kept here? I unfolded the letter. The writing was neat and clear but the letter appeared to have been written in haste. For the first time in the year that I had been married to her I was reading my wife's writing, and in a letter

144

addressed to another! I felt some pride—my wife's handwriting was better than average! I began to read as fast as I could, afraid of being caught.

And for a long time afterwards, every word of that letter echoed and re-echoed in my mind. When I recalled it I felt as if it was not something I had read but something she had told me, as we lay in the darkness of night. After some days I could scarcely believe that I had actually read so long a letter. I felt that the letter was a short one and my imagination had expanded it. But I do remember that it had been written in instalments because at several points the writing broke off and then began afresh. What I remembered of it later went something like this:

Dear Rama,

I got your letter when I was at my mother's place and perhaps I'll be able to reply only when I'm on my next visit to Mother. You'll think my saying I'm busy is an excuse but how am I to convince you that these days, I get not a moment's rest. Every morning I think I'll write this evening but I never get time, I swear. Shall I tell you my daily routine from morning to night?

I know you must be very cross with me, very offended. You must be thinking that as before, when I used to come and coax you out of your sulks as you sat by the pomegranate tree behind the school, so now too I will come to mollify you. But how can I explain to you, Rama mine, that now I can't come, I just can't come to you. Even if I want to I can't.

If only you could come here and see the naughtiest girl, the 'lioness' of the school. You were the one who used to tell me to join a circus. Now I realize how false, how futile all our desires are. What do we not desire! Is there any limit to our desires? The flights of fancy we indulged in at school, our sentimental dreams, our desires for all the good things of the world! Rama, why doesn't anyone stop us and tell us it is all a lie? Whenever one of the girls got married and I saw her husband I would think: my husband won't be anything like that! My husband will be a professor or an officer or the manager of a big company. We'll be together, he and I, just the two of us—no mother-in-law, brother-in-law, sister-in-law or nephews swarming around. We'll have a huge modern bungalow. Whenever I saw a piece of furniture that I liked I'd find a place for it in the house of my dreams. The colours, the polish, the curtains, the lawns surrounded by evergreen trees, the tennis or badminton court—I'd imagined them all. We'd have three or four servants. He'd wake me up very affectionately in the morning, and scold me for my habit of waking up late. We'd drink tea together, laughing, reading the newspaper. After he left for office I'd find it hard to get through the day. I'd visit the neighbouring women or invite them over. Every evening we'd go to the cinema or to visit friends. Endless were those fantasies I wove. I don't even recall all of them now . . .

But Rama, if wishes were horses beggars would ride!

Destiny grinds its teeth whenever we laugh, but rejoices when we weep. It knows that we may jump up and down like puppets but the strings are held by hands that know no mercy. If I were to wax poetic I would say that the lamps of all those childish dreams have been extinguished in the poisonous fumes of reality, and those fumes, like terrible serpents, now writhe all around me. At first I feared those serpents, Rama, but now I feel no fear. I wish one of them would sting me. Fresh troubles arise constantly but I am unmoved. I feel as if my heart has turned to stone. And had this not happened, Rama, how could I have survived? By now I would have swallowed poison or jumped into a well.

Look at me, carrying on and on about myself with no thought that I may be boring you. And yet, what have I written of myself? I know that if I write even a few words about myself this letter won't reach you. So I can't write more than this. Don't ask for more, I pray you. How can I tell you how I long to meet you, to embrace you and cry, to lie in your lap and tell you all that is in my heart? Let us see when God brings us together.

Always, only your
Prabha

I don't know how long I stood with the letter in my hand after I'd finished reading it. I was aroused only when it fell from my hand to the floor. Startled, I replaced it. When I closed the trunk I felt as if I were killing and burying a living creature. I wiped the tears from my eyes. Prabha, my Prabha, you don't know that these were my dreams too—all this was exactly what I too used to imagine. If you used to imagine your husband-to-be, did I not spend wakeful nights imagining how I would build my future? If your dreams were stifled to death, did not my future fall to the ground and shatter? But whom can I blame? You can write to Rama, blame destiny and suffocate silently, but if I too do this what will become of us?

Yet for some reason I continued to feel that my soul was burdened with the guilt of a murder, that something clung to me with its claws, like a bat. For a long time I stood banging my head against the door. Slowly the sun sank behind the tall buildings opposite. The din of the city escalated, a couple of kites hovered in the sky and a line of crows flew towards the sun.

That night, I asked Prabha, 'All right, Prabha, tell me the truth, what do you want? Be honest, don't try to mislead me, do you want me to study further or to take up a job?' And I remembered the stranger I had met.

Prabha sighed deeply. 'Can everything turn out as I want it to? One has to consider one's circumstances. But my desire is that you should study further, at least up to M.A.'

'And then?' I asked eagerly. Perhaps she would repeat the language of the letter.

'What then? Become a professor or get a good job.'

'But what will become of this house till then? Do you think I'll survive this bickering so long?'

'But it's not as if you're getting a job right now which can lift the family out of poverty,' Prabha said. Then she added,

'But don't blame me later! Do as you wish.'

'Why should I blame you, Prabha? Don't I know how difficult it is to get a good job without proper qualifications? I must do M.A., whatever happens. Even if I have to study while working. Of course, we'll have to bear some hardship.'

'What do a few more hardships matter? It's not as if we're living in luxury now.'

'I'll manage it all, Prabha, just keep encouraging me. I'll do everything, you will see. All my life I've felt very lonely, very pessimistic. No one ever uttered a word of encouragement or affection. If you can become my strength, my inspiration, I will fulfil all my dreams and yours too!' My eyes filled with tears of excitement and emotion.

'I have never intended to act as a fetter on your feet. Whenever you feel I am dragging you back, you must relentlessly move me like an obstacle out of your way and stand apart. Don't pay any attention to my cries.' Tears glimmered on her cheeks in the moonlight.

I went on in a more practical vein, 'Prabha, our first resolution is that we won't accept anything at all from this house. Tomorrow I will search for a job even more earnestly. You heard Babuji's and Amma's reaction when I asked for a sari.'

'Oh, never mind. What can they do, poor things,' Prabha said, dismissively.

'Why not? How do they find clothes for Bhabhi?' I grew annoyed. 'Just because the house runs on her husband's earnings? Why don't they say so plainly then? Why pretend that all the sons are treated equally? Anyway, we won't take anything from them now.'

'Where's the question of taking? One doesn't get even

what one asks for, and without asking . . .'

'Truly, Prabha, today I was very depressed. Had it not been for you I may not have returned home,' I said and clasped her to me. Clouds of drowsy delight gathered in the skies of her eyes, wide-open like those of an enraptured doe, and my weariness and despair dissolved in the cooling fountains of love.

4

I had told Prabha about the person I had met outside the employment exchange. His remarks kept recurring in my mind. I had been so impressed by his way of talking, his self-confident style and his anger, that I really regretted not having found out who he was so that I could have developed the acquaintance. His words had supported me in my pain. But I hadn't anticipated meeting him again so soon, although I did keep a look-out for him on the streets, hoping to bump into him once more.

As soon as he saw me, Diwakar said, 'This is what is called a long-lived devil. In English they say, "Think of the devil . . ." and in India a person who appears when you're thinking of him is considered long-lived. So which epithet do you prefer?'

Smiling sheepishly, I entered the sitting room and said, 'Whichever you like.' But I was taken aback to see someone sitting in the armchair. He was half-hidden by a newspaper. I gestured questioningly towards him.

'Listen, you can read the newspaper later. Let me

introduce you to a friend of mine,' Diwakar said, tugging at the newspaper. I thought the person quite impolite to continue reading the paper even after someone had entered the room.

But when a clean-shaven face appeared from behind the paper, I started forward, 'You?'

He calmly folded the paper and laid it aside. 'Yes, I. Diwakar talks so much about you that when I saw you the other day, I thought you might be his friend. I thought I might as well make your acquaintance before he introduced us.'

'Ever since then I've been regretting not having introduced myself to you. All that you said that day—' I broke off, trying to control some feeling akin to gratitude that was welling up in me.

Diwakar wrung his hands in mock despair.

'What's the use of introducing you now? Where did you meet each other? Anyway, Samar, this is the person I told you about—my Shirish Bhai Saheb. He did mention that he had seen you somewhere but I said you were nowhere to be found these days, and the police were out looking for you.'

Ignoring the joke, I said, 'If I had known you were Shirish Bhai Saheb—'

Interrupting, he said, 'What would you have done— beaten me up?' And he burst out laughing. 'Anyway, sit down and relax. I arrived a couple of days ago and have been waiting for you ever since.'

'I was caught up with some urgent work,' I said apologetically. Then I asked, 'Are you here on business or . . .'

'Well, yes, you could put it that way. I brought my sister.' He looked towards Diwakar, who was in his vest, a towel siting over his shoulder, ready to go for a bath.

152

'You brought her to meet Diwakar's mother?' I remarked inconsequently.

'No, not exactly.' He seemed to withdraw into himself. 'Or, yes, you could say so. Diwakar, haven't you told him the story? The fact is, Samar, my sister used to suffer from hysterical fits, and of late she has suddenly begun acting completely mad, the frequency of the fits has increased. The doctor said she must be admitted to a mental hospital as soon as possible, otherwise her condition would deteriorate. We got her admitted two days ago.'

'If you had been around we would have got you admitted too,' Diwakar put in.

I felt irritated with him for making a joke of such a serious matter. Looking with even greater concern at Shirish, I said, 'What did the doctors say was the reason for the fits?'

'What can the doctors say?' Shirish replied. 'The reason is always mental troubles, anxieties and repression. Doctors may find fancy names for it but we know the real reason.' He was silent for a while, cracking his knuckles. Then he said as if to himself, 'Not that it's anything new or out of the ordinary but she takes it that way. What can be done? It was the fault of our family. They married her off very young. She was barely eleven or twelve. Her husband was a student then. Now that he's completed his studies it's suddenly dawned on him that his wife is uneducated so he can't pull on with her. I had kept her with me and by getting after her night and day managed to make her pass her matric. But the silly girl is so depressed that one doesn't know what to do with her. If she hadn't gone and developed this illness she would have passed intermediate this year. I try my best to explain to her that she has no reason to fret. She won't listen. Keeps muttering to herself in her sleep.' The thought of his sister's sorrow choked his voice. He fell silent and began to fold up the paper.

'Hmm.' I felt as if he were recounting Munni's story. After a while I asked, 'That means you'll have to come here frequently.'

'Yes, at least twice or thrice a month. It's really very difficult.' He sounded drained. 'I'm just waiting for these politicians to pass the Hindu code bill or some such law so that I can get her divorced and remarried. Even if she can't be remarried, at least let her be rid of that useless fellow. But all they care about is votes. My family is opposed to the idea but I can't see her suffer like this . . .'

Yes, it is hard to see one's sister suffer but I was not sure divorce was the solution, so I asked, 'Are you in favour of divorce and of daughters getting an equal share in their fathers' property?'

In a calm and decisive tone he replied, 'Absolutely.'

'But that will shake up our whole society,' I said anxiously.

'What society? I don't understand,' he said, surprised.

'Our Hindu society,' I ventured. 'Terrible chaos will be let loose. The pure sacrament of marriage will become a source of entertainment for people. Marry one day and divorce the next. It will become like a children's game. Brothers will fight with sisters or sisters' husbands over the division of property. What will remain of the loving relationship between sisters and brothers?' I looked towards Diwakar, hoping he would lend me support. We both had argued about these topics for hours in the park.

'What kind of love?' His manner convinced me that he

154

was deliberately pretending not to understand me. Perhaps so as to get me to put forward all my arguments before he set out to refute them.

'The kind of love you have for your sister which makes you bring her here for treatment and come to visit her every week even at great inconvenience to yourself,' I said more forcefully. 'Because you pity her and love her. This is not a legal bond—it's your heart which impels you, your free will. If tomorrow this sister were to demand an equal share of your property, would you still pity and love her in the same way? Even against your will, you would then feel envious of her.'

'Well, you and I look at things differently,' he said in a somewhat harsh tone. 'I think even the situation you describe would be better than the one prevailing now. Fine, you pity or love your sister now. This is not a legal requirement or the result of social pressure. So, if you refuse to pity her, if you become somewhat shameless, the poor girl will have no recourse against you. She can weep, complain to a few friends, and curse her fate. If she had a share in the property, she wouldn't be forced to live the way you decide. It wouldn't be up to you to decide whether to envy her or love her. She wouldn't have to live or die at your mercy, on the crumbs you throw her. Don't brothers fight over property? They take their shares and live independently. If it were up to you to give your brother a share, if there were no law to compel you, then you would be free either to give him a share or to beggar him.'

I was taken aback by this argument. I had never considered these aspects. Still, I answered, 'Anyway you must admit that such new laws would create chaos. The laws framed with great

155

care by our ancestors for the good of society would be turned upside down.'

'So what?' He was unperturbed. 'What if they are?'

These little questions of his, asked in so cool a manner, began to upset me. Very cautiously, so as not to sound foolish, I said, 'Our glorious tradition of pure and perfect womanhood will be destroyed. Self-interest or mere gratification of desire will become the basis of marriage.'

'Pardon me, Samar,' he said in the same tone. 'Diwakar told me you are a thinking person, a reflective person. But now I see that there are two kinds of thinking. One is to judge issues by the test of reason and logic; the other is to become emotional about them. Don't mind my saying so, but your thinking is of the second kind.' Picking up the newspaper between finger and thumb, he said, 'You talk of chaos in society. Open your eyes and look around you—do you see order or beauty anywhere? This is today's newspaper—five thousand women of decent families in Lucknow district alone have filed petitions for divorce. You think all of them are mad with passion or have suddenly developed a desire for entertainment? Two women burnt to death, four jumped into wells, eight ran away or died of TB—we have grown so used to reading of cases like these that we don't give them a second thought. They leave us unmoved. Tell me, what is this wonderful system and order you are talking of? I can't speak about your family, but in my experience I don't know of a single family where women are not suffocated and helpless. I'm not talking of educated and courageous women. They too have problems, but of a different kind.'

All the time he was talking, I kept thinking of Munni and

156

Prabha. I felt as if he were talking about them alone, as if every word had reference only to my situation.

'Indian women are helplessly suffering and dying and you call it their power to endure, you worship it! Sita and Savitri—two names extracted from the history of crores of people over thousands of years! I ask you, should we not hang our heads in shame at the name of Sita? We embroider our banners with the undeserved shame and inhuman torture of an innocent woman, and worship them?'

At this, my face grew flushed. I felt as if he had abused me in public. 'So you think the laws laid down by our sages are useless?'

'I fully agree that they should be preserved in beautiful glass cases in museums, but if you insist on imposing them on today's society in the form of laws, I'll say, throw them into the stove as fuel to make tea, and laugh with joy to be rid of the load that was weighing you down and the sand that was caking your throat.' Enjoying my agitation, he took a cigarette packet from his pocket and began to search for matches.

Refusing the cigarette he offered, I examined his face carefully—was he too in the process of losing his mind like his sister? As he exhaled and blew out the burning match, I wondered how the smoke erupting from his head would look if his head were banged against the wall. Forcing myself to stay calm, I asked, 'Don't you think our Hindu religion is the best religion in the world?'

He smiled ruefully. 'I can see that you're quite cut off from the world, Samar. Are you aware that no one across the Arabian sea has ever heard this Sanghi language of yours? The world is manufacturing atom bombs and hydrogen bombs while you weep for your cowdung culture. Have you ever tried to evaluate other cultures and civilizations before talking with such arrogance? Rome and Egypt too have no dearth of ancient ruins and old books. No civilization has given half as much to the world as has the Chinese. You may abuse the Christians as much as you like for converting people but they are the only ones who go and live among alien races, enduring great hardship. They open schools and hospitals, they devote their whole lives to this work in the name of religion. As for you, if anyone gets inspired by all the talk about the world's welfare, he runs off to the Himalayas to practise austerities. If he is rich, he gives money to temples for sadhus to batten on, if he is poor he shaves his head and begins to live on milk and cream.'

'You're taking a very one-sided view, Shirish Bhai,' I said.

'I'm looking at the side which is visible to us today and of which all of us are victims. Perhaps rivers of milk once flowed in your land and gold rained down on it, but today you are the most uncivilized people in the world, and your religion the most unscientific. What a pathetic religion it is which ignores all the developments of human intellect and sets forth impracticalities as the goal of life, which imagines that all the knowledge and science of the world is to be found in the Vedas! When I hear such talk I am reminded of the nawabs of Lucknow who earn a living today by pulling handcarts.' And he laughed loudly at his witticism.

I said with an effort, 'It has never been our aim to concentrate on externals. That is why we never attacked other countries and never waged wars to spread our religion. Spiritual peace and upliftment have always been our aims.'

He burst out laughing again. 'What a beautiful web of

words woven to conceal your compulsions! That's what is called worship of poverty. It was not for philosophical reasons that you didn't attack other countries but because you lacked the strength. You never hesitated to fight among yourselves and to usurp one another's kingdoms. And Ashok and Kanishka, who had the power, did not spare outsiders either.' Then he changed tack and said, 'I am not interested in history or in abstractions—I will ask you a straight question. Ask anyone in your country today how much spiritual peace he enjoys. Spiritual peace is the property only of those who feed on milk and cream provided by charity, trusts and donations.'

I was burning with the desire to say something that would stump him. Suddenly I burst out, 'How did the universe come into being?'

He again broke into laughter. 'You have started a regular philosophical debate like the sages of old! The universe came into being like this—*Brahman,* the Universal Self thought, I am alone, let me become manifold. So he manifested his attributes, Nature appeared and the world came into existence. What's so problematic about that?' Blowing smoke through his nostrils, he tossed the cigarette out of the open door and smiled. 'Samarji, I don't say that the explanation today's scientists give of the origin of the world is the ultimate truth, but doesn't it seem more accurate than all this mumbo-jumbo? And then, is there any end to knowledge? As we get to know more, we will be better informed.' Getting up and stretching his limbs, he said, 'What a set we are—as soon as we meet we start worrying about the past and future of the world! I hope you haven't drawn the conclusion from our last meeting and today's that I'm a terribly talkative fellow.'

159

'No, no, you give me much food for thought and assessment,' I said, embarrassed.

'Then you are a half-baked Hindu. A true Hindu never thinks or assesses. He just keeps assimilating everything he can—whether it is spiritual knowledge or black money or bribes. Anyway, forgive me if anything I said offended you. I tend to forget myself when arguing. I say whatever seems right to me.'

'That's how it should be,' I said. 'I want to talk over many things with you.'

'Certainly, certainly! We'll meet often now,' Shirish said. 'Some things I'll learn from you, and some others you will rethink.'

'What can you learn from me?' I said shyly, looking down. 'Everything you said seemed new to me, I got to know many things.'

'No, no. I never consider anything complete. Everything develops, so no one's knowledge can be complete. One who has the desire to know is knowledgeable. He is knowledgeable only as long as he retains that desire; once he loses it there is no difference between him and a library book. Well, now that you and Diwakar have finished your exams, what do you plan to do next?' he asked with the solicitude of an older brother.

'That's the problem. I'm not sure.' I've never liked discussing my problems with someone I've just met.

'Study further, if you can. You are capable of achieving much,' he said.

I asked, 'What do you do?' Glancing at Diwakar, he replied, I'm a clerk with India's glorious government, earning one hundred and fifty rupees. It's very hard for me to get leave. So I'll come here every Saturday and go back on Sunday. That's what I've planned.' Seeing me get up to go, he said, 'I'll definitely meet you next time I come. I'm leaving this evening.'

'I greatly enjoyed meeting you,' I told him warmly. He was the first person I had met who, although he knew more than me, had talked to me with such affability. I was overcome.

He looked at me affectionately when I said this. We shook hands and I came out. Diwakar had been looking from one to the other of us, as if surveying two wrestlers. With every look he seemed to be saying, 'Well, what do you think of my brother!' I said, 'Just come out a minute, I have something important to tell you.'

He came out with me. On the street I said, 'Get me a job somewhere, pal, things are very bad at home. All my studies will go to waste and I'll end up as a clerk all my life. Help me spend some more time with you.'

Perhaps affected by the distress in my tone, he said at once, 'Really! why didn't you tell me before? I'll ask my father today and mention it to one or two others too.'

'Yes, please do. And let it be a job which will allow me some time to study. Seriously, I must find something.'

'Fine. Don't worry about it.'

On the way back I felt as if a vast churn were working in my head. My restlessness was not so much due to Shirish's answers as the ease with which he had an answer ready for every question. Truly, I had learnt many new things today.

5

I put my fingers into my ears as I came out of the house, determined not to listen to anything that was being said.

It was evening and a herd of cows and buffaloes was proceeding down the street, crowding the rickshaws and tongas out of its way and raising clouds of dust as it went, leaving a trail of cowdung behind it. These days the thought of going to the temple or the Sangh never came to me—it was as if I'd left all that far behind. Or as if the person who once went there was someone else, not me. It all seemed useless to me, a waste of time. I wondered how in this day and age people could waste so much time on such things.

I lay down in my favourite haunt, the park. This was where I used to lie in the early days of my marriage. People were out walking on the narrow streets and in the alleys. The way they talked and laughed, it seemed as if they had not a care in the world. Ayahs were wheeling babies around in prams. Whenever a young man and woman passed by, talking intimately and laughing, I would stare at them and grind my teeth, 'Look at them, behaving as if they couldn't care less where the next meal will come from. Must be living on inherited wealth and squabbling morning, noon and night, but they've come out for a walk as if they're off to the cinema. Idiots, have they nothing better to do?' And then I'd be angry with myself and also laugh at myself for my peevishness. What was wrong with me? Why couldn't I bear to see others happy? But I lay there unmoving and passive, as if opiated, or like a helpless invalid, unable to get up. I looked around through half-closed eyes . . . Boys playing cricket . . . a boy chasing a puppy . . . another couple . . . I felt as if I were watching all this from some other planet. But the voices from home seemed to have followed me here—bah, was that a home? It was a hell-hole crawling with worms.

'Why aren't you putting ghee on the rotis today, Bhabhi?' Amar had demanded as soon as Prabha set his plate before him.

'It's finished, Lalaji,' Prabha said mildly.

'I brought a kilo only a couple of days ago, and it's finished already?' His tone was sharp.

'It wasn't much.' Prabha was busy, and answered unthinkingly. 'After all, it's a big family.'

Amar replied rudely, 'Why don't you admit that you fed all of it to your husband? Why talk of the family? As if I don't know—anyone else in the family may or may not get any but Samar Bhaiya will get plenty in his food. But when it comes to me—'

'What do you mean, Amar?' I yelled. He wasn't aware that I was sitting just outside the kitchen, polishing my shoes. Glaring at him with furious eyes, I came into the kitchen, a shoe in one hand and a brush in the other.

As soon as he saw me, he fell silent and began nibbling at his food.

I kicked him hard in the back and said, 'You shameless fellow, have you no manners at all? Is there no limit to your impertinence? Shooting off your mouth all the time! And you a student of class ten!'

He looked at me, threw aside his plate, and stormed out, crying loudly.

Prabha stopped cooking and turned around to glare at me. 'Why do you keep sitting around and listening to what is being said? Who asked you to spring to my defence? Go out now. Don't come into the kitchen carrying a shoe—'

I yelled at her, 'Be quiet. He's grown so big and still doesn't know how to talk.'

Just then Amma shouted from her bed outside, 'Samar, come here! Do you think just because she's your wife, no one else has any right over her?'

Tossing down my shoe outside, I went pounding up to Amma. Amar was standing by her, crying.

'Why did you beat him while he was eating?' Amma asked, putting the last bead of the rosary to her eyes. 'Why don't you plainly tell us what you have in your heart?'

I shouted back, 'Can't he speak politely to his elders?'

'What did I say that was impolite?' Amar demanded, as brashly as ever. 'All I asked was how the ghee finished so soon when I brought a kilo only day before yesterday.'

'Look at him, telling lies to my face! Don't count too much on Amma's protection, Amar! I'm not done for, yet.' And I pounced on him with the brush in my hand.

'Don't you dare hit the boy!' Amma growled at me. 'I'm not

164

dead yet. As long as I'm alive I won't let anyone oppress him. Of course you now consider all of us your foes. I knew you would turn out like this. Raising your hand against your brother for the sake of that black-headed, inauspicious creature! You call him shameless but you have no shame yourself. Barely started talking to your princess and it's gone to your head— fresh fights and quarrels every day! Things were better when you weren't talking to her.'

'It's because I didn't talk to her that everyone began to misbehave,' I replied. 'No respect or concern for anyone. No notion of how to behave.'

'How would we know how to behave? You learnt all that overnight from that black-faced woman. It's only now that you've found your teacher. So now the pampered brat has set out to teach us how to behave! Till yesterday you didn't know how to walk, now you've begun to fly. Stay on the earth, son, stay on the earth. Who is shameless—he, or you who are always sheltering behind your wife, with no regard for your parents? You have no concern for your elders. We—' And Amma began to cry.

'It doesn't occur to you to do anything and if I say a word I'm sheltering behind my wife? Months have passed. Does anyone care when she eats or whether she gets any rest? I asked for a sari and all hell broke loose. Is Bhabhi incapable of doing any work at all? No, why should she? She's the older daughter-in-law, she's in the position of a mother-in-law! So she's a queen and all the rest are slavegirls.'

'Why should she be a slavegirl, I'm a slavegirl, I've fed one and now I'll feed two.' Bhabhi threw her crying child on the bed and emerged on the battlefield. She stormed into the

165

kitchen, dragged Prabha off her stool and said, 'Get away, madam, you must be suffering great inconvenience here. I'll do the cooking.'

'But I'm doing it . . . why are you angry with me, I haven't said anything . . .' Prabha continued to protest tearfully but a formidable strength had suddenly descended upon Bhabhi. She picked Prabha up and put her aside, sat down with a thump and began rolling rotis at great speed. For some time Prabha sat there stunned, her eyes full of tears, then she took the tongs and began roasting the half-cooked rotis over the fire.

'When he's asked to earn he says he wants to study, keep studying . . .' Amma's mutterings continued. Bhabhi snatched the tongs from Prabha and began hitting the rotis on the rolling board with all her might. Prabha sat there a few moments longer, confused, then she guiltily crept up to the crying baby. Bhabhi had dumped her roughly down in anger and she was crying herself hoarse. Prabha picked her up and began to rock her.

As soon as Bhabhi saw this, she stormed up to Prabha and tried to snatch the baby from her, saying, 'Let it be, let her alone. Let her cry. She won't die of a little crying. She must cry if crying is in her fate. At best she'll die and that will satisfy your soul. You can't stand the sight of my sitting with her . . .'

Prabha felt that the responsibility for the whole incident was being laid at her door. Tearfully she said, 'But I never said anything. Why are you saying all this to me?' She kept trying to hold on to the baby, who began to howl even louder at this tug of war.

I stood there, taken aback, watching all this. I felt I had been reduced to a mere spectator. I rebuked Prabha, 'Why don't you give the baby to her, Prabha?' Then I made good my escape, saying, 'One should not open one's mouth in this house. One word and everyone takes off like a rocket.'

Bhabhi snatched the child from Prabha, threw her down on the bed, and went back into the kitchen. That was how things were when I left. I don't know what happened next but I could guess the kind of storm Prabha must have had to face. My brain had turned absolutely numb.

Going over it all as I lay in the park, I felt myself become completely tense.

Suddenly I sprang up at the sound of a bullet fired nearby, as startled as if I were the target. I looked around and saw some men standing in a huddle in one corner. I rushed up to them. In the middle of a crowd of about ten to fifteen men lay a huge horse drawing its last breath, neck twisted and foaming at the mouth. A stream of thick blood flowed over the scorched grass and clotted in a pool. There was a hole in the horse's chest from which blood and some white liquid flowed out. Nearby stood a man in khaki pants and a white shirt, wiping his eyes. With one hand he leaned on a rifle propped up on the ground. I asked someone, 'What's happened?' He replied sadly, 'It's the head constable's horse. He loved it very much. It's been ill a long time and wasn't recovering, so he killed it.'

'Huh, loved it indeed! It fell ill so he killed it. Rode it all its life and now that it's ill he kills it. One day he'll kill his old father the same way . . .' I said, pulling an angry and disgusted face. I'd have said much more, but the other man looked at me scornfully and replied, 'You'd rather it should suffer and writhe in pain? It suffered just for a minute and that was the

167

end of its woes. Some can bear to see others suffer and some cannot . . .'

I came away, sat down by myself and smote my brow. What was wrong with me? Of course he was right. How was the head constable to blame? The other day I had misunderstood Shirish too. He was quite right. I am a blockhead.

When I got home at ten that night I felt my head was either empty or full of cowdung. I had a terrible headache. The house was absolutely still. Everyone had gone to sleep. The door was not bolted—either Babuji or Bhai Saheb had not yet returned. I stole up to the roof. April had gone by. Everyone was sleeping on the rooftops. I went into my room and lay down on the bed without changing my clothes. It was hot and stuffy. I was not at all sleepy. I gazed at the ceiling with vacant eyes.

Prabha suddenly appeared and sat down next to me. Timidly she touched my arm and asked, 'Won't you eat?'

I couldn't see her face. Somewhere inside me, I'd been dreading this moment. Without moving I replied tonelessly, 'No, have you eaten?'

'No . . .' she said, putting her hand on my brow.

And, suddenly, I buried my face in Prabha's lap and burst out sobbing, 'Prabha . . . Prabha, tell me, what shall we do, where shall we go?'

6

When you've heard some good news and are bursting with the desire to go home at once and share it, how irritating it is to have someone entangle you in conversation or in a highly complicated argument. You feel like standing up with a jerk, and bursting out, forgetful of courtesy and common politeness, 'Enough of this chatter. I have to go and give my wife this good news.' This was my predicament as I sat in Diwakar's sitting room.

Diwakar had asked, 'Do you really want a job?'

'Yes, yes, have you found something?' I sprang to my feet in excitement.

'Yes, but it's very far off,' Diwakar replied. 'More or less the other end of the city.'

'O tell me, tell me more! You talk of the other end of the city—I'm ready to go to the other end of the world!' I put my hand on his shoulder.

'On condition that you join third year.'

'Yes, yes, I will. Tell me.' I was getting irritated but kept smiling.

'It's the job of a proof-reader in a printing press. I fixed five to eleven in the morning as your working hours, so you can go straight from there to college.'

'Who are they? Where are they? Tell me everything, Diwakar! How much will they pay?'

'Calm down, my child! The press belongs to a friend of my father's. The salary's not much to begin with, but we can try to get it raised after a couple of months.'

'Tell me how much ... ?'

'Seventy-five. It can go up to a hundred in a couple of months. But why are you so agitated?' He couldn't help laughing at my childlike impatience.

'Oh, it's quite enough, Diwakar!' I said, overcome with gladness and gratitude. 'If it works out, Diwakar, I'll be a made man. You don't know how many troubles I have. Not a moment's peace at home ...' A turbulent tide rose and swept me on. 'When will you take me there? Come, let's go now, right away.'

Diwakar looked keenly at me for a moment and then said, 'All right, let's go.'

And when everything had been settled, I still could not believe that I had actually got this job at seventy-five rupees a month. I had begun to feel as if I was fated to be starved of money all my life. To get seventy-five rupees in a lump sum every month was like a dream that was scarcely credible. My poor brother's salary was only slightly higher than this even though he worked all day long. As we returned, my heart was flying ahead and saying to Prabha, 'Prabha, listen, I've got a job!'

I owed it to Diwakar, without him I would have continued

to rot. I went back with him to his house. We had decided that I would stay at the press from five to eleven and then go straight to college. Perhaps, if I were fortunate, we would not be allotted a first period in the third year time-table. Since fate had now smiled on me surely she would extend her kindness that far. Otherwise I'd have to miss the first period and wheedle one of the professors into giving me extra attendance. I felt like falling at Diwakar's feet.

'Diwakar, you have saved me, otherwise I'd have gone mad—that's the truth. You have no idea how bad things are at home.' I didn't know how to express my gratitude. My eyes filled with tears.

'Forget it, pal, I didn't do anything. To struggle against difficulties is heroism. You give me such fine lectures but are so weak yourself.' And to save me further embarrassment he changed the subject. 'But there's one problem. It's very far from your house. You'll find it hard to travel so far, and where will you eat?'

'It's not far—two miles at most. It'll be a good morning walk. Yes, food is a problem.' I thought a moment and said, 'But that's okay. Prabha will pack food for me. She'll have to wake up a bit earlier or else she can cook it at night. Diwakar, she was very anxious that I should do M.A. She'll be wild with joy.'

'Ah yes, tell me.' He suddenly recalled something. 'That day, you said to Kiran . . .'

I caught hold of his hands and said apologetically, 'These things happen! Let me get through this phase and then one day I'll tell you everything.'

'As you please. But won't she find it difficult to cook so

early in the morning?' he asked, trying to work it out. 'Because, to reach there at five, you'll have to leave home at four-thirty, which means getting up around three-thirty. It'll be really hard.'

'It'll be taken care of, Diwakar. You don't know her, no one knows how much hardship she has endured. She can do anything, endure anything for me.' And the thought of Prabha's sacrifices and sufferings for such an unfortunate wretch as me brought tears to my eyes. My lips trembled with emotion. I looked away and tried to control myself. It wouldn't look good if I started to cry like this before Prabha too. We walked on in silence. Then I said with difficulty, 'Diwakar, lend me some money.'

'How much?'

'Twenty will be enough. I'll repay you as soon as I'm paid.' I thought I wouldn't go home empty-handed today. How happy Prabha would be if I took her something! And she badly needed a sari.

'I don't have it on me. If Kiran has it I'll give it to you. Oh yes, Shirish Bhai is here, he was asking about you. Today is Saturday so he arrived by the afternoon train. Then he went to visit his sister—he must be back by now.'

I felt like saying, no, not now, I don't want to meet anyone. I must go straight to Prabha and give her this news. But I wanted to borrow money from Diwakar, and also I was so obliged to him that if he had asked me to accompany him to hell at that moment I would have agreed. As we walked along, I asked, 'Sunday will be a holiday, won't it?'

'Absolutely. If he asks you to come on Sunday he will pay you overtime.' Then he added, 'You don't know proof-reading. It'll take you some days to pick it up.'

'I'll manage, Diwakar, you think I'm a slowcoach like you?'
And for no reason at all, I burst out laughing.

I had just taken the money with trembling hands when
Shirish Bhai appeared. 'What, off as soon as you see me?'

'It was to see you that I came.' As I spoke I thought, I will
be able to buy at least two saris with the money. I asked, 'How
is your sister feeling?'

He settled tiredly into a chair. Sighing deeply, he said, 'All
right. It will take time. Diwakar, forgive me. I told you I would
take you along to see her, but I was so upset that I went off
without you. So, how are you?'

'Fine—'

'Well, well, what's this I see!' he broke in, 'What's become
of your topknot?' Diwakar leapt up, 'Yes, I didn't notice—what
happened?'

My face grew red. The day before, while getting a haircut,
I'd got the topknot cut off. I don't know whether fear of
Shirish Bhai was behind this or my having understood that it
was of no use. But after it was done I felt so embarrassed that
I hardly dared step out. I was constantly running my hand
over my head as if to smooth down my untidy hair, but in fact
to conceal what I had done. My family was sure to raise a hue
and cry; besides, my friends too would give me a hard time if
they got to know. The top knot's absence was not noticeable
because I had begun to hide it in my hair of late. But how long
could I deceive my family? I knew the remarks I would have
to hear. 'He has set out to become a fine gentleman!' 'Fashion
has gone to his head!' 'He's forgotten his religion!' I considered
wearing a cap. But that would only attract attention because
I had never worn one before. I was constantly on the alert,

wondering whether anyone had noticed that I'd cut off my topknot. Today I'd forgotten all about it in the excitement of getting a job. Now embarrassment gripped me anew.

'Just one debate made you forget all your piety,' Diwakar said teasingly. 'Fancy, I've been with you so long and I didn't notice it.'

Shirish Bhai came to my rescue. 'He puts into practice what seems reasonable to him. He's not an obstinate mule like you.'

'Good, he looks like a human being now. Earlier he looked like a cartoon,' Diwakar said, laughing. I felt too happy to take offence at anything he said. All I wanted was to get through these civilities as soon as possible and go to Prabha. She would be overjoyed.

Shirish Bhai lit a cigarette and changed the topic. 'So, you didn't tell me why Indian culture is so great.'

I was relieved at the change of topic. Ever since our last discussion, I had been thinking about the issues he'd raised, but hadn't been able to arrive at a conclusion. I was not sure I could put into words the little I knew. I replied, 'Self-knowledge and spiritual reflection, I think—'

He interrupted, 'These are big words and I don't understand their meaning. Even if you explain the meaning, I won't be able to understand of what use they are or why they are necessary. So please . . .'

I was taken aback but managed to say, 'In simple language it would perhaps be called knowledge of oneself and of the world.'

He interrupted again, 'The world is false, an illusion, and you are a part of *Brahman*. Your parents, brothers and sisters, wife and children, all are illusions to entrap you, and you an illusion to entrap them. Self-knowledge is to be found by breaking all these illusory bonds. Run off to a cave in the Himalayas and you will be rid of all these bonds.' He laughed loudly. 'Wonderful!'

I was stunned and couldn't think of an immediate reply. Putting his hand on my shoulder, he said, 'This philosophy of escapism and defeatism has brought you to the present pass. That a son should consider his father illusion and the father his son illusion—what could be more ungrateful and insulting? Is it not the height of ingratitude to call the woman who gave you birth the doorway to hell and the woman you are going to make your son's mother a pit of corruption?'

'But all these relationships leave you empty-handed in the end,' I said.

'Is that a reason to commit suicide? Wonderful, what a wonderful philosophy!' This time he was genuinely excited. 'What beautiful names for suicide—self-knowledge, absorption in *Brahman*, freedom from illusory bonds, a state of steadiness in wisdom! Why should you think you have conferred a great boon on this universe by appearing in it? A magician draws out all these philosophical abstractions one after another, like rabbits from a hat—*Brahman*, Maya, the three Gunas, and then off you run in pursuit of this knowledge of *Brahman* . . .'

'It saves you from useless troubles and anxieties,' I said.

'Ah yes—others are suffering and you have attained knowledge of *Brahman*. You sit apart, lost in meditation, while your family is overtaken by disaster. Now who will come to their aid? Is this knowledge of *Brahman* or a bottle of liquor that sends you into a state of unconsciousness? To hell with home and family—let them fall into a well!' Then he suddenly seemed to recollect something and added, 'Well sir, what if your parents had not cared to educate you or to feed and clothe you properly? Why then should you curse them when you grow up? Why don't you decide that they too had attained the knowledge of *Brahman* and had begun to consider you an illusory abstraction in their path?'

This really stumped me. I had never thought of the knowledge of *Brahman* in this light. Looked at this way, it really appeared like ingratitude and irresponsibility. I tried another approach, 'The knowledge of *Brahman* is not so gross and superficial. So many events that we call divine, so many phenomena that appear miraculous ...'

'Your talk of miracles and divine events puts me in mind of something,' Shirish Bhai said, smiling, 'I don't know how far it's true, but I've heard this story about Swami Vivekanand. They say that on one of his journeys he had to cross a river. The ferry had gone over to the other shore so Swamiji had to wait for it. Just then an ascetic appeared and they got talking. When the ascetic heard that the Swami was waiting for the boat, he castigated him, saying, "If such trivial obstructions are able to halt you on your path, how can you enlighten the world? You are Swami Vivekanand, and are thought of as a great spiritual teacher, a philosopher, yet you cannot cross a mere river. Watch me, I'll show you how rivers are crossed."

'And the ascetic walked on the water with ease. After taking a long walk on the surface of the water, the ascetic returned and said challengingly, "One does not become a swami merely by going to America and giving speeches. It requires meditation and austerities." The Swami was truly amazed by the ascetic's powers. He asked, "Mahatma, where and how did you attain this ability?" Smiling at the effect he had created and at the Swami's dullness, the ascetic said with pride, "It was not easy to accomplish it. I practised austerities in the caves of the Himalayas for thirty years." At this, the Swami burst out laughing.' Here Shirish Bhai paused to allow me to question him.

The story was so interesting and had been broken off at such a point that I could not help asking, 'Why? What was there to laugh at?'

'That's what the Swami explained. He said: "Mahatma, I'm truly amazed at this miracle you have performed. But the river can be crossed by paying two paise. And you have wasted thirty years of your life to do this. Thirty years that you can never recall, for a job that can be done at a cost of two paise! You've spent thirty years acquiring this ability and will spend the rest of your life demonstrating it. All your life you will do nothing but cross rivers and gain people's devotion. Could you not have spent those thirty years for the welfare of humanity? Even discovered some medicine that would have freed people from a disease?"

'I don't know if this story is true or apocryphal. But we cannot deny that while human beings were dying of hunger and disease, your Indian culture kept singing songs about human welfare. We roast and devour women and Shudras even while we raise slogans about the equality of all life. We could see the same *Brahman* in an ant and an elephant, but we could not treat Shambuk and Sita as living beings. What atrocities we heaped upon them!'

177

And all of a sudden I stopped hearing what Shirish Bhai was saying. I felt as if I were standing before Prabha, with my head bowed like a criminal. Did King Ram, the ideal for all men, never, in his own heart, stand thus, his head bowed by the weight of his crime? Did he never find himself speechless before Sita? I began to feel suffocated. I felt that I should be with Prabha now, at this moment, not here, engaged in debate. How to end this discussion and make my escape? But his arguments were so interesting that I was rooted to my seat.

He was saying, 'Our biggest problem is that we don't know our history. I don't know if other races have their authentic history or not, but certainly what we have is mythology, not history. The Puranas so blend poetry and history that it's hard to unravel the truth. When historical truths and facts are given poetic form, the sequence of their reality is changed and their significance oriented to another purpose. And then the Puranic myths have been poetically reconceived in every age so that one cannot find out what the truth was. Everyone knows that every age looks at history and mythology in the light of its own circumstances and problems. It bends them to suit itself—not merely interprets them afresh but puts a new spirit into the old form. You can well imagine what truth is left once it has travelled from ear to ear over hundreds of years. You must have witnessed how even a small incident is changed drastically when it passes from one person to another in the course of five minutes. In any case, poetry weighs history down with metaphor, symbol and irony.'

I was only half-listening to him. Noticing this, he said, 'Is my talk upsetting you?'

'No, no, why do you say that?'

'I felt perhaps something was troubling you . . .'

'The thing is . . .' I stammered, 'I'm in a bit of a hurry just now. I have some work at home. Your talk is so interesting that one doesn't feel like leaving. Of course much that you say is new so it startles me.'

'Oh, why didn't you tell me earlier that you had to go? What a strange fellow you are!' He stood up. 'Brother, I'm infected with the virus of argument. You must tell me when you are busy. I'm a talkative chap.' Laughing at this weakness of his, he said, 'Your results are due any day, aren't they?'

'That's the anxiety that is consuming me. God knows what will happen!' My heart sank at the thought. Smiling weakly, I said, 'My younger brother has appeared for matric. He's also mad with worry. I wonder whether he manages to get any sleep at night or not! One day he's off to light a lamp in the temple, the next day he is visiting an astrologer, and the third day he's making offerings to Hanumanji, on the fourth to Shivji . . .'

This time Diwakar spoke. 'Yes, yes, I wanted to talk to you about him. I often see him around when I go out. He's immature and going through a dangerous phase, you should watch over him, otherwise he will get into bad company. I don't like the look of the boys I see him with.'

'I know that, Diwakar, but I can't do anything about it. It's hard to explain but . . .' My head drooped as I recalled the incident of Amar's insolence to Prabha. I said goodbye to Shirish Bhai and came out.

Diwakar accompanied me to the door. As we stepped out he said, 'While you two were taking civilization and culture to pieces, I thought of a solution to your problem.'

'What?' Today, he seemed to be acting like an angel sent to solve all my problems.

'There's a train which passes here at four-thirty or five and reaches Raja Mandi in five to ten minutes. You can walk it from there.'

'Wonderful. I never thought of that. What an easy solution!'

'But it'll cost you two annas a day,' Diwakar said uncertainly.

Shaking hands as we parted, I replied, 'Forget it! I am not the kind who buys tickets. I'll evade the ticket checker so smoothly that he won't know which way his head's screwed on!'

And laughing loudly, I set off.

When the shopkeeper told me that one sari would cost twelve rupees, my enthusiasm was dampened.

I had planned to buy at least two. Anyway, one would do. Tossing the bundle from hand to hand, I raced along. If only the road were smooth and sloping like a mountainside covered with snow, so that I could slide along and reach home in a jiffy! Prabha would feel as if I'd suddenly descended from heaven, and would leap with joy when she saw the sari! As I walked, I smiled and murmured to myself. I tossed my head and pursed my lips as I made calculations on my fingertips. Then I burst out laughing at my crazy behaviour.

Now, God willing, if I got good results, all my problems would be solved! Nothing to stop me doing M.A. then!

God willing . . . if Shirish were here, he would take God to pieces too. Foolish fellow! What he says is true, but how will we exist without culture, civilization and religion! He says we are now at a point where no religion except humanity is required. But our religion is an eternal one. Imagine, we've been discussing all this for two hours! I was in a hurry to get to Prabha and he went on and on. How much the poor girl has suffered! This is the first gift I am giving her.

But soon my pleasure turned to grave anxiety. How would I give this to Prabha? This was a big problem that I had overlooked. It wouldn't look good to give it to her in front of everyone. Amma and Bhabhi would be upset. What I could do is go straight to Amma and give her the sari. I'll tell her I've brought it for her. She'll understand. After all, we've just had that talk about a sari. She herself will give it to Prabha. Yes, that's best. It will get me out of the mess. How much squabbling there is in our house over every small thing! But is my poor mother to blame?

After all, things are so difficult. Poor Bhai Saheb toils all day and earns hardly anything. Thank God the house is our own. If it were rented, we'd have to pay at least thirty rupees every month. Actually this sari from my first salary should go to Amma. If I give it to her how happy she will be . . .

But all these emotions were dispelled as soon as I reached our door. As I entered, Kunwar asked, 'What's this you've brought, Bhaiya?' Spontaneously, I replied, 'A sari for your sister-in-law. She needs one badly.' And off he went. I went straight to Amma and put the bundle in her lap. 'What's this?' she asked. I said affectionately, 'Amma, I've brought you a sari.' And at that moment I really felt that if Amma wanted to keep it, I wouldn't say anything. I could buy another for Prabha. Just then I saw Prabha sitting in a corner, grinding herbs for chutney. Then I felt, no, her need is greater than Amma's. As soon as I get my first salary, I'll definitely get one for Prabha. Let Amma keep this.

Amma smiled and said, 'For me indeed! Why don't you say you've brought it for your wife?' She began to open the bundle. Rocking the baby in her arms, Bhabhi too came up to see it.

'It's very nice!' Amma and Bhabhi exclaimed together. Just then, Kunwar came in. He watched for a few moments and then said, 'It's for Chhoti Bhabhi.'

'Yes, yes, of course. I understand that,' Amma said wisely, as if she had known this since her previous birth.

'Bhaiya told me at the door,' Kunwar said, to reinforce his point.

This put paid to all Amma's pleasure. I glared at Kunwar but either he couldn't see me in the dark, or he enjoyed setting Amma against me. Amma looked the sari over as if to complete a ritual, then folded it and held it out to me, 'Here . . .'

'You keep it, Amma, what will I do with it?' I was feeling annoyed both with Kunwar and with myself. I almost said to her, 'You give it to Prabha yourself,' but I kept quiet.

'Why don't you give it yourself to the person for whom you've brought it? Why drag me into the picture?' Amma said with such bitterness that I was forced to take the sari. I quietly went to my room and put it on the bed. That was the end to all my enthusiasm and joy!

That night at dinner I said to my brother, 'Bhai Saheb, I've decided to join third year.' I was afraid this would cause an explosion.

Bhai Saheb stopped chewing and looked at me as if he didn't know who I was. Then he said, 'Have you asked Babuji?'

'He will agree if you do,' I said, gaining courage from his reasonable tone. 'The thing is, Bhai Saheb, one can't get a good job unless one is well qualified. So many graduates and post-graduates remain unemployed.'

In injured tones Bhai Saheb replied, 'That is all very well, but think of the expense. Even B.A. costs something. I don't think Amar is going to pass, and . . .' I answered firmly, 'I'll manage my own expenses for B.A. You won't have to worry about that.' The announcement that I had got a job rose to my lips but I said nothing.

'But you are not alone. There are others too,' he said. Clearly, he meant Prabha.

'I'll take care of all that, Bhai Saheb,' I said in a half-obstinate, half-wheedling tone. 'Please speak to Babuji.'

'Well, do as you like. I'm not going to speak to Babuji. He's always in a bad mood these days.' Bhai Saheb was annoyed and fell silent. So I would have to suffer Babuji's wrath. That moment, too, arrived soon enough.

Prabha was pleased with the sari but somewhat upset too. She said gravely, 'You have annoyed Amma.'

'Well, what else could I have done? Was it my fault? I was ready to get you another one if she had kept this.'

'Oh really—you've become very rich all of a sudden!' Prabha said with laughing tenderness in her eyes. 'What happened—did you find some money lying on the road?'

Trying to make it sound unimportant, I said carelessly, 'I've got a job.'

'What? Really?' Prabha leapt up. Her eyes widened with surprise, pleasure and eagerness. 'What a deep one you are! Sitting there so long and not saying a word about it! And now behaving as if nothing at all has happened!'

Her excitement made me feel very good. But I kept up the

appearance of carelessness, 'Ye-es. What's so special about it? I would have told you sooner or later.'

Prabha was overwhelmed with happiness. Her pleasure was like an explosion of flowers on a tree branch, and it made me feel that something really important had happened. Excited, I wrapped my arms around her and covered her face with kisses. 'Yes, Prabha, I was teasing you. How worried I have been about whether I would be able to study further.'

When Prabha was able to catch her breath, she asked, 'How much will you get?'

'Oh, don't ask that. It's just about enough to keep my studies going. If it continues, I'll be able to complete M.A. at least.'

She caught hold of my shoulders and shook me. 'But tell me, tell me what the salary is.' Her exasperation tickled me no end. I lay down comfortably with my head on her lap and began playing with her plait as if I hadn't heard what she'd said, and continued what I had been saying. 'First of all, I have to get admission, and get a fee exemption. Then I'll somehow get lots of clothes for you. Two saris, blouses, a coat for winter.'

'You won't tell me what I'm asking, and you keep talking all kinds of nonsense.' Her exasperation was growing. She had my hand in hers. She put my finger between her teeth and said, 'Aha, now you'll have to tell me.' The pressure of her teeth increased.

'And listen, no need to take anything from this house, not a single paisa's worth. We'll buy for ouselves whatever we need.'

'Tell . . . tell . . .' Her teeth sank deeper into my finger. 'Ssee . . . ! Ow, stop, you'll bite off my finger!' I cried in pain.

'Then why don't you tell me?' She looked at me guiltily, ashamed of what she had done. Looking at the tooth marks on my finger I grew irritated and hit her on the back. 'Idiot, if I hadn't stopped you, you would have bitten off my finger.' Then I felt afraid that she would get annoyed. I felt like laughing at our childish squabbling. Pressing her close to me I tried to make light of the whole thing, 'Old enough to be a mother of three, and behaves like a kid. And has teeth as sharp as a mouse.'

She grew cross, and lifted my head off her lap. 'Why should I bear this weight, and get hit into the bargain?' She bit back a smile. I was afraid I might have hurt her.

At once, I came around. 'All right, all right, I'll tell you. But let me put my head back first.' And then I put my head back on her lap and told her everything.

That night we stayed up late, talking. I indulged in all kinds of flights of fancy. Again and again, I dwelt on my various dreams. It was decided that if I got good marks in M.A., I would become a professor. 'You're a lucky one,' I said to her. 'An illiterate like you will be known as Mrs Professor!'

Prabha grew annoyed. 'Fine, then get yourself an educated wife. Select one of your female students.'

'What about my own girl who will also become a student?' I said, cajolingly.

Forgetting her annoyance, she said, 'Yes, I'm telling you right away, don't make a fuss later. I'll definitely join college.'

'Do anything you like, Prabha! You'll be the queen of the house. Who can stop you then?' I got lost in my dreams again. 'We'll have a library with all the latest books, and we'll subscribe to two or three magazines.'

'But the house will seem very quiet without a radio,' Prabha said.

'Why quiet?' I said mischievously. 'We'll make arrangements in advance. By then, a walking radio will begin moving about the house.'

Prabha's face grew suffused with shyness. And at that moment nothing seemed out of reach. With my head on Prabha's arm, the biggest problems seemed small to me. I felt as if I would be able to overcome all obstacles. Prabha proposed changes in my plans and I in hers. We discussed everything from the flowers in the garden to the nameplate on the gate of our bungalow. Whenever we recalled how baseless all our talk was, we'd say, 'This is called counting the chickens before they are hatched, building castles in the air!' We'd be quiet a little while and then begin again. But what all our talk came to, finally, was, 'These hardships and difficulties will only last a short time. We must face them with courage. After that I'll make you a queen, Prabha, a queen!' And when she assured me she would silently endure all the hardships in the world, I was overwhelmed with gratitude and faith. When I remembered that we had not included the family in any of our blueprints of the future I said, 'I'll keep one brother with me and educate him. Not Amar, he's very rude. Kunwar is better. Amma and Babuji won't like to leave their house and live with us, they can come for visits. Bhai Saheb's burden will be lightened.' Prabha didn't say anything.

That night, the imagination was freed and the dreams on our lips yearned to burst into song. That night our two spirits united and became a rainbow that would take us from the present into the golden world of the future. We could clearly see ourselves walking hand in hand on that bridge. That night, the sky above glittered with blossoms of light.

We decided that as the next day was Sunday, I should go and survey my workplace, and then I would break the news to the family. But I would tell them clearly that Diwakar had got me this job on condition that I continue my studies. Just before going to sleep I realized that I hadn't talked at all to Prabha about the person who had got me the job. Nor had I told her about Shirish Bhai.

As soon as we woke up next morning, I said, 'Prabha, one of these days you must come with me to Diwakar's house. He has asked me many times to bring you.' I told her about the day we had gone to the cinema and I had told them that Prabha was at her parents' place. I told her about Kiran's remarks.

Prabha was embarrassed at the idea of meeting Kiran. She said, 'How can I go? You see how things are here.'

'You have to go with me. Things here will be bad whatever we do. Anyway, no need to worry about it right now. But we must not delay it too much. One day you must go and meet Shirish Bhai's sister too.'

'Who?' she asked, surprised.

And I gave a detailed account of Shirish Bhai—everything from our meeting at the employment exchange till date. Then I said, 'Really, Prabha, that man is amazing. He has his own way of looking at everything. It's as if he doesn't believe in anything. Takes everything to pieces! He says we don't have our own history. We have only mythology which is a mixture of religion, superstition and poetry. We can't make out how much of it is true. Plus we have poems written by hired poets who term a chieftain of five villages the crown jewel of the earth. He says our ancient texts, the Shastras and Smritis, say that laws came into existence first and human society afterwards. How and why should laws come into existence before human beings? Today, human beings do not need Hinduism, Islam, Christianity or any other religion. We need only one religion—humanity . . .'

Here I was suddenly interrupted. The door shook as if someone had kicked it with all his might. We froze as if struck by lightning. We got up with a start when the yelling and shrieking began outside. At first we didn't quite know what had happened. Then we made out that it was Babuji, shouting loudly, quite oblivious to the fact that the neighbours would hear him. Prabha had begun straightening her clothes and I, my knees trembling, peered through the cracks in the door. Babuji was standing there, roaring, 'We too were young once, but we could tell the difference between day and night! Lies around all day with his wife! Has no shame before his elders or before the children in the house! It's nearly ten and the gentleman hasn't woken up yet! What shamelessness! Giggling and squeaking all night, mad with youth. Unconcerned what the world may think. To hell with such blindness and immodesty! When he wasn't talking to her he was as scared as if she were a lioness, not a woman, and now that he's begun talking he's always hovering round her. The whole family has bathed and completed the morning's work, while here they are still lost in sport and mirth!'

We looked at one another as if a bomb had suddenly exploded. What should we do now? I peered out again. Babuji's lecture was still in full swing. 'Look at the cheek of this dolt! He'll study further! His lordship has a buried granary somewhere! Thinks he's the son of a king!'

Hmm. So the affair of the sari and the talk of studying further, had been reported to Babuji. When he went away after yelling himself hoarse, Prabha opened the door a crack and peeped out fearfully. Then she slipped out, shrinking and silent, and went downstairs. I sat there, trying to work up the courage to go out and meet everyone's eyes.

I felt as if we had been caught red-handed committing some highly immoral and indecent offence.

7

Overnight I found the atmosphere of home transformed. Everyone's behaviour seemed different. I had sensed this but it was Prabha who first put it into words.

One day I was late getting back. As I stepped in, expecting to be yelled at, I came face to face with Babuji. He was coming along with a labourer carrying a headload of firewood. Babuji had some vegetables in the sling bag on his shoulder. This was a habit of his. Whenever he went out to buy wood or wheat, he would take this bag along and buy up some vegetable vendor's last stock at a cheaper-than-market rate. He was free all day so he did all the household shopping. If it was left to us brothers we would end up arguing about who should go. Each one thought his studies most important and each dreaded some classmate or teacher seeing him laden with vegetables or rations.

I trembled with fear when I saw Babuji. Of late I had taken to slipping upstairs silently and sitting alone in my room. So, when I encountered any family member, it was either while entering or leaving the house, or when coming downstairs to bathe or to eat. I thought Babuji would now pick up the threads of his last harangue.

But when he saw me, he said, 'Try to come home on time, Samar. After all, Bahu too doesn't eat. She keeps waiting for you. Why don't you have lunch before you go out? Eating cold food is not good for you.'

I had forgotten that Babuji was capable of speaking in such an affectionate manner. My hair stood on end. I was prepared for a scolding but these kind accents struck terror in my heart. God knows what is going to happen! But Prabha soon relieved me of my fears. She remarked, 'The whole family is becoming very magnanimous towards us these days.' I was startled, and remembered the afternoon's incident. 'Why, what happened?' I asked.

'Nothing in particular. But I notice a change. Your mother and Bhabhi deliberately overlook things which earlier led to fierce battles. Amma constantly remarks that if you begin to contribute, the situation will become much easier. Yesterday she asked me whether I had enough clothes. Bhabhi bought her daughter an ice-cream and kept trying to persuade me to have one too.'

'Hmm.' I fell silent. Yes, this was the change I too had sensed, and this newfound gentleness displayed by my family made me anxious. When I didn't speak for quite a while, Prabha shook me. 'What's eating you?'

I sighed deeply, and replied, 'Nothing, Prabha. You tell me, how am I to explain to them that I can't contribute anything right now? They are pinning all their hopes on me but I feel it will be more than enough if I can somehow provide for our personal expenses. At least we won't be a burden on them then.

'We'll manage on our own. After all, I have to think about my B.A.—it's no joke. Diwakar clearly said he was getting me this job so that I could do my B.A. Won't he feel bad if I don't fulfil the commitment I made when I took the job?'

'Why should he feel bad?' Prabha asked, trying to gauge my thoughts.

'I asked him to get me a job only so that I could study further. This time, each book will cost fifteen rupees. Anyway, I won't buy books. I can read Diwakar's. If we study together, we won't need two sets of books. But even so, what is seventy-five rupees? I have to return twenty to Diwakar. As soon as college reopens, twenty-six rupees or so will go for admission fees and so on. And look at these clothes—are they fit for college? They've become absolutely threadbare. I should have at least one decent set of pants and shirt. To tell the truth, I don't have shoes, I don't have a pen, I use Bhai Saheb's razor— the needs are endless. And this month they have all descended together on my head. About twenty-five rupees will go on paper, exercise books, and stuff like that. Then I want to get you a sari and blouse . . .'

'Leave me out of it. I've told you I have more than enough. I'll tell you when I need anything. Nothing for me. It can be bought next month or any time later . . .' This time, Prabha was really agitated.

'Anyway, you can see how the account stands. Now tell me, what will be left of seventy-five rupees? Which item should I knock out in order to make a contribution to the family kitty? At the most, I won't return Diwakar's loan this month.' Then suddenly I recollected something, 'College will open on the eighth and I won't get paid before the fifteenth. I'll have

192

to take another loan because I'll have to buy all these things much before I get paid.'

And then we poured out our woes to each other at great length. Lost in my thoughts, I said, 'Prabha, I can see that Babuji, Amma, Bhai Saheb, all have pinned their hopes on me. But I can't tell them all my problems. Even if I do, they will not understand. They know I'll get just seventy-five rupees but to them it appears like a gold mine. You tell me, how am I to explain to them?' I drew a deep breath and continued, 'And these wretched results too are wringing the life out of me. Who knows what will happen? Will I be able to join college at all, or will all my aspirations remain unfulfilled?' And I saw gathering before me a vast, dark sea whose shores could not be discerned.

These days, the air was thick with talk of the results. Wherever one looked, one was sure to see a group of boys earnestly discussing how they had performed and what marks they expected. Or how the same examiner who had thrown Umanath out on his ear when he went to try and get his marks raised, quietly obliged Baleshwar, who had a high-up patron to put pressure on the examiner.

I kept out of it. I had developed a new self-assurance. Best cross one's bridges when one comes to them. But I had begun to sympathize with the other boys' impatience. Who knew what conditions they faced at home?

I had started going to work. I had thought that until college opened, Prabha could be spared some hardship. Once college opened, I would have to go straight there from work, so the poor girl would have to get up at three-thirty or four in the morning to feed me. But now, I could go to work without eating, and return home by noon. As it was, she worked like a bullock at the plough. I never saw her rest for a moment from morning until eleven or twelve at night. But, despite all my attempts to slip out of bed very quietly, she somehow or other always woke up too. On my insistence, she would go back to bed and pretend to sleep. But I knew that as soon as I left the house, she would get up and start the day's work. I felt terrible. Earlier she used at least to sleep till six but now she had to get up even earlier because of me.

My way of reaching my workplace was very interesting. Our city had two stations—one was near our house, the other near my workplace. There was a morning train which covered the distance in barely five minutes. The moment the train stopped I would be through the broken fencing that ran alongside the railway line, and start strolling down the road as if I'd been there quite a while. The first couple of days I was in a sorry state. I described it to Prabha, 'My heart beat so loud that I could feel it thumping. On the train, I was dizzy with anxiety. Again and again I would break out in a cold sweat at the thought that the TT might be round the corner, or that any moment a black-coated official might seize my arm.' But that was only the first two days. Later my courage grew and I developed many evasive tactics.

Until the train began to move, I would appear utterly unconcerned, as if I were waiting for another train. I would keep an eye on the TT, and as soon as the train started, I would get into the compartment that was farthest away from him. When it stopped, I would be the first one out on the platform, strolling along as if I'd been there a long time and had nothing whatever to do with this train!

So the train journey was a source of entertainment as well as a blessing, for even the thought of having to walk such a distance every morning petrified me. In summer one might manage it, but to brave the winter in my threadbare old clothes would have indeed been hard. I shuddered at the thought.

As for the work, to begin with I found it interesting but later it grew monotonous. Inditing all kinds of weird symbols on wet, ink-blotted proof-sheets from five to eleven made my head ache. And I would feel afraid—if this work was so exhausting and painful, how would I manage to concentrate on my studies once college opened and I had to go straight there from work!

In the first few days I was full of enthusiasm and corrected proofs at a speed that amazed the press workers. What was there to it—just read a page and mark the mistakes. But the manager returned all the pages I had read because they were full of mistakes. I was surprised—how come I'd overlooked so many even though I'd read so carefully? Gradually, I lost enthusiasm, and after I'd gone laboriously through the pages, comparing each word with the original, my head felt like a lump of wet clay. I had to work amid the clatter of the machines above which rose full-throated yells, 'Why is the note-type not registering?' 'What are you gaping at now? Put in the paper!' When the manager, hands in the pockets of his ink-stained trousers, came and stood near me, watching me proof-read, I would feel as uneasy and agitated as I used to when the invigilator came and stood near me during an exam. As he walked away, he would say, 'You're very slow, mister, the machine is standing idle. The corrections will take time too. Read them carefully, and read again and again. Proof-reading is like sweeping the floor. Each time you sweep, you manage to collect a little more dust from somewhere or other.'

The place was dismally overshadowed by blackness and ink. Sumera in one corner soaking something in water and pounding it, and the machine man in another, thickening ink on a makeshift brick oven. The nauseating smell of glue lingered in the air, and the thick greasy black waste dripping from the machines would wickedly scheme to get on to your clothes. The boy from the Sindhi hotel came in every ten minutes or so with glasses in his wire holder, to give tea to one of the workers or to answer Sumera's summons and provide refreshments for the clients who had come to see the manager.

But the people who worked there were so interesting that one could not get bored. At first I felt out of place, but soon I grew to like them. While they were composing type or distributing it into cases, they would recount with great enjoyment some girl's love story or the adulterous intrigues of a neighbour, or a strange narrative made up of a mixture of many films, strongly spiced with imagination. Whether the story was drawn from films or from life, the theme was always the same—sex. I noticed one boy in particular. He was usually silent and his face and manner created the impression that he belonged to a respectable family. His silence seemed to indicate that he was not prepared to descend to the level of the others. The old machineman went to see almost every film that came to town. And, every day, I would recount to Prabha the stories these men told.

When I returned home at noon, soaked in sweat, I would be dizzy with hunger, but, compelled by the heat, I would gulp down two glasses of water, which would take the edge off my appetite. I would have the food fetched up to my room. I didn't like the idea that Prabha should stay hungry so long on my account. So on the first day itself I said, 'What is this nonsense, Prabha? How can you be so foolish despite all your education? Why do you wait till one o'clock for me? Please eat on time—after all, you work so hard all day.'

'I eat at my usual time. Who says I wait for you? It's at this time that I get through all the chores.' She pulled a wry face. 'As if you are so good-looking that I'd sit around waiting for you! I'm not one to delay my meals, don't you worry.'

'Then why don't you eat earlier?' Her quick repartee was endearing. 'Good-looking indeed! I'm a lot better looking than anyone in your family, that's for sure. Each one of them looks like an ape!'

'Hey, hey, don't you say a word against my family or it'll be the worse for you. Just because I keep quiet, you think you will get the better of me.' She drew her eyebrows together and looked at me angrily.

'Well, let's see what you do to me,' I teased her.

'I'm going, you can sit here and talk rubbish to yourself.' She stood up and flounced away. 'Ammaji and Bhabhi make all kinds of unkind remarks when I come to sit with you, and then you talk such rubbish. I'm the only scapegoat around here.' Her voice grew husky but she swallowed and made a joke of the whole thing, 'You can be made to behave yourself only when Babuji throws a fit.'

I caught hold of her hand. 'Why would I have bothered about him? It was you who turned red as if you were bathed in vermilion.'

'Oho, and what about you—you were trembling and

couldn't get a word out, and now you sit around showing off!'
She couldn't help laughing at the memory.

'All right, forget it, have you nothing better to talk about?
Come on, let's eat.' I drew her hand to the plate and tried to
force her to pick up a morsel.

'O lord, you'll be the death of me. If anyone sees, I'll be
thrown out of the house. Eating together indeed!' She threw a
scared glance over her shoulder.

'All right, now stop talking nonsense and eat quietly!' I
rebuked her. In my heart I thought, how unfair that the poor
girl should wait so long and yet not have the pleasure of eating
with me. A picture of the future flashed before my eyes, when
she and I would sit together and eat at a proper table. She
would look out through the window, waiting for me to come
home in my free periods.

She smiled faintly, as if a similar picture had appeared to
her too. She got up and closed the door, 'All right, let's close
the door first . . .' Then she began to shrug and pout like a
child, 'I feel shy eating with you . . .'

'You'll get spanked if you pretend to be shy.' She tried to
get up but I pulled her back and made her sit down.

The whole family was stunned when it turned out that I had
somehow passed in the second division, but Amar's name was
nowhere to be seen on the list. I can still see before me the
scene that ensued. Amar sat in a corner, sobbing. Dejection
hung heavy over the house. The shock was so great that no
one felt any pleasure at my having passed. Everyone was
horrified by the thought that Amar's way would have to be
paid through yet another year. Babuji was pacing about, his

arms folded over his chest, 'I kept telling the sons of owls to work hard. But the wretches have no time to study. One has got out of hand ever since he got married. How he used to boast that he would definitely get a first division! Now have a good time with your second division. And as for you, Amarji, take note of what I say. I can't afford to spend money like water on you. You are so busy having fun with your friends that you have no time to study. If you want to study further, provide for yourself, otherwise go and beg on the streets.'

Prabha told me that while Bhabhi had expressed great sorrow at her Amar Lalaji's having failed, and had spent much time consoling him, she had said to her husband, 'A nice sort of mess this house is in. We toil day and night to feed and educate these hulks, and they never stop to think that we too have a child whose future we must consider.' Bhai Saheb had replied, 'Never mind. I am doomed to work like an ox and throw my earnings into this bottomless pit . . .' And he had broken down.

Bhai Saheb's sorrow moved me deeply.

Despite all the taunts and opposition I faced at home, I went with Diwakar and, with great difficulty, managed to enrol myself in college. When I saw the hordes of boys there struggling to get admission, and the tactics and contacts they brought into play to achieve this, I felt that to pass an exam was no big deal compared to success in this competition. It was so hard that I almost felt as if my life's ambition would be fulfilled if only I could cross this hellish whirlpool of admission procedures. I had no one to help me, and I saw first divisioners kowtowing to the principal and vice-principal. One was recommended by an MP, another was accompanied by a man specially sent by a magistrate. It looked as if each class would have at least four sections of sixty boys each. I had to waste three whole days on getting myself enrolled. I managed it because I was an old student of the college. It was the first year students who had the hardest time. And to get Amar re-admitted proved extremely difficult. But, surprisingly, the furore at home died down in a couple of days.

Now Prabha's real troubles began. I had to rush straight to college from the press at eleven in the morning, and my classes ended at three. Fortunately, military training had not begun in college, otherwise I would have been stuck there from four-thirty to seven-thirty, or else had to pay an eight anna fee. When that began, I'd have to leave home at four-thirty in the morning and wouldn't get back till seven or eight in the evening. The problem of my meals arose once more. Prabha said, 'Why do you bother your head for nothing? I'm telling you I'll get up at three o'clock and cook something.'

'As it is you work non-stop all day, and now this! You'll sleep at eleven-thirty at night and get up at three? What exactly do you have in mind?' I asked in mock anger. 'Tell me plainly, and I'll kill you off right away.'

'Oh, I won't die of doing a little work. And do you think I'll do it for free? I'm telling you, you'll have to repay it all . . .'

Her manner touched my heart, and I said joyfully, 'If I live, I'll pay back every penny. I'm doing all this only to be able to give you a decent life; do you think I enjoy working from four in the morning to ten at night?' Then I recollected myself and said, 'No, whatever happens, I won't let you get up at three. Why don't you cook the food at night and keep it for me?'

'But it'll go stale by morning . . .'

'No, it won't. And I'll eat it at ten, in the press. How can it go stale so quickly?' I thought I had managed to convince her. She said, 'And you'll go around carrying that tiffin box all day?'

'No, I'll leave it in the press and pick it up on my way back. It's very close by.'

But she suddenly reverted to her original position. 'No, no, it's no problem at all. I'll cook it in the morning. You'll feel better if you have a hot meal before you go. They say eating stale food dulls the brain and one feels sluggish all day.' Then suddenly she recalled something and added, 'Oh yes, Amma said that if you carry food with you, I should make at least four paranthas. Because you might want to share with a friend so you should have enough to make a decent meal.'

'Really! I didn't know she'd said that.' I began to feel anxious. 'Prabha, I understand this family very well. All this kindness is because I'm supposed to get paid around the tenth. If it were not for that, do you think they'd have kept quiet when I got new clothes made, or bought books, or paid my fees? I'd have been slaughtered on each occasion! But tell me, what am I to give them from my salary? Listen, I have an idea. Can you somehow give Bhabhi an account of our expenses this month?'

'Wonderful! So I get a beating and you watch the fun! You're real smart, aren't you? Amma will grind her teeth and say: "Now she's accounting for her husband's earnings."'

'Then tell me, how am I to get across to them? I've decided that we'll cost them very little in future, except for our food. But let's see how things work out!' A sigh escaped me, and hung damply between us.

We were silent for a few moments, then I jerked my head up and said, 'Prabha, I feel like giving up the whole thing and getting rid of all these problems. Why have we got ourselves into this mess? No peace by day, no rest at night. We're consumed with anxiety all the time. Running around in circles from four in the morning to ten at night. Why don't I just become a clerk somewhere and we'll have sixty or seventy rupees to spend each month. I'll leave at ten and be back by five. At most, I'll have to bring a few files home.'

Prabha gave me a sympathetic look. 'But the problem is not just money. You're earning that much anyway. The real problem is that we have too many dreams. Our plans for the future are so different!'

'Yes, that's the root of the problem. But those dreams are not mine alone,' I said, troubled. 'Tell me, what should we do with our dreams? If one has a heart, one must dream.'

'What's come over you today?' Prabha said with affectionate reproach. 'This is a phase of hardship, it'll soon be over. After all, it's we who will enjoy the happiness of our dreams being fulfilled. Why shouldn't we suffer a little for our dreams? And whether anyone else is with you or not, I am with you.' She put her hand on my shoulder.

And my heart overflowed with gladness. I felt like putting my head on her lap and bursting into tears. She seemed to me like a goddess from heaven who was under a curse that compelled her to spend some time here. Could I ever have faced all these problems without her constant inspiration? Never, never, I would have given in long ago. In a husky voice I asked, 'Prabha, tell me, do you never feel discouraged by all these difficulties and disappointments? Did you never

202

feel defeated, even temporarily, in the days when I was not speaking to you?'

'I?' She answered with great self-confidence. 'You don't know me yet. I have tremendous survival power. Even greater trials than these would not be able to move me. Before marriage, I used to feel afraid, wondering what would happen, and feeling that I wouldn't be able to bear any hardship. But now that I have experienced pain and trouble, I wonder, is that all, is this what I was so frightened of?' Somewhat embarrassed at sounding like a schoolmistress, she looked down. I felt as if a roseate radiance of energy were bursting from her face and forming a circle of light around her.

'No, Prabha, I am not defeated. I didn't mean what I said. You'll see, I will do it all. You don't yet know what I will do for you, what I can do for you . . .' With tingling hands, I took hold of her shoulders and raised her head. Looking at her face, her lowered eyes, a strange thought came to me—what if she were to become a mother in this interim period? And I felt that she had somehow sensed my thought and was blushing even more deeply . . .

8

Exhaustion has an intoxication of its own. I was lying on a small cot outside my room, on the roof, in an attitude suggestive of one lying in a boat. My head hung down, my arms were spread out, and my feet rested on the ground. Each limb dangled lifelessly. I could hear many voices downstairs. Huh, now Amar was to be married, was he?

Stepping inside the house, I'd been startled by a familiar voice. I peeped into the sitting room and saw my maternal uncle there. I was surprised. This was his first visit since my wedding. He was offended with us. I hesitated and then went upstairs.

But his voice followed me, 'Samar, aren't you going to meet me, son?' Perhaps he had been informed of my coming. Unwillingly, I came downstairs. He was still in the sitting room; perhaps he hadn't come inside because he wanted to show that he had not yet got over his annoyance. When I touched his feet, he put an arm round me, made me sit next to him, and continued talking to Babuji.

'It's for you to do as you like, to assess things for yourself. I know of this girl so I have told you. Because it's like this—a man acts for the best, but is misunderstood. When my sister spoke as she did at Samar's wedding, I felt like drowning myself in shame.' He sounded offended.

Babuji was sitting on a tuffet, pulling strange faces and extracting wax from his ear with a matchstick. He seemed to be deliberately keeping himself busy. Finally, he wiped his ear with his fingers and said, 'Forget it, Chandanji, why do you pay any attention to women's talk? They have nothing better to do than to wag their tongues.' Then he added in a mild tone, 'You must have seen the girl. What's the family like? Tell me frankly.'

Hmm, so a girl is being discussed! I listened quietly.

'No, no, that's wrong,' my uncle said, spreading out both arms like a peacock's tail. 'You see the girl for yourself, show her to Amar and to a few of your neighbours. Make all arrangements yourself. They asked me to talk to you, they were after me for three days, so I was forced to come, but I won't do any more.'

'Tch, tch, that's all right, brother, but . . .'

I couldn't restrain myself any longer. I said, 'Babuji, what's your hurry? He's just failed, and now you want to get him married. What if he fails again . . .'

'You be quiet, you don't understand anything and keep interfering!' Babuji rebuked me. 'Who's getting him married right away? The negotiations go on for ages. If only I can get everything done in my lifetime, I'll feel free and can go bathe in the Ganga. Who knows what will happen later?' His voice grew husky, and to control himself he drew on his hookah. My uncle had drawn on it and pushed it towards him. Taking a pull, he added, 'Pass and fail will go on. Life can't be stopped on that account. Well, Chandanji, don't take offence, but this time we don't want the kind of confusion there was at Samar's wedding. We must have a plain talk about the give and take . . .'

The humiliation of being rebuked by Babuji filled my heart with bitterness and my eyes with tears. You've had your way with me, now get Amar married too! As if we don't have enough squabbling in the house, take on the expense of one more person. He must be married, true, but why not let him stand on his own feet first? But no. To voice an opinion is a sin. They'll have a plain talk about give and take, but quarrel over it later all the same. They won't listen to any advice. They are the only ones who have a right to speak in the matter. We are either idiots or sacrificial goats. I have already been led to the slaughter and now it's poor Amar's turn. And I felt it was futile for me to continue sitting there. Much better to go take a nap instead. I tried to stand up but my uncle caught my hand and made me sit down again. 'Where are you off to? I've been waiting for you so long—where had you gone?'

I swallowed and said, 'To college, Uncle.' Amar came in with the baby, deposited her in Babuji's lap, and went away as if he were not at all concerned with what was being discussed.

Uncle said, 'Oh, so you've joined college?' Nodding his head in approval, he went on, 'Very good. Study as much as you can, son. Learning is the only true wealth.'

I kept quiet.

'And, how are things? You're looking very pulled down. What's the matter? Why don't you take care of your health?'

He laughed meaningfully. 'Have you given up going to the Sangh parades in the morning?'

'This prince doesn't open his eyes till nine in the morning. Is he to go to the parade in the afternoon?' Babuji spoke softly, while playing with the child, but I was stung by what he said. He was reminding me of that day's incident.

I felt like retorting, 'Yes, I don't open my eyes before ten in the morning, so what do you have to say about that?' But I somehow forced myself to reply, 'No, Uncle, nothing's wrong with me. This year it's so terribly hot a summer that one doesn't have the energy to do anything.'

'Ah yes, that's true, that's true.' Taking the hookah from Babuji and putting it to his lips, he went on, 'Now you should take some responsibility for the family, son! You must think about how you can contribute. One's duty to one's parents is uppermost. Now you are grown up, you are a family man, you should educate your younger brothers. How long can the eldest alone do everything?'

Babuji intervened again, 'Why should he worry? As long as he and his wife do well, the rest of the world can go to hell for all he cares!'

He was about to say something even harsher but Uncle stopped him. 'Just a moment. Let me talk, you keep quiet a while. He's not a child, he will understand. And son, your parents have educated you, got you married, how much longer will you depend on them? When parents struggle so hard to educate their children, they do it in hopes of something, don't they?' He again put his arm around my waist.

Babuji must certainly have complained to Uncle, otherwise how could he know all this? He must have offered to talk to me. This was a well-formed plan—I understood it. But it was perhaps the first time in two years that a family member was talking to me so affectionately, explaining the situation of the family to me. Although I understood what he was implying, his intimate tone melted me, brought tears to my eyes, and I listened quietly, curling and uncurling my big toes as I did so.

'Everyone gets married, but can one leave one's parents or brothers and sisters on that account? When utensils are kept together, they are bound to clash and clang. Women are fickle-minded, easily moved. A sensible man should not be misled by their talk. You are better educated than I am, you understand these things better. She has come from another house, another family, what does she care about your family ties! After all, blood is blood—a blood relationship cannot be broken. So, son, these are the perils of domestic life, one has to tread very cautiously.' He kept stroking my shoulder.

And someone inside me shrieked, 'Uncle, you don't know, you don't know how things are in this house. If you knew, you wouldn't come here, proposing to get Amar married.' These thoughts came to me, yet I sat there silent, like an offender, my eyes fixed on the ground.

'As for quarrels between mother-in-law and daughter-in-law, in which house do they not occur? I know of such quarrels even in the homes of millionaires. After all, in every house the stove is made of clay.' He continued affectionately stroking my back.

For some reason, and wholly against my will, I felt like bursting into tears. I had a strong desire to run and fall at Babuji's feet, to cry and ask his pardon for the excesses and discourtesies I had committed. Until today, I had never looked at things from this point of view. Truly, my behaviour towards them had been neglectful and wrong. But all I managed to utter, with great difficulty, was, 'Uncle, I want to study further.'

'No one wants to stop you, son! But one has to cut one's coat according to one's cloth. Isn't your elder brother doing his duty? My child, when you live with others, you have to consider all this. Now you are a family man, try to understand how the world goes. Keep your wife in her place, teach her how to behave respectfully and to follow the rules. If love leads you to place her above you, she'll learn nothing. Girls have to learn everything at their in-laws' house, in their own homes they do nothing but gambol and play.' And he continued in his butter-soft and honey-sweet language to teach me how to keep a woman under control. I knew that not all of this was advice; some of it was merely a repetition of the accusations levelled against Prabha and me. Several times, I was on the verge of contradicting him.

'And your father says you are giving up prayer, religious rites, everything. Is that what education teaches you, son? If people give up all rites, how will the world be sustained? Think of your ancestors. What difficulties they had to face and what terrible trials, but they were like lions, they gave up their lives but not their religion. How Hakikat Rai and Bandabahadur were tortured! We owe it to the splendour of our religion that we are sitting here today. Otherwise, we might have been in Pakistan, or else worshipping in some church. You are better educated than me. You well know that if the Germans had not stolen the Vedas from us, the West could never have produced so many inventions. To steal is easy, but we would have acknowledged their intellectual abilities had they invented radios and aeroplanes on their own.' And his eyes became moist at the memory of this glorious past. I was trying to think of a reply to all this when Babuji's loud voice suddenly brought the mesmerism to a violent end, 'You are instructing a stone, Chandan. It has been said: Give instruction to one whom instruction becomes; do not give instruction to a monkey.

'Your words will have no effect, Brother. They will be so much water on a duck's back. He'll listen quietly, but will do exactly what he wants to, what his wife tells him to. Why waste your time? He too must be in a hurry to go to his wife.' He paused a moment and added, 'I say, let him do whatever he wants to, we will endure what is in our fate, as we have so far.'

Uncle too was taken aback at Babuji's unexpected outburst. This was not in their programme, apparently. Patting my back, he said, 'No, no, our Samar is not a child. He understands everything, he's just a bit spirited. Isn't it so, son? Ask your father's pardon, son! He is older, after all.'

It was as if someone had pressed a switch and at once turned off the humility, meekness and timid sentimentality that had arisen in me. Babuji's words pierced me to the heart. I longed to throw courtesy to the winds and say something harsh. I brazenly raised my head, so far meekly bowed, stood erect and taut, and came upstairs without saying a word. Yes, I am as I am. What do you propose to do about it?

Standing on the roof, I was trying to decide whether to go out and roam around, or to go back to bed. Just then Prabha came out of the room, sewing a button on to a blouse she had taken off. She stood for a while, observing me, then came up and asked, 'What happened?' She touched my neck, 'Are you feeling all right?' I didn't answer or respond. She said, 'What did Uncle say?'

'He said my foot!' I exclaimed, exasperated, and then my eyes fell on her face. I thought, what has she done, why am I venting my irritation on her? She doesn't even know what happened. Softening, I said, 'He was telling me how a wife should be kept in her place. I know, Babuji must have complained to him. He is not an astrologer who can read everything in one's face. How did he get to know all this?'

Prabha stroked my shoulder lovingly and said, 'So what if he did tell him something—why upset yourself? Go out and take a walk, you'll feel better. He's older, it's his duty to explain things to you.'

'Who is he to explain things? Why doesn't he explain to the others?' I thought a moment and said, 'No, Prabha, the problem is that I am a very weak-minded man, anyone can get the better of me. He spoke affectionately and I nearly melted. Tell me, what have I done that he should tell me to ask Babuji's pardon? Shouldn't he say what fault I have committed so that I can tell Babuji it was a mistake and can ask to be forgiven? I have never been rude to him, never confronted him. Never talked against him. Why this constant refrain: His wife teaches him, his wife teaches him? What do you teach me, after all? Just because we keep quiet they think they can keep cawing away at us. Your wife did this, your wife did that. You get up at three in the morning and don't get to bed till midnight, shouldn't they realize that we have desires too? Does anyone in this house have any consideration for us?'

'It's all right. Why do you upset yourself by thinking of all this? It's a matter of a few days. It won't go on forever.'

But I continued in my own strain. 'Who is he to teach me religion? Why doesn't he try to understand it himself? Kill a person in the name of religion! Don't let him see which way the world is going. Sit in a temple and keep clashing your cymbals—everything else will get done of itself, God will do it. If anyone talks sense, call him an atheist and rush to bite him.'

Prabha got somewhat irritated. 'What if he did say something? Ignore it. Elders have the right to say anything they wish.' She added teasingly, 'He arranged your marriage. Doesn't he have the right to comment on it?'

'Great job he did,' I said. 'Look at how things are in this house—and he's come to arrange another marriage. Has his eye on Amar now. Fellow doesn't earn a penny. Like you, she too will yearn for a paisa to buy a thread and needle to stitch her torn sari. One brother started earning and they got me married; I haven't even started doing anything and they're entrapping the third one. What do they care—it's the girl who'll bemoan her fate.'

This time Prabha laughed aloud. 'If you're in this state now, you really will be more dangerous than these people when you grow old!'

The way she said this made me forget my anger and laugh too. I felt like patting her cheek and saying, 'You are a wicked one!' But I recovered my former gravity. 'No, Prabha, I know what the real problem is. Today is the eleventh. According to their calculations I should have got my salary by now. I haven't given them anything. And when I did not say a word about it even today, they lost their patience.'

'Oh yes, I didn't ask you. You must have got your pay

212

yesterday, what did you do with it?' This time, the maturity of a true housewife entered her tone.

My voice grew sharp once more. 'That wretch of a press owner didn't pay me. Better if I had taken up tuitions instead. May the wretch's children die! God knows what the son of a cur has in mind! I've already taken loans of sixty-one rupees. Now if I give the remaining eight to Babuji, even a bag of peanuts will be beyond my reach! A fine state of affairs! If I'm not paid tomorrow, I'm going to demand the money. Does he think I have a buried treasure at home, or what? I'll tell him he can keep his proof-reading with my compliments, if this is the way he intends to behave. I'll find another job. To hell with the job if the bastard refuses to part with his money . . .' At this, Prabha could not hold back her laughter—she covered her face with her sari and laughed away. I felt that her laughter was artificial, calculated to make me forget my pain. Then she said, 'You sound like a seventy-year-old harridan. What would anyone who heard you think.'

She gave me a push. 'Go and take a walk—you need some fresh air. But come back soon. I'll keep dinner for you.'

I went off, laughing at my own folly and at Prabha's reactions, but soon all that my father and uncle had said began to trouble me afresh. I was surprised when I realized that although my father had spoken in anger and my uncle in honeyed tones, yet the essence of what each had said was the same. One point of view but two modes of expression!

Lost in thought, I wandered the streets.

As I walked along, I suddenly felt as if I was being followed. When I turned round, there was Diwakar, overcome with mirth! There was someone else with him too. For a moment, before I recognized him, fear seized me. Then Diwakar said, 'Well, my friend, are you sure you know where you are going and why? We've been with you for two furlongs! The way you mutter and gesticulate to yourself! You appear to be quarrelling with yourself and getting ready to fight—what is all this?'

I felt highly embarrassed. I peered into the darkness and discerned Shirish Bhai standing unconcernedly nearby, smoking a cigarette. Each time he inhaled, a fiery flower glowed beneath his eyes. I hastily greeted him, feeling very awkward at the thought that both of them had been following me for quite a while. God knows what I had been saying to myself, what kind of gestures I had been making! What must they have thought of me! Somehow I managed to say, smiling sheepishly, 'Where have you been?'

'I've told you we've been accompanying you for half an hour,' Diwakar repeated brashly. 'We've been listening to your conversations with yourself.'

'Yes, I too felt you were reflecting on some very weighty problem. What was it? Some knotty question of Indian culture?' And Shirish Bhai laughed loudly. Then, observing my face, he asked sympathetically, 'What's the matter—is it really so terrible a problem?'

Had Diwakar asked this, I might have replied sharply, or evaded him. But I respected Shirish Bhai so I replied mildly, 'No, nothing important, Shirish Bhai! Once an idea gets into my head, it takes me a long time to get rid of it.'

'Look, when something is troubling one's mind and soul, one should always share it with someone else. That diminishes its power over one. Perhaps it is this need to relieve one's heart that lies behind the Catholic tradition of confession to a priest.' Coming close, he put a hand on my shoulder and added, 'But I'm not trying to persuade you to tell me your personal affairs.'

'Why, would it be a great disaster if one did enquire about his personal affairs or if he did talk about them?' Diwakar put his hand on my other shoulder.

Shirish laughed, 'But I don't like this police-like style of extracting a confession!'

Afraid that they might take offence, I said, 'No, no, there's no such problem!' I thought a moment and went on, 'Diwakar, you are well aware of the situation in my family. Something or other crops up every day. They've barely managed to get me married and now they're doing Amar the same favour. If I say a word I'm treated to a hundred sermons.'

Shirish Bhai asked, 'Do all of you live together?'

'My uncles live separately. My parents, brothers and I are together.' I said.

'Forgive me if I ask a few questions about your personal life.' And as we walked along, Shirish Bhai kept asking about my family and I kept replying without trying to conceal anything. When we got to the quarrel, I acknowledged sadly that the squabbling had started from the very day of my wedding. Then he asked about Prabha, her education, her temperament, her aspirations and the problems she faced at home. I was troubled by his way of asking these questions as if he were a doctor, yet I also enjoyed talking about Prabha's good sense, her education, her dreams. But finally he asked a question which I found myself unable to answer.

'Fine, you were married against your wishes, but now

answer one question truthfully. Do you truly love your wife now or are you impelled by your duty as a husband to think of her the way you do?' He seemed preoccupied with his cigarette as he asked this.

'I . . . I . . .' I stammered. At that moment I could not decide whether the feeling I had for Prabha was love, or remorse for my conduct, or only pity for the situation she was forced to endure. No answer came to me. Somehow I managed to pull myself together and say, 'I am studying further because she wishes me to. Had it not been for her, perhaps I would long ago have become a clerk at a salary of 100 or 125 rupees a month. She is very anxious that I should be well educated and hold a good job. Shirish Bhai, I can't tell you how much hardship she has endured for my sake. She gets up at three in the morning to cook for me, and toils non-stop till midnight.'

All three of us fell silent and I kept searching for an answer to his question. A thought flashed into my mind and I felt like expressing it to Shirish Bhai. 'She has forgotten herself completely for my sake—it is as if she has no joys and sorrows, no desires and aspirations of her own.' But then I realized that this suggested her feelings. It did not answer his question. And my heart melted for Prabha. I did not know how, in what words, to express my inner turmoil. Gripped by this restlessness, I looked at Shirish Bhai. He was stepping along, silent, deep in thought. I knew he would soon speak. Perhaps that was what I was waiting for.

The road was deserted. We had walked a long way. Had I paid attention to my surroundings I could have identified them, but I contented myself with reading the advertisements for clothes and shoes written in large black letters on a high wall that flanked the road. I felt as if a mist was beginning to enshroud me. It was around eight-thirty or nine. Earth and sky were awash in milky moonlight. Perhaps that was why the streetlights were not on. The streetlights generally stay switched off during the bright phase of the moon. How strange it is that wherever I may be on a moonlit night, when I think of Prabha I think of her huddled up, crying, on the roof. At this moment too, that scene on the roof came before my eyes.

'Samar, my friend!' Shirish Bhai's voice seemed to come from a long way off. 'When I think of your real situation, or Diwakar's or my own, I begin to realize that we will have to break this tradition of the joint family. To take your case, if you want to stay alive, if you want your wife to stay alive, the only way is to live separately. However hard it may be, live separately . . .'

This advice was so unexpected that I was stunned. Hesitantly, I said, 'I don't get your meaning, Shirish Bhai.'

'Don't take offence, Samar, but the truth is that all your wife's aspirations and your efforts will die a slow death in this atmosphere. One problem after another will keep cropping up, and perhaps you will spend your whole life merely dreaming of the day when you can sleep in peace and contentment.'

'You mean you are not at all in favour of the joint family?' Perhaps he was right about me personally, because it did seem to me as if my difficulties were infinite in number, but I could not quite swallow the fact that he should dismiss an entire family system in so summary a manner.

'Yes, you could say so,' he replied. 'The joint family cannot work in today's economic conditions. If it continues, it will give rise within it to many units consisting of smaller families. You cannot imagine the terrible consequences of the sentimentality that prevents us from splitting up. We become miserable wrecks, we fight and quarrel day and night, yet we insist on staying together. How many murders and suicides take place every day as a result of our preoccupation with honour, our refusal to maintain separate kitchens, and our selfish struggles veiled by a show of sentiment. Even if you overlook all this, one consequence is so terrible that it cannot be ignored.'

'What is that?' I was compelled to ask when he broke off at this point.

Knowing we were listening closely to what he was saying, he told us, 'The joint family may sound like a great ideal, but its greatest disadvantage is that no member of the family is able to develop an individual personality. All one's time is spent either creating problems or trying to solve them. Quarrels, conflicts, vindictiveness, guilt—all make the atmosphere so poisonous and suffocating that one can hardly breathe. The cause of all the troubles is financial, as you well know. As a result, we lead a constantly divided existence—outside, we fight economic battles, and indoors, struggle with familial discord. If a man is simple and straightforward, he gets ground to pieces by all this.'

Diwakar, who had been silent so long, suddenly turned around and asked, 'But this is the situation, not the consequence, surely?'

'I told you—the consequence is that your individual growth gets stunted. You get no chance to develop your strengths and your talents in the right direction. Or, one could say, you exhaust your energies in so many petty affairs that your mind and heart become incapable of fulfilling your dreams. You just don't have any energy left for your studies or for your intellectual development. This is one major reason why so few great minds appear in our country today. We somehow memorize some stuff, pass an exam and think we've achieved great things. What we memorize are the leavings of somebody else. Far from contributing to scientific, literary or philosophical developments in the world, we do not even get to know of them. What we know is the little that someone has swallowed and regurgitated, or what went out of date fifty years ago. How long can we keep masking this unfortunate situation, this failure of ours, by telling ourselves we don't need the scientific advancements and knowledge available in the world because we are the most knowledgeable race of all, and have given great things to the world? All we manage to do is produce one regiment after another of convention-bound fools.' He came back to his original advice, 'Well, Brother, the simple solution to your problems is that you should start living separately and at the same time fulfil whatever responsibility you feel towards your family.'

I was amazed at this man's analytical powers, surprised at how easily all that he said made its way into my understanding. Why had I not realized these simple truths earlier? Suddenly a question occurred to me. I asked, 'But, Shirish Bhai, wouldn't this be gross selfishness? Parents cherish such high hopes of their children when they bring them up and educate them. They think their children will support them in their old age, will help them in illness and trouble, will carry on the family line. Wouldn't it be selfish of the children to separate as soon as they become capable of doing so?'

He hesitated a moment, then said, 'It certainly would appear like selfishness. But would it not be better if parents allowed children to develop freely so that the idea of their duty to their parents could grow up naturally in their hearts, rather than trying to tie them down and denying them the opportunity to develop their personalities? I think such problems do not arise when there are only one or two children. The joint family becomes a curse when there are many children, and the family is not well off or has severely limited sources of income. In such a situation, parents think they have the primary claim on their son while the wife thinks whoever's son he may be, he is certainly her husband and she has a primary right over his earnings. To fulfil your duty, it's best to live separately and bring up one or two of your younger brothers and sisters. That way you will lighten the burden on your parents. Also, practical experience shows that when people live separately, their relations do not sour. If brothers insist on living together, they will separate sooner or later, but with bitterness, after a fight, and often all relations are severed, they stop speaking to each other. Parents should, of their own accord, first equip the children adequately and then leave them free to test out their abilities. Parents should, help children find their freedom. Parents do not realize how harmful their sentimental desire to keep everyone living together can be.'

If only Prabha had been there to hear all this!

All the way back, I thought how I would recount it to her. If I tried to explain it to Babuji, I would get nothing but more abuses, 'Who are these friends of yours who give you these fine ideas? Of course this is what you are bound to pick up from such good-for-nothing friends.'

My uncle left without even having a meal at our house.

9

Is it love I feel for Prabha, pity for the difficult situation she is trapped in, or merely remorse for my misdoings? The question that had arisen at that moment would perhaps have continued to churn in my mind for a long time had something not happened which shook me to the core, and made me feel as if I had always been standing alone, with no one close to me.

'You've worked very hard today. Let me press your feet,' Prabha said, sitting down next to me on the bed. I immediately snapped out of my drowsiness and drew my feet away.

'No, certainly not. You rest. What if I did work a little today? You work much harder all day, every day.' Looking up at the sky, I asked, 'It must be ten-thirty or eleven—have you been in the kitchen all this time?'

'What to do—Bhai Saheb came in late today. I really feel very sorry for him. He's so simple and good, never goes out or mixes with anyone, just keeps working all day.' Swinging her legs as she sat on the bed, Prabha went on, 'I served his food, washed the dishes and the kitchen, kept things ready for the morning. It was very hot so I had a bath . . .'

'Oho, that's why you're sitting pretty like a little princess, clean clothes and all. I felt something was different today. What's this perfume? What have you got on?' I drew her to me.

Prabha blushed, looked away, and said, 'I had a little musk, so I couldn't resist it.' Freeing herself, she added, 'Really, I very much feel like pressing your feet today. When I saw you carrying buckets of water upstairs, I thought, Right now, he's determined to carry bucket after bucket, but at night his legs will ache.'

How much Prabha cares for me! I felt very happy. Stroking her back, I said affectionately, 'No, Prabha, if my legs begin to ache at this age just because I've done a little work, what will become of me at Babuji's age? Look at him, he carries fifteen kilos of wheat home from market . . . How hot it was today!'

All evening I had been feeling the heat, so I had brought up buckets of water from downstairs and drenched the whole roof. We slept in a secluded corner between my room and the outer wall. Unless someone specially came this way, we were sheltered from the eyes of anyone coming up or going down. Bhaiya and Bhabhi slept on the other side. Amar, Kunwar, and my parents slept out in the open, near the stairs. Today, I had wet the whole terrace and also poured a bucket of water over each of the cots that lay baking in the sun all day. So it was somewhat cool now. I lay with just a pillow on the wet cot, looking up at the star-studded sky. Sometimes one star would leap from its place and go to join another group, drawing a line of fire as it went. With wonder I would tell myself that, to look at, this journey had taken but a moment, yet in reality it may have taken thousands of light years. Was there no way whereby one could journey to all these stars in a lifetime? How do the inhabitants of those worlds live? Then I would feel frustrated—we, who know so little of our own world, how can we know all about the entire universe? The other day, Shirish Bhai had said, 'Far from contributing to the scientific developments in the world, we do not even know what others have done . . .'

As I was thinking along these lines, my eyes closed. Some part of my mind was aware of the clinking of dishes and the sound of voices downstairs, by which I could guess the various goings-on in the house. I could hear the murmur of Bhabhi's and her child's voices from the other corner of the roof, and, far away, snatches of a film song. Will we sleep on the roof when we have a separate house of our own? But we will have a lawn there . . .

'What are you thinking?' Prabha nudged me with her elbow. I could feel her hands stroking my calves. I came back to consciousness with a jerk, yawned, and asked, 'Have you finished eating?'

'I must have. Why worry your head about it?' she replied, pouting.

In a tone expressive of my concern and yet inability to help, I said, 'No, Prabha, don't take it like that. You know the problems here as well as I do. What I would like is for both of us to always eat together. You will see, once I become a professor and we have our own house, you'll never have cause to complain. Here, I can't ask you every day whether or not you've eaten. If I do, we'll soon have another uproar on our hands.'

Prabha burst out laughing. 'I was only joking, silly. I've

eaten much better than you have today. Didn't you notice the sweetmeats you got a little of—did you think they were made specially for you?'

I liked the sound of her laughter in the silence of the night, as if a string of tiny silver bells had been set tinkling by a gust of wind. The memory of Babuji roaring at us the other day struck us both at the same time perhaps, and her laughter abruptly broke off. To divert our attention, I asked, 'What's so special about today? I thought those sweets had been sent us from the house of some friend who'd got married.'

Then I realized that after stroking my legs Prabha had gradually begun to press my feet. Holding her hands back, I asked, 'What has come over you today? I told you I don't like this. I should press your feet—you are the one who works like an ox all day.' Then I changed the subject, 'So, what were we celebrating today? Has uncle fixed up a match for Amar, or what?'

'No, no. We kept a fast today—Bhabhi, I and Mrs Awasthi who lives next door.'

'I see. That's why you are so eager to serve your husband today,' I said jokingly. 'In what connection were you fasting, little goddess?'

'What has that to do with you? These are women's affairs.' In case I should take offence she added, 'Shouldn't I do something to help you study well and get a good job?'

Her hands continued to press my feet. I was beginning to find it pleasurable now so I didn't resist too forcefully. Doubling my arm under my head, I turned towards Prabha and said, 'As it is you work so hard, Prabha, and now you want to start keeping fasts and rituals too. Why don't you ever think

224

of your health? If you fall sick I won't even be able to afford proper treatment for you.'

Prabha tossed her head. 'Does anyone fall sick from keeping a fast? Fasting improves one's health. You have no idea how many benefits one derives from fasting.'

I said somewhat dryly, 'Perhaps one does. I don't believe in all this and I don't like hearing about it.' Somewhat startled by my own harshness I added, 'To fast one requires proper diet—fruit, milk, dry fruits—one might derive some benefits that way. But not to drink a drop of water all day—is that a fast or a punishment?'

To evade this Prabha said, 'Nobody fasts every day. It's just once in six months or a year.'

'The question is not one of frequency,' I said. 'I don't believe in all these superstitions. You never told me that you believe in them. At one time, I did have faith in all this. I used to go to the temple, make vows and keep fasts. But now I no longer have any such faith.' And I thought to myself that perhaps this change had come about from keeping company with Shirish and Diwakar.

Prabha's voice grew husky. 'I don't believe in it either, but when living with others in one house, one has to do many things one doesn't want to. Bhabhi was keeping the fast. What a scene there would have been if I had refused to keep it. Anyway, I kept it with good intentions. Now don't start fighting with me about it.' Then she tried to explain, 'A fast merely provides an occasion to recall a resolve one has made.'

'Occasion, my foot.' I grew annoyed. 'First you do what I don't like and then you try to hand me a line. I've said I don't believe in all this. You work so hard all day and to top it all . . .'

Two or three tears ran down her cheeks and fell on my legs. 'I beg of you, don't say anything today. You can scold me tomorrow.'

Her pleading manner, her tone and her tears suddenly aroused a storm in me. I drew her to me and held her close. I was flooded with remorse—the poor girl had stayed hungry all day for my sake, for my future and hers, and here I was, scolding her. She had not fasted with any bad intention. If someone really believed in it, shouldn't he have the freedom to do so? One person may prefer sweets and another salty snacks. Is it right that I should force someone to prefer sweets? Really, sometimes I take things too far. For some reason, Prabha continued crying for a long time and I kept reassuring her, 'I was only teasing you. Don't get upset about every small thing, Prabha! Don't I know that one has to do many things only to please the world?'

Yet tears kept flowing down her cheeks and on to my breast. No, these were not tears of anger or of sorrow, they were an acknowledgement of the significance of life itself. They were the breath that Prabha could not breathe. She had surrendered every breath of her life and her being to me. My eyes grew moist. The smell of musk rising from Prabha's body spread to every pore of my being. At that moment I felt there could be no greater happiness in life than to have found such a wife. Misty-eyed I looked up and saw the sky above glittering with stars. I wondered what these stars, the witnesses of my bliss, must think of me. Perhaps on one of those distant planets, at this hour, in just such a house, on such a roof, a couple, tired by the day's work, lay in an embrace, and among the stars they saw in the sky was this earth of ours . . . and at this moment, this idea of mine had come into their minds too. And in a flash I felt—this star-laden sky, these many directions, all are part of ourselves, our being, they too are us. And, patting Prabha's cheek, I kept softly kissing her lips and eyes, saying, 'No, Prabha, don't cry, listen, don't cry any more now.'

What troubled the child that she woke at night and kept crying? I was awakened by Bhai Saheb's roar. He was scolding Bhabhi, 'Throw her out on the street if she won't be quiet. Take her away and let me sleep.' It seemed as if Babuji too had woken up. Bhabhi took the child to Amma and tried to quieten her. I tried to go to sleep again; when I couldn't, I asked myself, 'What time is it?'

Prabha had woken up too. She had to wake up early because I would be leaving at daybreak. Taking out her watch from under her pillow, she said, 'It's only one-thirty.'

'All right, go back to sleep.' And I lay quiet, looking up at the sky, trying to make out the Seven Sisters and the polestar. One corner of the sky glowed as if reflecting a powerful light somewhere. I recalled that a searchlight from the aerodrome used to be seen here before. A tongue of fierce light used to pass across the sky, licking up the darkness. The roar of a railway engine and the retreating sound of the train's wheels brought back to me that night when I had sat in my room reading *Sohrab and Rustum* by lantern light, while an angry Prabha lay in the corner. How far behind I had left those days! Who knows where I shall be lying this time next summer! What will the routine of our life be like when we live separately? I felt a strong desire to tell Prabha all that Shirish had said.

Touching her arm I said, 'I can't sleep, Prabha.'

She seemed to have been lying awake. She said, 'Talk to me then. But don't go off later into so sound a sleep that you fail to get up on time. You haven't told me anything of that friend of yours for quite a while.'

'Which friend? Diwakar?' I asked eagerly. 'His wife keeps asking after you, but you refuse to go and see them. Do let's go one day. And Shirish Bhai is here too these days .'

'Which Shirish Bhai? The one whose sister . . .'

'Yes, yes, that one. Poor fellow is very upset. The doctors have declared his sister incurable. Yesterday he said many things which were really an eye-opener for me.' Since I couldn't sleep I might as well tell Prabha about him, so I launched off. 'First we talked about the joint family. He's strongly opposed to everyone living together. He says it prevents development of the personality. A person's talents and strengths do not expand. People forget their obligations because of constant bickering and animosity. He thinks one can live separately, develop oneself and also fulfil one's duties to the family. You tell me, what duty are we doing by living with the family? All we are doing is accumulating bitterness in ourselves. Neither are we doing our duty nor do we have good feelings. If we lived apart, we could strive to preserve at least one of the two, if not both.'

Prabha looked up at the sky with unblinking eyes. She said, 'What you say doesn't sound wrong.'

'Exactly what I said to him, Prabha! I said it sounds right, but my soul cannot accept it. It seems like gross selfishness.

Then he talked for a long time about the soul and about inherited patterns of behaviour. He said there is no such thing as the soul. Practice, influence, tradition, imitation, all combine to build certain patterns in the mind. These patterns obstruct any new action. We think our soul is stopping us. As if the soul is a watchdog chained at a doorway to bark at strangers and to wag its tail at those it is familiar with. A vegetarian's soul shrinks at the idea of eating meat, and one who does not eat onions feels that to eat onions would be to go against his soul. Now, either we must believe that those who eat meat and onions have no soul and a soul is the special property of a favoured few, or we must accept that the soul is just another name for conditioning. There was a time when the souls of orthodox priests revolted at the idea of drinking tap water and such people carried mud around with them too to scrub their hands with. Should we then say that the soul only existed in bygone times? In fact we give the names of "soul" and "conscience" to our own traditionalism, our own mental laziness and folly which prevent us from accepting anything new. If only we acknowledged that all this is only conditioning, we could change our attitudes.'

Prabha listened intently while I, propped up on one elbow, explained all this. I thought to myself that she would soon pick up many ideas if I kept explaining them to her like this, from time to time. Once I got a proper job, I could also help her study further. When all my colleagues are graduates and post-graduates, and their wives well-educated, Prabha too will have to be educated enough to mix with them. Well, this can be considered a mental preparation for the time when she will be able to join college. At least I won't have to feel embarrassed at the thought of introducing her to Shirish Bhai. I gave her time to reflect and ask questions. She said, 'When one listens to such ideas, one understands their logic. But if you tell me today to go out with you on the street, wearing a sari in the new style and with my face uncovered, I won't have the courage to do so.'

I felt pleased that she had grasped what I was saying. I said, 'Then the notion of conditioning is correct, isn't it? Shirish Bhai used a very good metaphor when he was talking of conditioning or of the conscience. He said that the inherited patterns of behaviour with which the mind is stocked are like travellers comfortably seated in a railway compartment. When you try to get into a compartment that is full, all those sitting inside try to push you out, stop you from entering. But you are in need so you fight your way in. Once you manage to get those inside to accept your presence, their opposition disappears and you become one of them. In a short while, the situation changes so much that the place you had to fight to secure is treated as yours by right, and even if you step out or move around, your seat will be kept for you. But now a new problem arises. As soon as you become one of the insiders, you too begin to oppose the entry of new people. You completely forget that you too have had to encounter such opposition . . .'

But Prabha suddenly changed the subject. 'But what, after all, does this Shirish Bhai of yours believe in? I really want to meet him but I feel very hesitant too. How will I talk with him? I won't dare open my mouth.'

'Of course you will! I'll definitely take you to meet him,' I said. Then I answered Prabha's question, telling her that I had asked him exactly that. 'Shirish Bhai, you oppose everything;

230

what, after all, do you believe in? He laughed loudly and replied: I believe in whatever is left when one has done away with God, religion, conscience and the soul. I said: That means you do not believe in anything. He replied: If all that is worth believing is contained in these four or five words, take it that I do not believe in anything. I probed further: How can that be? How can one develop if one believes in nothing? What direction will one take? He said: A human being always develops, in every situation. One gives up the old and takes on the new. It is enough to believe this. The human foot faces forward in order that we may walk forward, may advance. A ghost's feet are supposed to be turned backward, which indicates that one who lives in the past is a ghost. And, to tell the truth, all that you call Indian culture and the pride of India appears to me at one level to be the culture and civilization of these ghosts who live in the past. I have lost faith in everything.'

Then I said to Prabha, 'After this, Prabha, he said something which made my blood boil. Were it not for the great respect I have for him, I would have slapped his face there and then. But I restrained myself.'

'What did he say?' Prabha asked with anxious curiosity.

'He said: Samarji, I feel we are the descendants of a set of fraudulent, good-for-nothing impotent rogues who lived only in the past. They took no account of social problems nor of the value of their own time. They lived isolated from the rest of the world, constantly applying sandalpaste on their foreheads and worshipping themselves, intoxicated with their belief in their own greatness. We never stop to consider what is great and heroic about those whom our ancestors worshipped as heroes. Their heroism consisted in battling the social problems of their time, in risking their lives to answer the challenges of their times. They did not become heroes by sitting and chanting the name of Ram.

'Well, however that may be, it does not seem right to talk like that about our ancestors. They were worthy people, after all, I said to him.

'Shirish Bhai answered: You may be content to say so, but I cannot help cursing myself for being so ineffectual. Those ancestors of ours were museum pieces of this cowdung culture. We are their descendants, so we are an army of straw puppets, fit only to be burnt or to clutter up the place with waste. One day we will be burnt up and reduced to ashes. The least we can do is to temper in this fire the little iron and gold we have among us so that it gets refined and becomes strong.' Suddenly I broke off. Where would Shirish Bhai's influence lead me? These days I seemed to have altogether stopped thinking in my own language. He cast a long shadow over my mind. As if analysing this influence, I said, 'Sometimes when I observe this man's anger I too get excited and wonder why I am not able to think as he does. Why do I not get stirred up by the situation as he does, why am I becoming so dull and lifeless? But at other times I feel sorry for him, and feel that the poor fellow is upset and unhappy, that is why he has become a permanent rebel. However that may be, his ideas and his style of talking do influence me greatly.' And I fell silent, recalling his gestures and mannerisms.

I felt as if Prabha had fallen asleep while listening to me. First I thought, let her sleep, she is tired with the day's work. And I began to remember how I had felt earlier this evening when I was returning after having talked to Shirish Bhai. I had felt as if all my former notions had been wiped away, as if they never had been mine at all. These new ideas alone resounded within me. As if the chambers of my mind had been closed for thousands of years and had become damp and suffocating, full of cobwebs and rubbish of all kinds. The air in them was rotten and poisonous. Silence and solitude consumed themselves there. But now someone had kicked the doors open with heavy boots. The damp, stifling atmosphere was gradually changing. The dust of many years rose in an angry cloud, and sounds reverberated all around as if someone had thrown a brick at a beehive. As I entered the house I had said to myself, 'Now I am not a ghost living in the past. Now my intellect is cleansed, freed of rubbish and waste. But now what dream shall adorn these empty rooms? What heavenly songs, what songs of dawn, shall be played here? What great age is that towards which we little wheels shall move in unison, with one rhythm? When will that era begin? Will it come in our lifetime? Will we really witness it? Will we feel it, and know that this is the era for which we have yearned through many wakeful nights ...'

And I tried to distract my agitated, restless desire for a new age by carrying buckets of water up to the roof. Now, once more, I began to feel restless, wanting to tell Prabha all this, or to go over it all in my mind. What should I do? Prabha seemed to have actually fallen asleep. I thought of pulling a strand from the bedropes and tickling her ear with it, 'Here I am, wide awake, and you are fast asleep!' And then I felt like tickling her on the stomach instead. I knew that always made her jump and squeal; the danger was that she might squeal too loud. But I couldn't resist the desire so I suddenly began tickling her, 'Hey, Prabha, get up, I'm awake, and you went off to sleep while talking to me.'

'Huh? What happened?' Prabha suddenly leapt up. 'When did I fall asleep?'

I would have continued the teasing, but suddenly I felt something tied to her waist. A round pill-like thing tied by a cord. Pinching it, I asked, 'What's this?'

'Nothing, nothing, let go of me.' She was agitated and spoke as if pleading.

'I won't. Tell me what it is, first . . .' I caught hold of her and tried, by feeling it, to discover what it was. It was somewhat like a betelnut.

'I beg of you. Let go. It's nothing.' She tried to unclasp my hands but I wouldn't let go. She seemed so upset that I redoubled my enquiries. She said, 'I had some stomach trouble so Ammaji got me a medicine.'

Clearly, an evasion. I said sternly, 'Medicine is to be eaten, not to be tied here. Tell me, or I'll break it off and throw it away.'

'I'll die if you do!' She kept up her pleading.

I was getting angrier every moment. 'So you won't tell?' I growled. Then she said fearfully, 'Bhabhi and Ammaji insisted. I kept saying I don't believe in it, but they began to abuse me. So I had to agree, to please them.'

I interrupted, 'You had to keep the fast to please them, I understand that, but what is this you had to do? Why don't you tell me plainly?'

'They said . . . they said . . .' Prabha stammered and grew tearful.

'What did they say, why don't you speak?' My anger was getting out of control.

'They said the holy ash given by Sayyad Baba will cure it,' she said, shielding her face with her elbow as if I were about to slap her.

I took hold of her shoulders and shook her. 'Cure what? Why don't you tell me clearly? If you were ill, you should have told me.'

Prabha began to cry. 'Mrs Awasthi said her Pramod was born four years after her marriage, after she went to Sayyad Baba . . .'

When I took this in, I let go of her and burst out laughing like a lunatic. 'Oh, I see, so that's it! That's why these fasts are being kept! Sayyads and prophets are being worshipped! Sayyad Baba's ash at your waist and perfume on your clothes!' And I ground my teeth so hard that the sound was audible. 'You want a child, do you? We don't know where our next meal is coming from and you want to hang a rattle around your neck . . .' And, with a jerk, I broke off the bundle of ash and threw it into the alley. What castles in the air I was building a moment ago! While this, this is the reality . . .

Enraged, I knocked my head on the bedpost, while Prabha, head on her knees, cried, 'What am I to do, tell me? They are after me all day. Bhabhi and Amma keep cursing me, calling me barren. Bhabhi doesn't let me go anywhere near her daughter. She doesn't want even my shadow to fall on her . . .'

Each time I knocked my head, I said to myself, 'How alone I am!' I thought Prabha would be with me, but this . . . is this the Prabha who once scrubbed the dishes with the sanctified lump of clay? What is she today? Was it on her that I relied when I dreamt those glorious dreams . . .?

10

'Why have you been sitting here since morning? Don't you have any work to do? Aren't you going to college today?' Prabha asked tenderly.

Languid and depressed, I had sat down on the parapet after returning home from the press. This corner was shady, sheltered by the roof. I was very quiet, hadn't talked to anyone. I sat still, watching a chattering squirrel. I looked so tired and dejected that Prabha came and touched my wrist to see if I had fever. I looked at her with vacant eyes and still remained silent. What she had told me the other day had shaken me to the core, and now everything around seemed unreal. I felt I was imprisoned in an endless mesh of fraud and falsehood. As I cut through one strand, another takes its place. Prabha now—has she too turned out like the others? Did I weave all those golden dreams for her? Whenever I saw her, these questions spontaneously arose in my mind.

I looked down at the courtyard. A big basket of bangles stood there. It was lined with thick cloth to keep the bangles from breaking. Long chains of bangles of all kinds—blue and green, red and gold—lay carefully coiled in it. The bangle-seller was not clearly visible from where I sat. If I leaned out, I could see her hands tattooed with flowers and leaves. I could make out that the hands she was adorning belonged to Bhabhi. She has a black birthmark behind her thumb.

Prabha suddenly took fright at my silence. She sat down on the floor, put her hand on my shoulder, and said, 'Why don't you speak? Tell me, has something happened? Have you had a fight with someone?'

'Nothing.' My voice, issuing from my dry throat, sounded lifeless. I sat unmoving, looking away with vacant, wide-open eyes. The huge question I had so long suppressed suddenly came before me—Now? What will happen now?

'Please tell me.' Prabha came closer, caught hold of my hand and asked pleadingly, tearfully, 'Are you still angry with me?' Silvery tears swam in the half-open, lotus-bud-like eyes. She kept looking at me, as if begging to be forgiven.

Startled by her tone, I slowly turned to look at her, then looked away again and said in a stifled voice, 'Prabha, I have lost my job.'

'Lost? How?' she sprang up, as if all the consequences had flashed before her eyes in an instant.

Just then, Amma called from below, 'Bahu, O Bahu!' And, very affectionately, 'Come down a moment, child!'

Prabha leaned over and replied, 'Coming, Ammaji!'

I told her, 'That wretch said he wouldn't pay me for the first fifteen days, because I was learning the job. And he said I would have to sign a receipt for seventy-five rupees but I'd be paid only sixty. I fought with him over that. Part-timer in name but actually a full day's work. And then this!'

'Why, what does he mean? How dare he give you less than what you sign for? Why don't you go and tell Diwakar? He's his father's friend, isn't that so?' Prabha frowned. 'This is sheer injustice!'

'Of course it is.' I smiled painfully, then sighed and said, 'What can I go and tell Diwakar? I'll try to do something or other. Tomorrow, I'll go for the last time. Let the rascal pay me at least for fifteen days. I have to repay all those loans I took, counting on this job.'

Amma's voice again, 'Where are you, what are you doing? You can talk later, come down now.' I was astonished to find that her tone was still gentle and loving.

'What's the matter? Why don't you go? Amma's been calling so long,' I said.

'What shall I do? She's calling me to buy me bangles. These days, we're being pampered, you see!' Prabha was agitated. 'Hmm,' I grew serious, and said firmly, 'No, Prabha, no bangles for you. We mustn't encourage anyone's false hopes, nor must we accept anything from anyone.' My face grew devoid of all expression. When Amma called again, Prabha was forced to go. I watched in silence. When she was halfway down, she returned and said softly, 'Look, don't worry. So what if the job is lost, don't be so upset. I have a watch, gold bangles and earrings. What else are they for? They're just lying locked up in the trunk. I don't need to wear them every day. I'll come in a little while and take them out. We can always get others made later. Your studies must continue . . .' And she went down. At any other time, I would have been overwhelmed, tears would have come to my eyes, but now I heard her and sat still, without a thought in my head.

I heard Amma's voice below, in affectionate rebuke, 'Don't we have any claims on you? Yes, yes, put them on! Which ones do you like? Choose for yourself.' So Prabha was downstairs now.

'No, no, Ammaji, I don't need any. I've got lots in my trunk upstairs.'

'So what? Can't you wear a few new ones? Everyone has lots kept by. We too must earn a living, mustn't we?' the bangle-seller said, and from the clinking, it appeared she had begun to open strings of bangles and display them. I heard a few broken sentences, 'These will look very good, they show up well on a fair wrist.'

'Wear them, Prabha, don't make such a fuss, wear them to please Ammaji.' Bhabhi's voice.

And then silence. I sat still, listening. I was sure she would not wear the bangles. Huh, now they think of giving her bangles! All this time, she was as good as non-existent for them. I leaned forward to look. Amma and Bhabhi had worn their bangles and were looking with cheerful anticipation at Prabha. Prabha was sitting with one arm propped on her knee, the hand extended to the bangle-seller. The other hand, laden with bangles, was on her foot. The bangle-seller was squeezing the hand she held to pass the bangles over it. Some pieces of broken glass lay scattered around. Prabha's face was turned away, twisting with pain. Her eyes were closed and whimpers broke from her lips. With the free hand she tightly clenched her feet.

The sight set off an explosion within me. I could scarcely control my fury. 'I had forbidden her,' I kept repeating to myself. Jaw clenched, I went downstairs and stood right in front of the bangle-seller.

239

Prabha had slipped on the bangles. Her arms shimmered with their bright, glassy colours. She looked at me and her face went pale. She tried to cover up her fear and laughed, forcing the words to her lips, 'See, how do they look? Amma and Bhabhi chose them.' At that moment she perhaps forgot that she never speaks to me in the presence of Amma and Bhabhi.

I glared at her with all the bitterness I could command, then I pounced on her and caught hold of her wrists. My hands seemed possessed by some demon. Shaking with rage, I slammed the wrists together. The bangles shattered and fell in pieces to the ground. I raised my head and laughed loudly, like a madman, then tossed her hands away as one throws aside a crushed insect. Slivers of glass had pierced my palms and fingers. My hands were covered with blood and trickles of blood were flowing from her wrists too. At the sight of the blood, I laughed even louder. Then, without looking around, I went back upstairs in a relaxed and unconcerned manner.

Without turning round to look, I knew that the bangle-seller, Amma and Bhabhi were gaping at me, thunderstruck.

Babuji waited a long time, hoping I would raise the matter myself. Finally, that night, he gave up and asked, 'Samar, didn't you start work on the tenth?'

I answered carelessly, 'I have lost my job, Babuji.'

Amma intervened, 'He's not asking you for money, why talk of losing your job?'

I answered brazenly, 'He's not asking outright, but I know what he means.'

At this Babuji exploded. Throwing up his hands, he

shouted, 'You know, so what will you do—hang me on a gallows? A lot he knows! I asked a simple question; instead of answering, he runs to bite me.' He slapped his brow. 'I know how your mind works, son! I've observed you from childhood. Now you're openly threatening me with having asked for money? Look at the cheek of this fellow! I brought my first salary and gave it to my father—that sense of duty can go to hell, here he accuses me of asking for money. Wretch! Did we bring you up and educate you for this, that you should dishonour us in this way? Trample on us, bark and run to bite us like a mad dog when we talk to you?'

I asked in a controlled and sorrowful voice, 'Babuji, what have I said that has made you so angry?'

'What else do you want to say, my prince? Do you think I'm blind? Can't I see your attitude? Now you are educated and married. What do your parents matter? Let them go to hell, let them fall into the oven and end up in the furnace! Don't let that stop you having a good time!' He was yelling at the top of his voice.

'I told you, Babuji, that I didn't want to get married. All of you forced . . .'

The whole family had collected by now and was standing huddled together, looking on fearfully.

'Marriage . . . marriage . . . marriage!' Babuji spat out the word with revulsion, since he could think of nothing else to say. He was trembling with excitement. 'Had we known that you would turn out this way we'd have buried you alive as soon as you were born. How you have gladdened our hearts! We have educated you and turned you into an elephant, now you will trample us. Yes, son, this is the way of the world. What glory you are bringing to the name of your ancestors! He's just begun to sprout wings. No one in the family matters to him. He's the lord of his own will. Let others bark—they are dogs, they will get tired and stop barking. This morning we bought bangles, so his majesty smashed them. No one has any right now over you and your wife. You came to earth readymade, straight from God's hands. I kept thinking, why have a fight? He's a sensible boy, he'll come to his senses, but as long as he gets delicacies to eat, why should he bother about anyone? Study for himself, clothes for himself, adornments for his wife. All he thinks of is himself. Unless someone checks him, he'll keep sitting on others' heads.'

When I couldn't bear it any more, I asked, 'What adornments have I bought for my wife, Babuji?'

'You will keep answering back, will you?' Babuji was almost incoherent with rage. Trembling with fury, he leapt on me despite Bhai Saheb's and Amar's attempts to hold him back. Before I knew what was happening, a shower of kicks, blows and slaps descended on me. Gasping and panting, he continued to hit me. 'Here . . . here . . . answer back now! Answer back, I say! I may be old and nearly dead but I will set you right. You have gotten completely out of hand.'

I did not resist as he beat me, nor did I say a word though I was quivering with suppressed rage. This acted like fuel to his anger. I neither cried out nor tried to escape. Bhai Saheb and Amar had caught hold of him but he was now trembling in fear.

'Get out of my house, get out! Don't let me see you again. You base, mean fellow, go and drown in some well or pond! I've been observing the symptoms for a long time, now that he's started studying . . .'

'Enough now, Babuji, calm yourself,' Bhai Saheb said. Both of them were pulling him away. He was foaming at the mouth, his eyes were dilated and abuses flowed unceasingly from his lips. The women, trying to hold back their tears, were whispering among themselves, 'What's happened? What's the matter?' A couple of women from the neighbourhood had also arrived. With them, clinging to their saris, were their children, who had begun to cry at the scene.

'Yes, Babuji, I will leave,' I said in a husky voice, slowly raising my bowed head.

As soon as he heard this, Babuji flung aside the restraining arms and sprang back towards me. 'I knew it, I could see it. If you are the true son of your parents, get out now, right now, this moment! You will go in your own sweet time. Come, I'll show you the way. Bring his things out. Send them both off. They are nothing to us. They died when they were born. Get up and go, sir! Take your things and find a place for yourself. I fold my hands to you.' He brought his hands together with a loud report as he folded them. Then he caught my arm, shook me hard, and said, 'Go, sir, go on, take yourself off. There's no place for you here. Don't you ever set foot in this house again. Go and die where you like, lie on the streets outside, we don't care, we cannot afford to keep stud bulls . . .' By then my brothers had again caught hold of him, and were leading him away, trying to calm him down.

All the women were crying shame on me. Amma gave me a couple of slaps, 'Why don't you be quiet, Samar? Don't you speak another word! Going on answering back his father, shameless fellow!'

At this, I answered very angrily, 'Enough, Amma, I

wanted to hear it plainly said and I've heard it today. I don't want to live in this hell—no rest at night, no peace by day! Parental affection is a display put on for your own ends. I will live anywhere, in a well or on the road, but not here. I'll leave tomorrow. Reign alone in your royal palace.'

Even in that excitement, anger and uproar, I felt somehow that what I was saying was very improper. One should not speak thus to a father. Another very strange idea, which seemed quite unsuited to the occasion, came into my head. Was it possible that Ram and Sita too had left home because of a fight like this? Someone inside me laughed at the idea as it arose. Babuji heard what I said and tried to turn back but no one let go of him. He was taken out to the sitting room. At that moment I vowed to myself that I would live on the street or a footpath, but not here, never here. Anywhere else, anywhere with a roof above and a floor beneath but not in this hell. Beg, steal, the world is a big place . . .

The crying and screaming died down, and the whole family with one voice continued to condemn me, to abuse me for my rudeness, but I sat silent, my head buried in my knees. Only one thought in my mind—not here, not here. At any end of the world, in any corner of the earth, anywhere at all. Only one picture flashed before me—myself walking ahead, carrying a tin trunk, Prabha following slowly, and, perhaps, Kunwar behind her, trying to stop us (Lakshman!?).

All night I tossed and turned as though I was being grilled over a red-hot fire. Strange noises buzzed in my ears and every time I shut my eyes a peculiar stupor came over me. I lay suspended between sleep and wakefulness, feeling as if my heart had been replaced with a heavy stone whose weight oppressed my breath. I don't know how one feels during a heart attack yet I kept wondering if my heart were failing. My body was numb, as if I were wrapped up like a mummy. Or as if some crablike creature had me clasped in its thorny, hairy arms, and, with its snout piercing my head, was sucking my blood, drop by drop. I cried out and flailed my limbs but I was mesmerised by its eyes which were like burning coals, and it continued to devour me. A strange, all-consuming silence cried out in my brain and I felt myself drowning, as if someone had laid me on the water's surface and was pressing me down with a foot placed on my chest. I felt as if it had rained all night. Every now and then I would wake up to see if the downpour had stopped.

Suddenly, someone touched me and I sat up in alarm. Yet I seemed to have been expecting that someone would touch me and I would get up at his behest and follow him, leave this place and go out. With great difficulty I opened my eyes to see who it was. Prabha was very hesitantly and fearfully touching me with her bandaged hands, 'It's four o'clock. Aren't you going?'

Then I remembered that several times during the night Prabha had touched my forehead or massaged it with something. I sat up. Washing my hands and face, I wondered why I was feeling so strange. Why was I going through all the routine motions as if under a spell, as if acting against my will? Why did I feel as if these hands and feet were not my own? As if I had gone far away, and was on some distant height, from where everything appeared misty, unclear, unreal. While washing my face, I suddenly turned and asked, 'Did it rain at night?' We were alone downstairs. Prabha was at the stove and I at the tap. Lighting the fire, she asked, 'Rain? What rain?' And at this I suddenly remembered—I have to leave this house today, I have no attachment to it. I must find a house today, anywhere, however difficult it may be.

Prabha had packed my tiffin in a small aluminium box. I picked it up and crammed it into my pocket. As I put on my coat, the palms of my hands hurt—perhaps because of the pieces of glass that had pierced me yesterday.

I put out the light and went slowly down the stairs. I felt that my legs were trembling; even my footsteps sounded different today. Everything seemed unfamiliar and strange. When I reached the last step I turned and looked up— perhaps Prabha was watching me descending. But there was no one there. Everyone else was still asleep.

Just then someone knocked at the door and I jumped with fright, as if I were a murderer and the police were standing outside. For a moment I stood undecided, looking around in agitation. Should I open the door or not? Then I shook off the hesitation and moved forward.

The knocking continued and someone called out, 'Telegram!'

I opened the door. A khaki-clad peon with a red cycle stood there, telegram in hand. I signed and took it. Then I watched him cycle off. The telegram was addressed to Babuji.

Day had begun to break. I turned the telegram over in my hands, and felt like going and handing it over as it was. Then, for some reason, I tore it open. A typed slip pasted on a pink paper, 'Munni expired.'

I read it once, read it twice, yet could not understand what this brief sentence meant. Hearing the word 'telegram', Bhai Saheb and Babuji had come down, looking worried. 'Where is it from? What does it say?'

With a soft, unnatural laugh I held out the telegram and said, 'It says that Munni died. It doesn't clearly say that she was killed . . .'

And without waiting for their reaction I went my way, as if unconscious and inanimate. Later, perhaps, there must have been much weeping and wailing in the house . . .

I knew on which side of the train the platform came, so I sat on the other side to stay undisturbed. Sitting by the window, I gazed at the dawning day with vacant eyes—today even the sunrise looked very strange.

My mind was dark and still like an electrically-run factory in which a fuse suddenly blows, so that everything is suddenly plunged into a fearful stillness. A voice resounded in my brain to the regular rhythm of the train's clatter. It hammered on my nerves and struck my ears—Munni is dead—Munni is dead—Munni has been killed—Munni has been killed.

As if a soft timid sound like the fluttering of bats in the dome of a huge ruin should resound terrifyingly, and its echoes build into wave upon wave of stillness that flood the atmosphere and then plunge all things into the profound stillness of death. And then again impenetrable, unfathomable darkness.

What is happening to me today! I ran a hand over my brow, and hit my head gently.

The train stopped with a jolt. I had to get off at this station. I glanced at the platform and then peered through the window at the scene on the other side. Three pairs of shining tracks, and a platform beyond them. It was clear daylight now, but the station's lights were still on. A sweeper was cleaning the far side of the platform and clouds of dust billowed around him. He had a cloth tied over his mouth. I sat as if I had no intention of alighting. When the train whistled, I suddenly remembered that I had to get down here. I hastily opened the door and jumped on to the track bed.

I had just put a foot on the line when I saw a train approaching from the opposite direction, perhaps from Delhi. A huge engine came closer every instant, passing under the distant roadbridge. Clouds of smoke burst from it and the gleaming tracks shivered, as if a terrible demon were ambling forward.

Suddenly a thought sprang up—what if I throw myself before it? The picture of the head constable holding his gun flashed before my eyes. And I felt as if a powerful electric shock had thrown me before the engine, and in the indivisible fraction of a second before I fell on the lines, the cobweb-like mist overlying my consciousness was torn apart and I awoke as if from a dream—what have I done? But by then the ice-cold tracks have me in their grip and the advancing engine touches me. I clench my teeth and grab the engine. Prabha's innocent face comes before my eyes. But the engine drags me on—one second, two seconds. My hands lose their strength, my grip weakens and I want to scream aloud. 'Prabha-a-a!' And the heavy clamorous wheels of the engine revolve over my open mouth...

The picture formed so vividly before me that I felt I might perhaps act on it. But I had removed my foot from the track and the train had stopped in front of me. Right in front of me was the empty space where two bogies are linked. Broad cables and heavy iron rods linked one to the other. A man leaned out of a window, brushing his teeth. I stood between the two trains as if caught between two walls.

I thought, what if I get into this compartment? And the next moment I saw myself in a labourer's outfit, on a steamer setting out from Bombay for foreign lands. But soon that picture changed to one of an ascetic with a long beard and saffron robes. I saw myself in an ashram, lying wrapped in a blanket, and in a hut under a huge tree in Rishikesh. A long time passes and then a woman in widow's white comes with many other old women and stands before my hut. No, while bathing at Har-ki-Pauri, I see a woman and say, 'That's Prabha!' I recognize her but she doesn't recognize me because of my beard and thick blanket. Then I saw people beating me up with sticks and shoes because I had gone up to a young woman while she was bathing and had called her 'Prabha, Prabha!'

And then all the pictures get blurred and merge into one big picture. My picture, printed in a newspaper. Dear son Samar, your mother is very ill, she wants to see you.

The train in front of me whistled. I woke from my stupor with a start. The wheels of the train revolved slowly in front of me. What if I jump into the space between the two bogies? Or if I leap up into the compartment?

The train behind me had also begun to slide forward— the two trains were drawing away in two opposite directions. I felt as if I were standing on a rapidly spinning wheel while someone chanted inside me—Jump down! . . . Leap up! Jump down! . . . Leap up! . . . Confounded, I looked up—the sky too had begun slowly to revolve above me.